# Cliffhanger

T. J. Middleton is the pen name of Tim Binding,
acclaimed author of *In the Kingdom of Air*, *A Perfect
Execution*, *Island Madness*, *On Ilkley Moor*, *Anthem*
and *Man Overboard*. He lives in Kent with
his wife and daughter.

# T. J. Middleton

# *Cliffhanger*

PICADOR

First published 2008 by Picador

First published in paperback 2009 by Picador
an imprint of Pan Macmillan Ltd
Pan Macmillan, 20 New Wharf Road, London N1 9RR
Basingstoke and Oxford
Associated companies throughout the world
www.panmacmillan.com

ISBN 978-0-330-45751-4

3 5 7 9 8 6 4 2

A CIP catalogue record for this book is available from
the British Library.

Typeset by SetSystems Ltd, Saffron Walden, Essex
Printed in the UK by CPI Mackays, Chatham ME5 8TD

Visit www.picador.com to read more about all our books
and to buy them. You will also find features, author interviews and
news of any author events, and you can sign up for e-newsletters
so that you're always first to hear about our new releases.

*To Andrew*

# One

It sounded simple enough.

'Audrey,' I said. 'Audrey, why don't we go out, for a stroll?'

'In this weather?'

'Clear the cobwebs,' said I, pulling on my boots, and she shrugged her shoulders and said, 'Why not?'

'Cause I'm going to shove you over the bloody cliff, Audrey, that's why not.

I thought it, but didn't say it, natch. She looked at me funny though.

'All these years,' she said, 'living by the sea and you barely setting your foot out the front door, and now you want us to go for a walk. It'll be pissing down before you know it.'

'Then I'll make us a couple of hot toddies when we get back. Light the fire. Open a bottle of bubbly. We can stretch out, make an evening of it.'

'So that's what this is all about. Well, it's been a while.' And she smiled, hoping that I'd smile back. Well you would, wouldn't you?

So I had to change it. Make her angry.

'That's one way of putting it. Dying of thirst and being stuck in the bloody desert might be more appropriate.'

Her face froze.

'Change the record, Al.'

'Well, it's always me that's got to come cap in hand, isn't it. I mean when did you last suggest it yourself? I can't remember and I've a better memory than you. And even when you do it's as if you're volunteering to go over the top. You should get out more, live a little.'

Well, that got her going. Let off a couple of rounds in my direction, words pinging against the walls. It worked, though. She stormed out that front door, down the rutted road for all to see, head bent into the wind, her oilskin, yellow, like what the lifeboat men wear, flapping around her legs.

I waited a couple of minutes then slipped out the back.

I knew where she was going, where she always went, up the path to the beacon and then along the top, where she'd stop, where the path runs down into the little dip, and you can stand a bit sheltered and look across to Portland Bill, and the sea all crashing below. I don't blame her going there. It's a nice spot. I've been there once or twice myself.

The thing is there's two ways to get there. The back way, across the fields, is longer, hugging the hedges and then along the cart tracks – not that they are cart tracks any more, what with tractors and combines and farmers slumming it in last year's four-wheel-drive, but if you've known a place for a long time, that's how you remember it best. When I was a kiddie there were horses down that neck of the woods; horses and Jersey cows and men with long scythes to cut your grass. Not that many years ago.

Sixties, early seventies. Things didn't change at such a speed then. Not like now. Now you make your decisions fast, and act on them without hesitation. That's what I've learnt.

I had only really decided to do away with Audrey the month before. It had been brewing in my mind, how great it would be if only she weren't here, but it only came to me sudden like that that's what I should do, get rid of the old dear. And as soon as it popped into the head, it seemed the obvious thing to do. Why not? She'd had a good life. Not a great one, but nothing much to grumble about. Regular money. A bungalow with two en-suite bathrooms. A grown-up daughter in Sydney. Great kid. Never phones, of course, but then they don't, do they? They just push off and leave the two of you stuck there with nothing to look forward to, save the prospect of staring at each other from opposite armchairs the rest of your natural.

Not healthy.

So, sorry dear, you've got to go. But nothing nasty like poison or strangling or wiping that look off her face with a baseball bat. Something that's almost over before she's noticed. A shove in the small of the back, and while she's falling not even sure that it was deliberate. Gone, before all the bad thoughts and the terror can set in. By the time she's said to herself, 'Oh Christ I've fallen off a cliff, I'm going to die,' and started screaming, it's over. She's dead and we are all very sorry and Carol comes over for the funeral and stays a week to make sure I'm

OK and Mrs Poke Nose from next door comes in with some ready-made grub, and then it's all over, finished and I can get on with the rest of my fucking life. My fucking life.

A nice spot I believe.

Anyway, to get back. Out I pop and checking that no one is about or watching through their windows, skirt along, hurrying like because Audrey is a strong walker. Big legs, tall, strides around more like a camel than a woman really. No grace to her. In the early days I didn't mind her size, her strength. It was part of who she was, fierce, kind of challenging. In the early days, when her blood was up she used to put me over her shoulder, carry me about, throw me down on the ground, get on top of me, like a sweaty Amazon. I used to like it, goad her into it. Kind of disgusts me now, all that muscle gone to seed. Anyway, going the back way there are a couple of vantage points when you can see the proper path as it climbs the Beacon before disappearing behind the burial mound or whatever that pimple on the top is, and sure enough, there she is, striding up the path, her hands stuffed deep into her pockets, head down, bent forward like she's looking for her contact lenses. She had a head of steam on her, that's for sure, so I had to step it out a bit to get there first. It didn't take me long.

At the back of the Beacon, facing the sea, there's this flat dip running to the cliff's edge, a gorse bush huddled under the pimple, a big one. You can go under it if you've got a mind to. It's hollow inside, like a tent. Sheltered. Private. I've been there a few times too. Got the scratches to prove it.

So I gets there. And waits. And waits and waits.

Desperate for a fag, but dare not. And then I hear her, and she's crying, really crying, a sound like I'd never heard before. That should of warned me, of course, but then I peeked through and there she stood, with her back to me, not four, five foot from the edge, as she always did. Why do people do that, stand near the edge? Not that I'm complaining. I mean standing near the edge is where I wanted her to be, but I never understood it myself, that need. Asking for trouble. Anyway there she stood, as close to perdition as a human might dare with the hood all up and a wail coming out of her and I thought right, Al, this is it chum and I just ran up and pushed her and she stumbled forward and then was gone. Just like that. I mean it was incredible. Not a cry, not a murmur, just her arms flapping in the air like she was a goose trying to land on water and then she tipped over and was gone. Disappeared. For good. It was so fucking simple. To think that just the flick of a hand could change everything. Just one push and the whole world had changed. My life had changed, her life had changed. No more quarrels about this and that, no more banging of the saucepans, no more cold shoulders after a night on the piss, when a man's thoughts turn horizontal. Not that I ever forced her. Never raised a finger to her in my life. Never would. I don't believe in that sort of behaviour. Show me a man who does and I'll show you a twenty-four-carat coward. This was different. This, as they say in the movies, was business.

Anyway, there I am. In front of me a bit of cliff and the sea. Above me only sky. I'm alone. No one's seen me. I've not been here. I skirt home dead careful, taking my time, listening out for the sound of a thoroughbred Shogun clip-clopping along or Mrs Poke Nose ferreting about in the undergrowth. Not that anybody was going to be out in that weather unless they had to. By the time I got back it was really mixing it. Making sure the coast was clear, I hopped over the fence into the back garden and snuck into the house.

'Bonsai!'

Don't know why I said it, but I did, said it as an exclamation, something to shout out loud, alone. It was my house now.

'Bonsai, you old bastard,' I said and swung into the living room like it was the Ponderosa, like I owned half of Texas. 'Cause that's what it felt like. That it was all in front of me, all mine.

Audrey was in front of the fire in her dressing gown, her hair wet, her bare toes wriggling against the heat, two little glasses of whisky, a kettle sitting on the grate, and a bottle of champagne poking out from the ice bucket.

'There you are,' she said. 'I was wondering where you'd got to.' She patted the rug beside her. 'Get those wet things off of you. Stretch out.'

I nearly shit myself.

# *Two*

The bungalow where I live, well there's a row of us, about thirteen in all, down along a path scuffed with stones. We got a baker, a plumber, a taxi driver (yours truly), someone who works in a gym over in Wareham, and at the far end Police Constable Corn-Plaster's one-man police house. In between live remnants of the rival fishing families, the Stokies and the Travers, who would row across the Channel just to see the other lot drown. The Stokies live next door, and back when I was a kid, when me and my old mum used to come down here, Kim's father was a kid too. Nasty piece of work Kim is, like his dad was, bullet-headed, but a part of village life, lobster-potting, hiring out the rowing boats in the summer season, doing his neighbours down as best he can. The Stokies never liked us much, coming down in the summer to use as a holiday home a bungalow very much like the one they had to live in all the year round. I can understand that now, the resentment, but then I couldn't. I was a scrawny kid, a bit shy I guess, and I looked forward to it, coming down here with mum and the cat, and being away from home, and the cunt who was my father. Not a good man. When me old mum died, I never saw him again, not even when he was pegging out himself. Rang me up he did, in the hospital, saying that he'd been taken poorly and I said to him that I'd be there the next day, gave him the time when the train would arrive, how long it would take in a taxi from the station, knowing all along that I wasn't going, that I just wanted the bastard to wait, get his hopes up, only to realize that I wasn't coming, never would and he could die all on his fucking lonesome. And he did too, and when I went to get his things, a watch, a wallet, his ring, the nurse banged the stuff down in front of me like I was the most thoughtless bastard a father could have and I thought, you don't know the half of it, sister. So just to make her feel even better I stuffed the lot in my pocket and asked her where the nearest pawnshop was where I could get a good price for it all, and if there was any decent clubs nearby, where a man on his lonesome might go prospecting. I found one too that night, despite her purple indignation, went there all togged up, and picked up one of her own, a nurse from the same hospital, and took her temperature from every vantage point I knew. My didn't the mercury rise.

In the morning I have the same routine, get up, make Audrey a cup of coffee, then hop down to the bakery and bring back a couple of warm rolls. Nothing like it with a bit of cherry jam. Audrey has muesli. Well she would, wouldn't she. She has yogurt too. In my mind there's only one use for yogurt, and Audrey hasn't needed that sort of treatment since her knees realized they had so much in common. That morning, the morning after so to speak, I didn't go down as per usual. I was uncertain as to what to do.

She lay there sleeping, her back to me, not a stitch on her (itself a rare occurrence), and I was looking at her thinking, well what do I do now? I still wanted her out the way, but I could hardly go pushing her off a cliff again, could I? I mean two bodies dressed in yellow oilskins lying at the bottom of the local beauty spot and Police Constable Corn-Plaster might think there was a pattern forming. The funny thing was, put out though I was, I liked the old dear more then than I had for a long time. After I'd got over the shock of seeing her stretched out by the fireplace, we hadn't half gone at it. Well, what else could I do? Like a piece of doner kebab I was, couldn't feel a thing. Halfway through the tanks opened up across the range, and we stopped to watch the fireworks. They'd put up a couple of tank dummies in there a couple of days before, and were blasting them to smithereens. It happened around once a week, the night-time exercise. It went with the territory. When we was courting we used to hop up over the range gate whenever we could, have a roll in the grass. There's gates and notices warning you about mines and unexploded shells, but the locals take no notice. There're no shells there. It's just to keep everyone out, 'cause when they're not tanking, there's no one about to see what you're up to. Sometimes when they were firing, us older kids used to chase down the broad path to this ruined cottage, half the walls knocked out, the floor just a bed of grass, stuck in the middle of it all, the tanks on one side of the valley, the dummies across the other, the cottage just below them. We'd stay there, caught in between, hearing the shells scream over, slamming into the dummies, the ground lifting up like an earthquake, the smell in the air like the end of the world. Christ it was terrifying, but you could scream your head off, do what you liked and no one would hear. Fuck the pictures. That was our excitement.

Half an hour we watched that night, our hands all over each other. If anything Audrey went harder at it afterwards. All the time I was jabbing away I was thinking, well who the fuck did I push over the cliff then if it wasn't you? Still it helped in the stamina stakes, being so pre-occupied. If I'd been there I might have enjoyed it. The trouble was of course that pushing her off a cliff was exactly what was needed. It smacked of an accident. People fall off cliffs all the time – but two in a row in the same spot, wearing the same clobber? I don't think so. What else could I do? Drown her in the carp pond? Electrocute her golf clubs? Nothing straightforward sprang to mind. What I needed was a Plan B.

I touched her on the shoulder. It was like I'd thrown a switch. She turned over and heaved herself on top. No preliminaries. She just grabbed at it and worked it in. She must have been waiting for me to wake up, the condition it was in. There was more suction applied than you find on your average Dyson. Christ I thought, I should try and bump you off more often.

'First last night, now this. What's got into you?' I said, genuinely interested.

She looked down, as if she could hardly recognize herself. She leant back, showing me all the working parts, like she was a young woman again. It was as if she sensed something had changed between us. Shameless she was.

'I don't know. I haven't felt like this in a long time.'

'Just as well,' I joked, 'unless you want me in an early grave.'

'I thought that's how all men want to go,' she said.

'That's as may be, but I don't believe it's covered in our insurance policy.'

'Perhaps I should have a clause inserted.'

'Perhaps you should.'

'I feel as if I could insert clauses all morning.'

'I was afraid that might be the case.'

'Clause one and two now, and perhaps, after breakfast, the preamble to clause three. Have you got much on today?'

I hadn't anything until an evening booking to Le Cassoulet in Dorchester. The Burgesses were hungry again. Audrey looked quite put out.

'Don't they ever eat in?'

'Would you with their money?'

'You should up your rates, Al, for evening work like that. They can afford it.'

'They're tight-wads. Ian would undercut me given half the chance.'

'Ian's a cunt.'

I winced. Audrey using language like that. It wasn't right. A sure sign of things going askew.

Come breakfast time I needed more than a couple of white rolls. We both did. I brewed a pot of strong coffee, put half a pound of pork sausages, a plate of fried mushrooms and four poached eggs on the table and watched Audrey chomp her way through. She might have put some clothes on, but the itch was still there I could tell. She had that look on her. If I'd taken it out she'd have speared it with her fork and smothered it with Coleman's.

'So what have you planned for this morning?'

I threw my hands up. 'Audrey, please. I'm nearly fifty.'

'I wasn't thinking of that,' she said. 'The shower needs fixing.'

And she standing under it, soaping herself with that lascivious look on her face. Not bloody likely.

'I thought I might go down to the Cove. Hitch a ride with Kim. Bring back a lobster or two. We haven't had lobster for a bit.'

'We had it last week.'

'That's what I mean.'

What I wanted to do of course was to go out and see if I could spot Audrey's doppelgänger floating in the seaweed.

'I thought you weren't talking to him.'

'That was last week. This week we're the best of mates. I fixed his Peugeot for him. After that I'm meeting up with Reggie. He's got a couple of hares, from over the artillery range.'

'God, this road,' she said. 'Every profession except a candlestick-maker. Even the oldest.'

'Now, now,' I told her. 'You mustn't believe the gossip. Iris likes company, that's all.'

Then I remembered. I couldn't go with Kim. Ted Grogan had rung me a couple of days back. He'd put his back out and the osteopath over at Wareham had managed to find a slot for him. He needed me to drive him over. What with one cliff and another I'd quite forgotten about it. Naturally I'd assumed that after Audrey's death, I'd be expected to take some time off; come to terms with my grief, ha-ha. Ted was the local coastguard. Spent the day sitting in his little hidey-hole up above the cove looking out across the Channel. Ships run aground? Lilos in difficulties? Audrey's lookalike washing in and out of the briny? Ted was your man.

'Audrey, you know what? You're right. I'll give the Vanden Plas a bit of a one-two. Tart it up for this evening. Sod Ian. I'm going to up my rates.'

So I spent the morning with my pride and joy, taking it down to the car wash, getting the boys to wash and wax it, coming back, vacuuming the inside, wiping down the dashboard. I could see Audrey through the window, sitting at the table polishing the front doorstop, an artillery shell that her grandfather had brought back from World War One, the only thing she did polish regularly. Up and down she went, greasing it up, spitting on the sharp end, trying to catch my eye. You must be joking, I thought. At about half ten she popped her head round. Ian had a job on he couldn't cover. Some officer from Wool station to the tank range. Typical of him, to use the house phone, not my mobile. Didn't want to talk to me, see. Just wanted me to get him out of shtook. Ian had the concession with the army base, ever since he set up on his own. Made my blood boil that, considering our history. Normally I would have told him to stuff it, but I didn't want to be around the house longer than necessary. Not after last night. Not after this morning. So I took it.

I stood just inside the ticket office, holding the sign. The train was fifteen minutes overdue. Major Fortingall was the name Ian had given out, and Major Fortingall was what it said. Big bold letters on a card about two and a half foot long. Audrey done it. It was a gift she had, right-handed, left-handed, she could script her letters any way you wanted. If she hadn't been an honest woman she could have been a forger. This one was done with a felt tip, kind of flowery italic, nice enough, though I must confess I felt a bit of a pillock holding it. Wool station doesn't have quite the traffic of Heathrow Airport. There were only four passengers coming off the train that morning; a couple of hikers, all togged up in their bobble hats and knee-length socks, Blind Lionel, Wool's unisex barber, and one other.

He was a young-looking geezer, good-looking in a fresh-faced, smack-him-in-the-mouth sort of way, only with a pair of glasses thicker than our double glazing. Audrey's very keen on double glazing. Keeps the noise out, she says. Keeps the noise in too of course. If I had to do her in at home, in the bath or the brand-new kitchen that had set me back six grand, no one would hear a thing.

He stood at the entrance, gazing round, expectant. He was carrying a little black case, and an overnight holdall. I waggled the sign, but he looked right through it, as if he was looking for someone else.

'Major Fortingall?' I enquired. 'I've come to drive you to the gunnery.' He wrinkled his nose like I was a newly laid dog turd.

'You're not the usual chap.'

'I'm not, am I. Sorry about that. Ian had someone important, apparently. The car's outside.'

He handed me his bag. It looked lighter than it was.

'Staying long?' I asked, still trying to be civil.

He shook his head.

'Running gear. Thought I might chase a couple of miles after I'm finished with this lot.' He waggled his case.

I shifted the bag onto my other hand. I hate runners. I don't mind people going to the gym, hitting the weights, running the treadmill, getting hernias on the rowing machine, but joggers, out there for everyone to see, with their horrible panting and glazed eyes, shouldn't be allowed. There are exceptions to the rule, of course. Eighteen-year-old Lycra-covered D-cups for instance.

'Well, don't stray too far off the paths,' I told him, 'or they'll be picking you out the gorse bushes next Easter. Ker-boom!'

'I thought those signs were just to keep the tourists out.'

'You never can tell with unexploded mines,' I told him. 'Take it from me. I've been living with one for the past twenty-two years.'

He didn't even smile.

'Let's get a move on,' he snapped. 'I'm late as it is.' He looked at me as if it was my fault. It's funny how people nearly always do that. The train's late, there's a traffic jam, they've forgotten their passport. It's always your fault.

I took him at his word, put my foot down, took the bends in fourth, made his glasses swivel. At the guard-house the sentry came out, Wacko Jacko, one of the regulars at the Spread Eagle. Liked to mix it. They all like to mix it, the squaddies, but some like to mix it more than others.

'Major Fortingrass, reporting for duty,' I said cheerfully. The Major leant over my shoulder.

'Major Fortingall,' he corrected. 'For the CO.'

Jacko ran his finger down his clipboard. You could see his lips moving.

'Admin,' he said. 'Third block on the left.' He had a nasty, threatening voice, Jacko, with a touch of obscenity about it, like he was talking filth even when he wasn't.

'I know where Admin is, chum,' I told him. 'I live round here, remember?'

'Oh, I remember, pal.' He tugged at his left ear. Had we had words the last time he was let out? I couldn't remember.

I drove round, parked by the entrance. I reached round and handed him my card. *Al Greenwood, At Your Service, Day and Night.*

'Will you want picking up later?' I asked.

He didn't reply, just slipped it into his pocket and hurried up the steps.

'And a very good afternoon to you too, General,' I shouted after him. Fucking military. Sometimes I think Ian's welcome to them.

I went back home. Audrey was nowhere to be seen. I had a quick kip in the back of the car, then at twelve fifteen drove round to pick up Ted.

Ted Grogan: small man, wiry, hair like a well-groomed Brillo pad. Always liked him. Honest man. Brave too. Come the summer he'd spend half his time dangling from the end of a rope, rescuing the arseholes who thought they were Dorset's answer to Sherpa Tenzing.

Ted lowers himself in and sniffs the polish. He looks wrung out. Nods a bare greeting and snaps the seat belt to. I flick the transmission and off we glide. It's a lovely car for gliding, the Vanden Plas. I look across. His hands are shaking.

'Late night?' I said.

'You could say that. She's run off.'

'Who, the missus?'

'Don't be daft, Al. Miranda.'

I kept the car on the road, natch, but there was a quiver in the wheel. Just for a second.

'How do you mean, run off?'

'I don't know. We had a row. She told me she and Kim were going to make it permanent this time. I let rip, pushed it a bit further than I meant to. Told her I'd wash my hands of her if she went back to that bastard. Three times this would make! She burst into tears and ran out.'

'To Kim's place? Gaynor wouldn't like that.'

'That's just it. He says he hasn't seen her for over a week.'

'What about Iris?' Iris was Ted's ex-wife, Miranda's mother.

'She hasn't seen her either. No one's seen her. She could be anywhere.'

I didn't like the sound of this, not one bit. I liked Miranda. Miranda liked me. I'd always liked Miranda.

'When did all this happen, then?'

'Yesterday afternoon. Half four, five. She picked up her bag and stormed out. Pelting down it was, you must remember. Force three it was. North-easterly.'

I kept my eyes on the road, trying not to grip the wheel any tighter. I could feel my knuckles turn white.

'Have you tried her mobile?'

'Course I've tried her mobile. I've been leaving

messages on it every half-hour. It's switched off. She's not answering.'

'What about the police. Have you been in touch with them?'

'I called them an hour after the pubs shut, after I'd checked with Iris and Kim. But a woman of twenty arguing with her dad? And half the men in the camp on a two-day furlough? They told me to wait a few days.'

'So?'

'So bollocks to that. You're taking me to Wareham police station. There's a fellow there, DI Rump. I want him to come down, take a look, start asking questions. Kim Stokie for a start. He's got a temper on him, everyone knows that.'

He turned awkwardly in his seat.

'Were you home yesterday? In the afternoon?'

'What, Sunday? Sure.'

'Did you hear anything from next door. See anything?'

'No, not that I can remember.'

'No arguments, no shouting.'

'No.'

'What about Audrey?'

'Don't think so. I'll ask. This Rump character. He might not come right away, you know. They have a point.'

'He'll come. He owes me. His father got into difficulties once, on the Race. You must remember. Kevin his name was, Kevin Rump. He's dead now.'

I remembered. The Race was a stretch of water that ran from St Alban's Head to Portland Bill. You got stuck in that and it wasn't good for you. Not with the size of some of those pebbles on Chesil Beach.

'You've brought a photograph, I hope. They'll need a photograph.'

'Iris is bringing one. We're picking her up, outside the barracks. She's been up there, see if Miranda's friends know anything.'

Miranda worked in the NAAFI. Ted and Iris had always hoped that some young officer would whisk her from it all, but it had never worked out that way. Plenty tried, but as she told me, she only had eyes for Kim. Not that Kim believed her. If he was cheating on his wife it stood to reason that his girlfriend must be cheating on him. Especially when she had all that fresh spunk on tap. Come Saturday night down the Spread Eagle and some young blood tipped his cap at her, the room would be flying with fists and glasses. Kim didn't always come out the best of it either, which made him even more certain that something was going on. Two and a half years we'd had of this, and it didn't seem to be getting any better. They couldn't work it out. As Iris said to me once; he couldn't be that good in bed. No one could. I kept quiet. It wasn't for me to butt in.

Iris was waiting by the tank. She got in, leant over and kissed Ted on the cheek. I put my hand out and she pressed it hard.

'Iss.' Iss was my nickname for her. I shouldn't have used it, but habits die hard.

'Al.'

We started off again, in silence.

The thing about Ted's wife is that years ago, long before they split up, for a couple of years before Miranda was born, Iss and me, we had a bit of a thing going. We took precautions, as best we could, but though we never talked about it, and it all ended as soon as she became pregnant, it always struck me that there was the possibility that Miranda could be mine. Nowadays it would be easy to find out, but we both wanted that particular can of worms well and truly sealed. Ted knew nothing about it and we wanted it to remain that way. Ted was a good father. Miranda had been a happy kid, and had turned into a good-looking young woman, tall and proud, with a set of hair like something you see in shampoo ads. That didn't come from *any* of us as far as I could fathom. But Iss, Iss was a social girl and Ted worked distinctly anti-social hours. They broke up when Miranda was about ten. Half the week she stayed with her mum, half the week with her dad. That worked well until she got to about fourteen, when Iris's social life had got a bit hectic and Miranda went to live with Ted exclusively. In the last couple of years Iris's private life had quietened down considerably, but a reputation like hers is hard to live down. They all got on though, Ted and Iris and Miranda, for all their ups and downs. Perhaps if Audrey and me had done something similar, it would never have got to this. Carol might not have decided to live on the other side of the world and I wouldn't be looking to do her mother in.

I looked into the mirror. Iris was chewing on her handkerchief. I nudged Ted's knee.

'It's probably nothing, Iss, you know that, don't you. And if Ted's made her see sense, well that's worth a sleepless night or two, wouldn't you say.'

She looked at me, with a weary look, like I was a stranger.

'You got that list of what she was wearing?' she asked Ted.

He put his hand to his head. 'Jesus, I forgot.'

'For Christ's sake, Ted.' She took out a neat little lady's pen and the photograph from her handbag and prepared to write. 'Well, come on, then.'

Ted squirmed in his seat. 'Jeans. Blue. A red top, that dark one, the one you gave her last Christmas, I think. I don't know. I wasn't paying attention.'

'Anything else?'

Ted shook his head. 'The last thing I saw was her tearing down the path, throwing one of my weatherproofs over her shoulders.'

'Which one?'

'The yellow, the one with the tear in the pocket.'

I knew it. As soon as she asked the question, I knew it. The yellow. Christ, the yellow.

Iris wrote it down. I could hear the pen moving across, scratches on my heart.

'That's good,' she said. 'Someone must have seen her in that. You can see those things a mile off.'

We drove to Wareham, him with his thoughts, Iris with hers, me with mine. How I kept on the road I don't know; instinct, I suppose, because I don't remember a single second when I was conscious of driving. Miranda out in the rain, Miranda in one of Ted's yellow oilskins, Miranda howling by the edge of the cliff. It couldn't have been Miranda. Miranda was twenty-two. Audrey was two years over fifty. You can't do that, not even when they're wrapped up, mistake a young woman like that for a middle-aged one. Everything about them is different. They walk differently, they stand differently. Even the aura around them is different. I couldn't have killed Miranda. I just couldn't. She was my girl even if she wasn't. I couldn't have killed Miranda. That wasn't part of the plan at all.

# Three

Originally the taxi business had belonged to Audrey's dad. There'd been three of us, Gil, me and quite some time later Ian Newdick (yes, I know). It was a good little business, built up over the years; the army camp, the holiday-makers, people like old Mrs Poke Nose with her weekly trip to the hairdressers, we had a fair mixture. When Gil fell ill, I took over running the business, married his daughter too. Well, it kept everything nice and simple, screwing the whole family. Then four years ago, Ian left and set up on his own. There was no call for that. It was ungrateful, considering how Gil and I had taken him in under our wing. When he first mooted it, I went round to try and make him see reason, his wife Bettina smirking at me behind one of those Tina Turner coffee mugs. Simply the best, my agitated arse. I pointed out, not unreasonably, that two taxi firms in a backwater like this did not make a whole lot of economic how's-your-father, but he wasn't having any of it. 'Best to go our separate ways,' he said, putting his hands round his wife's shoulders, all lovey dovey, as if they did that sort of filth in private.

'We're going to be a husband and wife team, aren't we, Tina,' he announced.

A husband and wife team! I'd never heard of anything so perverted in my life. Imagine Audrey driving the Vanden Plas, spouting God-knows-what claptrap to my customers. Anyway, that's what happened. Ian bought himself a people-carrier, one of those cars that look like a suppository on wheels, and a four-door Hitachi. Don't ask me where they got the money from. They had little uniforms made too, light grey, with a suit and tie for him and a suit with a perky little grey beret for her, to set off her perky little tits. Fair made me puke, seeing them drive around Dorset got up like Lord and Lady Fauntleroy.

In the beginning I put in a little retaliation, late-night bookings that vanished into thin air, nails in the tyres, the odd Maris Piper shoved up the exhaust, but after a while it began to drag, and besides, even Police Constable Corn-Plaster was getting suspicious. The unwarrantable thing was that in no time at all their business started to take off, while mine started to flat-line. There was bugger all I could do about it. It were the twin peaks that were doing for me, simple as that.

Then I had a brainwave. Miranda. Tina had a nice enough pair, but compared with Miranda's they were just grassy knolls, some place to rest your rifle on. Miranda's were more like a ski jump. You got vertigo just looking at them. Matter of fact Miranda had everything, looks, length, hair like Jane Russell stretched out on a bale of straw. She had a laugh that made you feel ten years younger and a smile that dropped off another five. She was bright with it, clued-up, interested, seven GCSEs under her twenty-four-inch belt and a clutch control that could move from second to third like a Vaselined finger slipping up your alimentary canal. Tina changed gears like she was stuffing the Christmas turkey, all fists and elbows. You couldn't talk to Tina, you wouldn't want to. Tina was thick. You'd cop an eyeful, then stare out the window wondering how many brake pads she got through in a week, while with Miranda you'd be leaning back, laughing and joking, listening to a kind of young, strong, feminine sense that made you wonder why the world wasn't full of Mirandas. Only Mirandas. So, I offered her a job, straight up. No poxy uniform; she could wear what she bloody liked, an unwashed fertilizer bag if that's what took her fancy, it wouldn't have made any difference. I bought a second car, a silver Renault 25, classy, nice and quiet, stuck her in the driving seat. The Deadwood Stage I called it, driven by the smartest crack of the whip this side of Purbeck.

They couldn't jump in quick enough. It wasn't just her looks. It was the way she did it all, held the door open, leant over to buckle the old ones in, *talked* to them. They'd tell her *everything*, man trouble, woman trouble, little Algy running with the wrong crowd, out it would all come, and she'd joke and sympathize, even offer advice. I ask you, a twenty-two-year-old kid offering advice! Six months in and the Newdicks were walking around looking like they'd had something painful inserted the wrong way up. I was grinning all the way round the back of my head.

Didn't last, of course. You can guess why. Audrey. Audrey didn't like Miranda. Not surprising that, because the truth was Audrey didn't like most people. It's what attracted me to her in the first place, all that acid in the battery. Miranda she didn't like for a number of reasons. Number one: Miranda was good-looking; number two,

Miranda was popular. But the big one, the ten-inch spanner in the works, was that as far as I was concerned, Miranda was a temptation too far. Or rather too near. The seventh month in and the Sunday after Miranda and me had sat up till dawn, sharing a bottle of bubbly after working a late-night wedding party, Audrey put her foot down. Miranda had to go. I couldn't tell her that as far as leg-over was concerned, Miranda was strictly off limits.

'Look,' I said, 'you deal with her, if you want to. I'll keep well away. But don't let's get rid of her, I beg you. She's a fucking goldmine. There's nothing between us, Audrey, I swear on my mother's grave. Never will be.'

She looked at me, one of those cold hard stares that make you think of fish heads.

'I didn't know you had a mother,' she said. 'By the end of the month, Al. I mean it.'

So I got rid of her. Why? The business, the double garage, the Vanden Plas, well they were all in Audrey's name, weren't they. Her father, bless him, had left the lot to her. All I had was the house, and even that wasn't all mine. In my mum's day it was on a fifty-year lease. When we bought the lease out, it was Audrey's money that paid for it. So the house was in her name too. My mum's bungalow! So, I had no choice. Miranda got the chop. But not quite. I started to meet her on the q.t. She welcomed it. I'd drive out to the disused camping site and park round the back. I had an old caravan there, set in one of Alan Sparrow's fields that ran down to the cliff. It was a good place for assignations. I'd make a pot of tea, get out the biscuits, and wait for her to turn up. She'd tell me all her troubles, I'd tell her mine. We understood each other. Iss was wrong. Kim Stokie could touch her like no other, she said. Made her come alive. Twinkled her eyes when she said it, made us both laugh. A chip off the old block, I thought. And now, thanks to me, it looked like she was never going to come alive again. Never going to do nothing again, except haunt me.

I waited by the car while Iss and Ted went inside. Could hardly light the cigarette my hand was shaking that bad. I tried to picture it again, the woman bawling her eyes out, looking out over the cliff, the yellow oilskin flapping in the wind, me rushing towards her, without thinking. Did I notice anything, her hair, her legs, her build? Come to think of it, when I pushed her, she did seem, what, *firmer* than what I'd expected. It was only the back, and after she'd gone I didn't pay it any attention. But yes, there was a bit of muscle on those shoulder blades. Audrey doesn't have muscle. Audrey has something resembling Trex pastry.

They came out about an hour later, Ted taking great gulps of air like he was drowning. Perhaps he was. Iss was more composed. She walked straight over, sat in the front and lit up. Normally I don't allow that sort of thing. Smoking in the Vanden Plas is strictly verboten, but I didn't say anything. Time and place and all that.

'What he say?' I asked, half dreading the answer. She half turned in the seat.

'Never mind that. Out with it?'

'Out with what?' Before she could reply Ted opened the rear door and slid in. His breath was short. He was taking it bad.

'What he say?' I repeated. 'Anything useful?'

Ted blew his nose, stuffed the tissue in my side pocket. I didn't appreciate that. His daughter might have gone missing but that was no reason for him to litter the car with snot rags.

'He's coming over, later this afternoon. Take a few statements, make a few inquiries. They'll ask around Wool station too, see if anyone saw her there.'

'That's good. What about the camp, the NAAFI?'

'That's not really his territory. First on the agenda is that bastard Kim. If he's done anything . . .'

I tried to reassure him.

'To be fair, Ted, Kim might have a bit of a temper on him, but he's never used it on a woman.'

'There's always a first time.' He tapped me on the shoulder. 'He'll probably want to talk to you too.'

'Me?'

'You and Audrey. Living next door.'

'Right. Yes. Of course.'

We drove back in silence. I had some thinking to do. OK, it wasn't Audrey I had pushed off. It was someone else. And Miranda had gone missing. I had to deal with all that as best I could. But there was another question that I hadn't asked myself before. If Audrey didn't go up to the Beacon, where did she go? What did she do, to have her coming back with her hair all wet and that grin on her face and her privates acting like they'd just been plugged into the mains?

When we got back, Iss wanted me to drop Ted off and then run her back to her place, but Ted insisted she went in with him. He didn't want to be left alone, poor sod. She fussed about in her handbag and as she climbed out, leant over and gave me a kiss on the cheek. Not quite like old times, but it brought back memories, her on her knees half out the seat.

'There's something digging in my back,' she said. 'Feels like one of those collapsible umbrellas or something.'

When they'd gone I put my hand down. It was a packet of fags with something scrawled in lipstick on the front.

'5.00 TA. CarP.' TA stood for tomorrow afternoon. CarP stood for the Caravan Park. It's where Iss and I used to meet up, all those years ago. Talk about scene of the crime.

I went back. Audrey was sat in front of the kitchen table peeling onions, a glass of whisky by her side.

'It's a bit early for that, isn't it?' I said.

'The longer it cooks, the better the taste,' she said.

'I didn't mean the soup, Audrey.'

'I know what you meant.' She swept the onions into a pan and turned to face me, her eyes a little shot. It wasn't her first. 'Well, how was he?'

'Well, his back's better, but he wasn't good. Miranda's disappeared. Went for a walk yesterday afternoon, and never came back. He's worried sick.'

'Maybe she's come unstuck at last.' She took a sip of satisfied whisky and walked into the front room.

'The funny thing is,' I called out, 'she went out the same time as you, around four. Wore the same clobber too. Yellow oilskin.'

'Half the village wear yellow oilskins. It's a bloody uniform round here.' I followed her in.

'The point is, Audrey, Ted's been to the police, reported

her missing, given a description as to what she was wearing and that.'

'And?'

'And they'll be asking everyone if they saw anyone wearing a yellow oilskin yesterday afternoon.'

'They'll have their little notebooks busy, then.'

'What I'm saying is, it would help them if you told them where you went. To eliminate wrong sightings.'

'Eliminate wrong sightings? My, aren't we the eager policeman today.' She swirled the whisky in her glass.

'Well? Are you going to tell them or not.'

'I might. Pour me another whisky.'

I poured her another whisky. There was a tension in the air, as if we were both walking on eggs.

'If you must know, I went up to the Beacon. Didn't stay long. It was too blowy.' She was staring at me as she said it. 'What about you?'

'What about me?'

'When I came back, the house was empty. I thought you'd gone to drown your sorrows.'

'It wasn't opening time, Audrey.'

'That's never stopped you before. So where did you go?'

'Nowhere special. I just stood in the road to see if I could see where you might have gone.'

'You weren't standing in the road when I came back.'

'No. I'd gone round the back.'

'What on earth for?'

'I was in a mood, Audrey.'

'Well, you snapped out of it pretty quick, didn't you?' She had that look in her eye again.

'Audrey.'

She flapped her dress between her legs.

'Draw the curtains,' she said.

This was getting silly. All through it, she kept looking at me as if we were performing in front of Wednesday karaoke night, rather than on the Easy-slumber Sofabed that pulled out in case we had unexpected visitors. Not that we ever did. Halfway through I seemed to lose direction, though she seemed happy enough. Afterwards, I had to sit up, to get my breath back. She lay sprawled out, her legs across mine, balancing the unfinished whisky on her not inconsiderable stomach. Three thirty on a Tuesday afternoon. It didn't seem right.

'So, what do you want me to say, Al?' she said, taking a satisfied sip. 'To the police?'

'I don't want you to say anything. There's not a lot *to* say is there?'

'Well, we had a row, both went out, me in a yellow oilskin, you in a mood. There's that.'

'I don't see what the row's got to do with it.'

'I don't see what's any of it's got to do with it. I mean I'm hardly Miranda's double, am I?' She eased her body up and shifted her legs apart. I tried not to look.

'Well, when you're covered up in a raincoat . . .'

'What, she becomes fatter or I become thinner?'

'Well, at a distance, you're just a human being, Audrey, like Miranda, like all of us.'

'And close up, Al, what am I then?'

'Audrey, what is this?'

'Nothing. I just don't like all and sundry knowing our

little ways. Did you see anyone when you were out, looking for me, in your mood.'

'No, did you?'

Instead of answering she reached out and patted poor old Tonto, like it was a pet. It was Audrey who had given it the name Tonto, because she said it led a man who never wanted to show his real face, and the name had stuck. A neat explanation, though I always thought it was because I once shouted out Hi Ho, Silver! in the back of her dad's Humber Snipe. That of course was the Lone Ranger, but she was never very good at westerns, Audrey.

'We'll keep it to ourselves, then, shall we?' she said. 'This place is too much like a goldfish bowl as it is. Mouths opening, mouths closing.' She leant across and stuck her tongue in my mouth, like she had a live eel in there. I thought I was going to choke. I pushed her off. She lay back, all loose and languid, and wiped her mouth.

'What I don't fully understand is . . .' I hesitated. It was a dangerous subject, considering what had been going on. I was loath to fan the flames.

'Yes, what?'

'Well, when you went out, I'd have thought a bit of you-know-what was the last thing you had on your mind. And yet, when I came back, you were . . .'

'In the mood?'

'Very much in the mood. More in the mood than . . .'

'I usually am.'

'You could say that.'

'I did say that.'

'The thing is, I was wondering, what it was that put you in that mood.'

'I bet you are. Find out what and you'd bottle it, if you could.' She laughed, as if she was remembering something.

'So, are you going to tell me?'

'Jesus, Al. This visit to the police station has turned you into a proper little Inspector Morse. No, I'm not going to tell you, simply 'cause there's nothing to tell. I went out angry, came back randy. That good enough?'

No it bloody wasn't, but I didn't say anything.

'Don't get your hopes up, though. It won't happen every afternoon, I can promise you that.'

'Experience would tell me that would be an unlikely occurrence.'

'But not an unpleasant one.'

'Unpleasant, no. Unsettling, yes. It's been two days in a row, now.' I leant forward, conspiratorially. People say things after a bit of the other, and we'd had quite a lot. 'Go on, Audrey, tell me the truth. Between you and me, where did you go, yesterday?'

She stood up, pulling her skirt back on. Mood change.

'I told you, Al. To the Beacon.'

'Why don't I believe you?'

'I don't know. Why don't you?'

Because I was there, pushing someone off it, that's why.

I went out to put the car away. There was a bag on the back floor. In his hurry to get away, Major Fortingall had left his running kit behind. That meant I'd have to take it up to the camp. I never liked going round there uninvited. Still, it might get me the return journey, one in the eye for the Newdicks.

I opened up the door and hauled it out, ready to put it in the boot. I don't know why, considering he told me what was in it, but I couldn't resist it, see what sort of pillock he was. As I zipped it open, they almost hit me in the face. They were crammed in so tight; black lace bras, frilly knickers, a snake's nest of stockings. Underneath lay another uniform, dark blue, all his little badges on the top pocket and underneath that more tart's clothes, short skirts and flimsy blouses, a bag of lipsticks and eyeliners, a pair of Mary Quant-type high heels, all black and white squares. Not a Nike in sight.

'Major, Major,' I tut-tutted, unwinding another bra from a pair of regulation socks. 'Privates on parade takes on a whole new meaning.'

I turned it in my hand. Take some filling, I thought, a bra like this. Behind me, someone coughed.

# Four

I don't know about you, but I hate surprises: surprise presents, surprise birthday parties, people jumping out of cakes, strippergrams, any of that nonsense. I mean whose benefit is it for? Not yours, not mine. It's the same with practical jokes. When I was a kid, there was always some joker putting flour bombs over the classroom door, stretching clingfilm over the bog, ducking you in the swimming pool, that sort of carry-on. My answer to it was quite simple. I kneed them in the nuts. They got the message.

Audrey wasn't averse to little bolts from the blue either; the crochet work she brought along on our honeymoon; the orange tan she got in Poole that glowed in the dark. Once she gave me a surprise do for my fortieth, when her old man was still around, in the village hall down the road. Told me I had to pick up some client there, and when I walked in, there they all were, Audrey and Gil, the Newdicks, the Grogans, the Stokies, half the village, glasses of Asti Spumante in their hands, warbling Happy Birthday. What a horrible song that Happy Birthday is, how horrible people look, their mouths gaping and smiling while singing it. Makes my flesh run cold, every time I hear it, like a death sentence read out in public, reminding you of all the time you've wasted, all the blind alleys you've run down, everything that's gone wrong in your life all wrapped up with presents and cards and lighted candles. Why don't they just throw a can of petrol over you and have done with it? At least that way you'd only have to endure it once. But no, the moment you walk through the door, out it comes and you have to stand there, pretending to enjoy it. That's another thing I don't like, not being prepared. I wouldn't have minded so much if I'd been told. I could have dealt with it then, got myself in the right frame of mind. But I wasn't. It was sprung on me without warning, another flour bomb over the lintel, another ducking. So I span round, ready to walk out that door and go on a three-day bender, and there she was, Miranda, standing right behind me. She was still just a kid, but she was, how should I say, advanced for her age, not just physically, but how she read the world and all its wicked thoughts.

'Don't,' she said, fixing me with that little-girl stare of hers.

'Don't what, darling?'

'I know what you're thinking. Don't do it. Stay here. Be good.'

It pulled me up that. I don't think anyone had ever asked me to do such a complicated thing before in my life. I tickled her under the chin.

'Anything for you, Monkey-face. You know that.'

So I stayed. And I was good. God was I good. I flirted with all the ladies and joked with all the men. I did my famous little dance routine, like what the Russians do, kicking out your legs with your arms folded, while they stood round, clapping. I made a little speech and at the end of it gave Audrey a great big kiss. I was the life and soul, but Jesus it was hard work. I must have sweated off a pound and a half of suet, my nerves were that bad. When we were back home, flat out in the dark, one more present to go, Audrey leant across and said, 'Well, Alfred Greenwood. You seemed to have enjoyed yourself.' I put my lips to her ear.

'That, Audrey,' I whispered, 'was the worst fucking evening in my entire fucking life,' and she laughed and snuggled up close, the flab of her arm across my face, and it came to me then, the loathing I had for her, every wobbling inch. It was like my head was suddenly clear, full of a pure, brilliant understanding, and I joined in the merriment, my mouth half smothered, laughing even louder, the whole bed, the whole house, the whole fucking world shaking with the clear crystal rage of it. I think I knew then, deep down somewhere, what the outcome was going to have to be. Her or me. Me or her.

Audrey didn't give me many more surprises after that, until that last one laid out by the fire. Now they seemed to be coming thick and fast.

I whipped round. Kim Stokie was leant up over the garden fence. Inside, Gaynor, his wife, was staring at me from under her peroxide crew cut, out the kitchen window, her pink, rubber-gloved arms thrashing about in the sink. Looked like she was drowning kittens. She had a wall eye, Gaynor, one that never went anywhere, a bit like its owner. Once carried over the threshold ten years ago, a bride of eighteen, Gaynor had never set foot outside the house again. She got a disability allowance, but Kim had to do everything, walk the dog, do the shopping, even go on holiday on his ownsome. I resented that. Audrey had complaints like the Common Prayer Book, one for every day of the year, but never one as agreeable as that. Come holiday time, Audrey always managed to rally round, until she got there, that is. Then normal service would be resumed, only eight floors up with added VAT.

'I want a word with you, Al,' he said.

'Yeah?' I threw the bra down quick, shut the door. I didn't think he'd seen anything, but you could never tell with Kim. He was a cunning little c. 'What is it? The Peugeot still playing up?' I crossed over. 'You heard about Miranda? Ted Grogan's worried sick.'

He shrugged it off. 'That'll teach him to stick his dick in where it ain't wanted, won't it? She's buggered off, that's all. Sooner or later she'll bugger back.'

He glared at me, willing me to takes sides. I said nothing.

'Any road, I ain't here to talk about Mandy.' He waggled one of his fingers at me. He was slow, but he had big red hands, raw like a skinned fish.

'Audrey came round yesterday. In a terrible state she were.'

'Audrey?'

'In a terrible state, Gaynor said.'

'You weren't there then?'

'Course I wasn't. I was working.'

'Right.' Working in Kim's dictionary had a very broad definition. 'When was this?'

'In the afternoon. Wanted to know if we had any whisky. Desperate, Gaynor said she was, like a dog with rabies. Half a bottle she borrowed off of us, half a bottle.

I don't like it, people coming round uninvited. Gaynor don't like it neither, all the dirt she brung in. What Audrey need half a bottle of whisky for? She getting sloshed in the afternoons now?'

'No, of course not,' I protested, though even as I said it, I was thinking he might have a point. Come to think of it, he did have a point. Audrey was putting it away rather consistently these days, afternoons included. Late afternoons I'll give you, but afternoons nevertheless. My mind being on other matters, I hadn't really noticed. It was an interesting development. Putting it away too much leads to all sorts of unpleasant consequences: loss of appetite, self-esteem issues, the odd headlong plunge from the top of the stairs. Maybe a two-storey bungalow would be the answer to my problem. Get it built, have Audrey come a cropper, bury her and sue the builders for negligence. I'd get a lot of sympathy for that. I could hear myself now, all poised and pious. 'She wanted a better view, and now she's got the best view of all, from heaven.' I dug my hand into my back pocket and brought out my wallet. He shook his head.

'It's not about the money.' As if. With Kim, it's always about the money.

'I know it isn't, but I'm with you on this one. I'll be frank, Kim. I have been a bit worried about Audrey recently. She's that age. I've suggested she see the doctor but . . .' I shrugged the male shrug. He nodded in sympathy. 'Go on, tell me, how much?'

You could see his mind ticking over. Ten pound for the whisky, something added on for the mental aggravation, not too much, but not too little.

'Fifteen should do it.'

'Let's call it twenty. Have one on me. Tell Gaynor I'm sorry.'

Kim smiled broadly. He has a peculiarly flat face. Rumour has it his dad had fetched him one with the steam iron once when he was a toddler. Makes sense to me.

'You going lobster-potting this week? I'll give you a hand if you like, if I'm free.' I still wanted to get out to that cliff.

'Wednesday. Wednesday morning. About six thirty.'

'I'll be there. And if you hear from Miranda,' I added, 'let me know, eh? She's a good kid.' His face changed abruptly.

'Good kid! You don't know the half of it,' he snorted and stomped back into the house.

I stood there watching after him. There was something in the slouch of his shoulders, like a man who's had his life pulled out from under him. What didn't I know? Miranda told me everything. Those afternoons in the caravan, I'd felt almost human, like I was connecting with someone at last. Religion, politics, I even turned her on to Leonard Cohen; 'Suzanne', 'Bird on the Wire', 'Songs of Love and Hate', she was like me, she liked a bit of a dirge, liked all that dark swirling underneath the surface. Things running sweetly wasn't really in our make-up. We needed something else. She knew all about me, fishing out of territorial waters, and she understood. She once asked me, what makes us cross the line. I took hold of her finger and placed it on my wrist.

'Because of that,' I said, ''cause we want to feel it racing through us,' and she nodded. We, what's the word, resonated. And now Kim was telling me, what, that I didn't know her, my Miranda?

Audrey was standing in the doorway. I glanced back to the bag in the car. It wouldn't be a problem, but I'd rather she didn't see it. She had the phone in her hand.

'You got a caller,' she said. 'That major you picked up this morning.' She put her hand over the phone. 'Butter him up a bit, Al. You never know, miracles might happen. He might put more business your way. Sod Ian. We need the money.' She pushed the phone into my hand. 'I'm off out. Will you be here when I come back?'

I nodded, then shook my head. I didn't know where I would be. A mere twenty-four hours had gone by and I was beginning to feel the strain. One murder, God knows how many paddles upstream and Miranda missing. And I was still no nearer to finishing the old girl off. Further away if anything. Audrey half turned as I walked by, her fingers patting my backside as I went in. I heard her humming to herself as she started down the road. Jesus, bring on the bromide. I cleared my throat.

'Major Fortingall. How nice to hear from you. Are you requiring a lift back to Wool station?'

'Never mind that. Do you have it?'

'Have what, Major?'

'My holdall. My running bag.'

'Your running bag?'

'Yes, I must have left it in your car.'

'Really?' I was enjoying this. I could imagine him squirming at the other end of the line.

'Yes. You put it on the back floor.' He was beginning to get impatient. I found myself breaking into a yawn.

'Pardon me. Yes, I did. But I don't think it's there now. I'll go and have a look. I won't be a moment.'

I put down the phone, went outside, sat on the step and lit a cigarette. The afternoon was bright and crisp, like it was hung out on a washing line, folds of green, patches of yellow, all clean and fresh in the summer breeze, everything in its place, the dome-shaped hill, the broad chalk path, the dip in the land where the cold sea lay. You wouldn't have thought there'd been a storm the day before, or that I pushed someone into the arms of their Maker at the height of it. I got up, opened up the rear door and picked up the bra and the Major's holdall and brought them inside. I took up the phone, walked into the bedroom and threw the bag on the bed.

'Sorry, Major, there's nothing there. I'm sure I saw you carrying it in. Perhaps someone's picked it up, on the base. You know what they're like there now, with unattended articles? You better pop round to security, before bomb disposal send in a robot to blow it up.'

He didn't appreciate the advice.

'Don't be ridiculous. I'm telling you, it's not here. I remember leaving it in your taxi.'

'Well, it isn't here now and it couldn't have been stolen. I keep the car locked at all times.' I unzipped the bag again, stirred the underwear with my fingers. 'This running gear inside? Anything particularly distinctive about it?'

'Distinctive, no, I don't think so. Just the usual things, trainers, shorts . . .' He came to a halt, fresh out of ideas. I threw him another lifeline.

'I did take the car to be valeted, after seeing you. I do that after most trips you know. Customers appreciate it. Could be the garage has it. I could ask them if you like?'

'I would. As quickly as possible. It's most inconvenient, my bag disappearing like this. I'm off on leave tomorrow.' There was rising panic in his voice. The idea of this lot wandering around unattended didn't appeal. Given that he'd brought it to the camp, it begged the question where he'd intended to wear it. Out on the firing range? In the privacy of the parade ground? Monday nights in the officers' mess could get a trifle tedious, I suppose.

'No worries on that score, Major Fortingall. I'm more than happy to bring it round to your living quarters if I do come across it. I wouldn't want to deprive you of your daily workout, even on holiday.' I could hear him jumping out of his seat.

'No! There's no need for that. I've got a spare set. Just leave me a message and I'll pick it up the next time I'm here.'

'Fine. If you just give me your number, I'll call you if it surfaces.'

He hesitated, thinking it through, not wanting anyone to know about the bag, desperate to get it back. Eventually he coughed up. Told me if I found it in the next two days not to call after eight. If I found it after that I wasn't to call him at all. He'd call me when he got back. A dead giveaway.

He rang off. I punched in the number. A woman's voice answered, young, friendly, plenty of bounce.

'Mrs Fortingall?'

'Speaking.'

'I wonder if I might leave a message for your husband, about something he's mislaid.'

'Mislaid?'

'Yes. My name's Greenwood. He thought he might have left his bag in my taxi. I'm afraid to say I haven't been able to locate it. If you could just pass the message on.'

'I'm sorry, I'm not with you. I've been away for a couple of days. You mean his case, his work case?'

'No, no. His bag.'

'Bag? What sort of bag?' Her voice had changed. Hints of the Spanish Inquisition.

'Just a bag. Full of running gear.'

'Running?' Time for the thumbscrews.

'That's what he told me. He was going running after his appointment.'

'Running?' She was beginning to repeat herself, bless her little cotton socks. 'I'm the one who goes running.' A jogger. How unfortunate. Still, the same rule applied. As long as her bust passed muster.

'Could it be your bag, then?' Perhaps I had the Major down wrong after all.

'No. Mine is in the hall. I'm just about to do my daily stint.'

'And a very nice day it is for it, Mrs Fortingall. I wish I had the time to do the same. Nothing nicer, jogging along with a fresh sea breeze in your face. Tell your husband if anything does turn up, I'll drop it round. The officers' barracks is it, just off the main road?'

'Chevening Road. Number thirty-two. I'm sure he'd be very grateful.'

Oh, he'd be grateful all right.

I killed the call. Poor Mrs Fortingall. She didn't deserve this sort of treatment. I hauled the bag onto the bed to take a closer look. I was looking for some sort of financial return here, I'll be frank. I tipped it all out on the bed: six bras, six pairs of knickers, three ribbed jerseys, a clutch of T-shirts, fancy tights, a couple of those three-quarter-length numbers that stop halfway up the thigh, one fish-net, another with little black butterflies running loose. Ooh-la-la. There was one top, scooped with a dinky bow on the front that reminded me of Miranda. She had worn something very like it, the last time we were in the caravan. That was what, four weeks before all this kicked off. I'd just made my mind up about Audrey, the how and the when, ticking through the ramifications, any potential problems, and wasn't my normal self. Miranda had been in a bit of a state too. She'd sat and eaten a whole packet of biscuits, talking ten to the dozen. I'd found it difficult to concentrate, looking out the window to where the fields ran down to the cliff. It wasn't all that far to the spot where I planned to do it.

She'd been full of questions that afternoon. Did I regret not having any more children? How did we both feel, Carol living on the other side of the world? She admired Carol for doing that, for doing what she had to do, even though she understood it must have been difficult for her, leaving us behind. Though I didn't say it, I remember thinking that I didn't think it had been difficult for Carol at all. I had always thought that Carol had hung around Earl's Court just so that she could nab the first half-decent Australian willing and fuck off out of it, to Sydney or Melbourne or wherever he came from. It was deliberate. You only had to look at the boyfriends she had, Australians, Canadians, that twerp from New Zealand who worshipped Tolkien. Only one Brit among them, and he fell off a mountain.

Single children, that's what Miranda had been on about that day. Questions, questions. Carol, didn't she run off with a married man at the end? No, he wasn't married. He was *about* to be married.

'Still, the principle was the same, wasn't it,' she had insisted. 'I mean, it must have upset you.'

I could see where this was going. I put my hand on hers. It felt good, being a father figure, giving advice.

'Miranda, sweetheart, you might want to run off with Kim, but believe me, Kim will never leave, whatever you promise him. He can't. I'm not talking about Gaynor, here. I'm talking about Kim, his make-up, who he is. He's about as capable of leaving this place as one of his lobsters is of picking up his shell and strolling out of the pot.'

'I know that,' she said. 'I've always known that.' Her eyes were all wet of a sudden. She took out a handkerchief, one of the ones I'd given her for her eighteenth, the golden embroidered $\mathcal{M}$ in the corner, blew her nose.

'God,' I said. 'Look at us, sitting in this poxy caravan, me knocking on fifty, you nearly twenty-three, staring at the outside world like we're serving a prison sentence.'

'Perhaps we are,' she replied. 'Perhaps it's time to

break out, drug that guard, jump over that wall, start a new life in Brazil or New South Wales.'

She got up and started to rinse out the cups. I could have kissed her. I could have taken her in my arms, whirled her round right there and then, told her what I was going to do, set myself free, start over again. I'd take her with me, if she wanted. We could go together. I'd set her up, wherever she fancied. She could do what the fuck she liked, I wouldn't mind. I'd look after her that's all, watch her back. But I didn't say anything. I took up a tea towel and started drying up, hanging the cups up on their little brass hooks.

'Not me, Monkey-face. Brazil? I wouldn't know where to begin.'

'What, with all those half-naked women parading up and down the Copacabana?'

I put my finger to my lips, like I was in a bad play.

'Hush your mouth. Audrey will hear you. She's got special antennae for words like that, like a Scottish mosquito looking for campers. Half-naked women! I'm not even allowed to buy the *Sun* any more,' and she laughed, Miranda's laugh, her whole body laughing with her, limbs and eyes, everything running like an engine with the throttle open. It made you want to jump on board, just to feel its power whipping through.

I was smiling at the memory of it, when something poking out the inside pocket of the holdall caught my eye. A handkerchief, a little white handkerchief, the thread of the monogram shining like a beacon. I pulled it half out, I realized that there was something wrapped up inside, a brooch maybe or an earring. I unfolded it. In the middle lay one of those vicious-looking wisdom teeth, with a bloody great fork at the end like a pulled mandrake root, the ends all dark with dried blood and bits of flesh. It had scratches round the side where a pair of pliers had wrenched it out. It ponged a bit too. Looked more at home in the Tower of London than tucked up in Irish linen.

'Al. Where the hell are you?'

Jesus Christ! I slipped it into my pocket, stuffed the clothes back and rammed the bag under the bed. I sat back, trying to look casual, when I noticed the black bra, sat up on the other side of the counterpane, like a tarantula ready to leap onto my gonads. I screwed it up and stuffed it into my pocket, the clasp catching on my wrist, but would it lie still? Every time I pushed it down, it sprang back up, like it had a life of its own.

'I'm in here,' I called out, finally putting it to rest. I could feel my heart hammering against my ribs. A tooth in one side, a bra in the other, and all the other gear tucked under the bed. It would take some explaining, a scenario like that, to someone like Audrey. She walked in. She looked put out.

'Taking a rest, Al? Stamina not what it was?'

I patted the old chest. Bang bang BANG Bang BANG Bang BANG. 'Just about to get changed. The pond needs checking. You're back early. I thought you were going for a walk.'

Audrey walked round the bed. Major Fortingall's bag bumped up against the back of my heel. In my right-hand pocket the black widow was re-asserting itself.

'I was, but then I remembered you said the police

would be coming round. I'd rather get it over with now than have them coming round God knows when. No telling what they might catch us doing.' She sat down, on the wrong side. In my pocket, spider woman was wriggling its naked way out of my pocket. For some reason Sigourney Weaver popped into my head.

'Besides,' she added, 'I don't want you seeing them on your own. You might say something foolish.'

'Audrey. I thought we agreed.'

'On what, exactly?'

'That we didn't see anything. That you didn't see anything. That I didn't see anything. That you went to the Beacon and I went looking for you. In a mood.'

Audrey sniffed.

'Is that what we agreed? It all seems very complicated to me, Al. I don't see why we have to say anything about either of us going out at all. After all we *didn't* see anything, did we? I certainly didn't.'

There it was again, that look on her face, defying me to not believe her. Where did she bloody go? I tried to sound reasonable.

'Yes, but someone might have seen you up on the Beacon. The path's very exposed. You don't want to be caught out in a lie, Audrey.'

'Oh no, that would never do.' She patted my knee. 'All right, then. If it makes you happy. I went out. You went out. Neither of us saw anything. Pity we didn't go out hand in hand though, then we'd both have alibis.'

'We don't need alibis. We're not under suspicion here.'

'Not yet.'

'What do you mean?'

'I don't know if you've noticed, but there's a lot of randy young men in this neck of the woods. All cooped up, all raring to go. An attractive young woman in the vicinity, out on her own, disappearing into thin air?'

'What, you think . . . ?'

'I don't think anything Al. I'm just saying. If she can't be found, then they'll start looking. And if they find anything untoward, clothing, jewellery, they'll start questioning again, probing. So, are you happy, being out?'

'I was out. No point in denying it.'

'If you say so.' She paused, her head twisting, looking down.

'What's that?'

It was said lightly, but I knew it was too late, the moment I felt her fingers on its tentacles.

'What's what?'

'This.' She pulled it out slowly, like it was attached to my liver.

She dangled it in front of my nose. Others had done the same, but not under quite the same circumstances. I was in for it now.

'Now, now, Audrey. Don't jump to any hasty conclusions. It's not what you think.'

'It's a black bra, that's what I think it is, size . . . 36, D-cup, see? Not many of these floating around the village. Not on any washing lines I've seen.'

'People leave the strangest things in taxis,' I said. 'You know that. Remember that chap who left his leg on the rear window. And the couple from Dagenham who . . .'

'Yes, yes, I remember them all.' She sniffed it. 'It's been washed.'

'Has it?'

'Yes.' Her face softened. 'On the back seat, was it?' I shook my head, trying to keep it as close to the truth as possible.

'On the floor, under the front seat. I thought, it might have dropped out that Major's bag, that's where he put it. Though what he was doing with it, I tremble to think. Still, you never know with these army types.'

'Hmm.' She handed it back. 'OK.'

'What?'

'I believe you. You found it in the taxi. I believe you. Is that so surprising?'

'Well, now you come to mention it, yes. A fancy bra in my pocket, one like this, I thought you would have jumped to conclusions.'

'I have. I've jumped to the conclusion that you're telling the truth. And you know why? Because it's washed, Al. Recently washed, recently tumble-dried. If you'd had a hand in it, so to speak, it would have come off a recent body. It would have smelt, smelt of perfume, body odour, your tobacco-stained drool. But it doesn't. Al's been a good boy for a change.' She handed it back, at a distance like I'd caught a conger eel off Kim's boat. 'So what are you going to do with it?'

'I'm not sure.' I turned it in my hands as if it was the most natural thing in the world. It was a strangely liberating experience, fondling a young woman's under-garment in front of her. 'Hang it from the rear-view mirror? Put a note up in the post office, "One black bra for sale, recently washed and tumble-dried"? Perhaps you'd care to model it.'

'Don't push it, Al. I've got a better idea.'

'Oh?'

'Put it in the post. Mail it to Ian. Write a little note with it, something to the effect of "Your wife left this behind last trip. Worth every penny, signed, A Grateful Customer". He won't like that.'

'That's a very twisted thought, Audrey.'

'It is rather, isn't it. It might affect their business, if he thought she was carrying on behind his back. And if he does start voicing suspicions, she's got a terrible temper on her. Nearly as bad as mine.'

I couldn't let that one go. 'No one's is like yours Audrey. Yours is of burnished steel forged in the fiery furnaces of Valhalla. Siegfried himself couldn't cut through it, not even if Brünnhilde had laid herself out on a plate in all her glory.'

'I thought she did lay herself out on a plate in all her glory.'

'On a rock, Audrey, surrounded by fire, gas mark eight. And she didn't exactly lay herself out. Her dad did.'

'He'd fit in down here, then. And then what happens?'

'Siegfried gets the goods. Has his Teutonic way with her. Doesn't do him any favours, though. This other bird slips him one in his drink, date-rapes him and he ends up chopped liver. It's surprisingly modern, the Ring.'

I didn't get changed. The pond didn't get cleaned. The police didn't come. We just sat in the front room, Audrey and me, waiting for the sun to go down. Mrs Poke Nose rang, to remind me of her trip to Wareham the next day, eleven forty-five sharp, her voice all clipped and officious, like she had a stop watch in her hand. She needed me bright and sparkling. Yes, Mrs Poke Nose. No, Mrs Poke Nose. Multi drills and cotton swabs and saliva drains stuck in the Poke Nose mouth. That would make a nice change. I put my hand in my pocket, touched the mystery.

At around seven Mrs Burgess rang to say they weren't going to Dorchester after all. Brian had a tummy upset. I'd forgotten all about them, to be honest, but they didn't know that. It pisses me off, when people do that, blow you out the water at such short notice. No consideration for the working man, that's the trouble with the world today.

'It's very late in the day to be cancelling, Mrs Burgess,' I told her. 'I've a living to make here, you know.'

'Brian can't help developing a tummy upset, Mr Greenwood,' she said, like she was sitting on a horse, looking down her nose at me.

'Well, perhaps next time you could ask him to develop it a little earlier, when I haven't turned down three other bookings, all with their bowels in perfect working order. I am sure the restaurant is of the same frame of mind. One upset tummy, two upset businesses. Smells bad to me.' I slammed the phone down.

'Nice,' Audrey commented, her voice melodic in the gloom. 'A very nice touch you have with your customers.'

'Fuck the customers, Audrey. They've no right.'

'That could be your motto, Al, "Fuck the Customers". You could paint it on the side of the Vanden Plas. It would be what is known in marketing jargon as your USP.'

Later she got out a bottle of plonk and we drank it down, glass by glass without saying a word. We didn't want dinner. We didn't want sex. We didn't want anything, not even a row. Every now and again I would look across to where she sat, looking at her nails, examining her ankles, staring out the window over to that bloody hill. Something had changed between us, but it was hard to say what. It was like I felt I could never take her unawares again, that killing her now would be twice as difficult, not in the aftermath but in the act itself. Push her off a cliff? I wouldn't get within a hundred yards. Even if I could, it wouldn't do any good. I couldn't do her in now, not until I knew where she'd been that afternoon. I tried to imagine what it was that she had done, where she had gone in that three-quarters of an hour that she'd have to lie to me about. It was galling to admit, but it prolonged her life, this not knowing. Not simply curiosity, you understand, but self-protection. It wasn't safe, me working to finish her off in total ignorance. If only she had gone to the Beacon. If only I had pushed her off, then none of this would have mattered. But I hadn't and it did. It mattered a lot. It mattered almost as much as Miranda.

I lay awake that night, staring at the Artexed ceiling, my mind spinning round and round, in and out, Audrey by my side, back in one of her long nightgowns, sleeping slow and regular, without a care in the world. Whatever she'd done, wherever she'd been, it didn't seem to be bothering her. How fair was that? I was the one taking all the risks, but where was the reward? A man plans his life, does the best he can, and then fate steps in and knocks it all to pieces. Fate or Audrey, it was hard to tell which. But I knew which I preferred.

# Five

In the morning, before Audrey was fully awake, I pulled on my old clothes and went outside to give the pond the once-over. It had been bugging me all night. It had been two days since I'd looked at it.

The carp had been Audrey's present to me on our twentieth wedding anniversary, the only present from her I ever really took to. Watches, bracelets, a week in Alderney looking over the old prison camp, didn't mean nothing to me, but my two dorsal-finned treasures, well I'll always be grateful to her for that. She introduced me to a wonderful world that day.

She'd got me up early, fed me a glass of champagne and a plate of devilled kidneys, then, while I was still in a good mood, led me outside. We had a pond even then, but nothing in it to speak of, just a few reeds and a stone nymph in the middle with one kneecap missing.

'What am I out here for, my own?' I demanded. 'I know I promised to do the lawn, but fair's fair.'

'Look down,' she said, 'into the water,' and I did, and there they were, swimming back and forth, their blue reticulated backs, the deep orange red on their cheeks and flanks, the pure white of their heads, flashing past. There was a lustre to them, a depth to their colour, a lack of blemish, as if they had been given several coats of silk emulsion. They shone, all radiant, the loveliest things I had ever seen. I wanted to reach in and stroke them, feel them slip through my fingers.

'They're called Asagi,' she said proudly. 'A very traditional variety. I bought them in Poole last week. Top quality the man said, bred in Japan. Do you like them? They weren't cheap.' She was all nervous. Apparently Ian and Tina (we were still friends then) had thought them a terrible idea.

'Like them? Look at them, Audrey, look at them! This is inspiration on your part, down from the Gods, that's what this is. I could chuck you in with them, I could, they're so perfect,' and I grabbed her, pretending I was going to.

'Get off me, Al, you crazy man,' she protested, but she liked it, we both did, the tussle of old love.

Of course, back then, she didn't know what she had let us in for. She thought all she had to do was to chuck them in the pond, and that would be that, but I soon found out that it wasn't. I bought a book about them, read it through and through. They were pedigrees, my fish, not some poxy low-life happy to swim about in sewage. They had breeding. They had to be treated right.

The first thing I learnt was that carp are very prone to stress. Stands to reason really. Most beautiful things are. Film actresses, models, the blunt end of my penis. Stress leads to the carp's immune system breaking down. Stress a carp and he's likely to come out in gill rot and ulcers. To keep them stress-free, the water's got to be just right, the right consistency, kept at an even temperature of around 22 degrees centigrade. For that you need an in-line electric water-heater, and a probe to check it; then you need water pumps and air pumps and UV filters; you need to test the water every week for carbonate hardness and ammonia toxicity and you need to pass it through a vegetable filter to absorb the nitrates. Then you have to watch their feeding patterns, change their diet according to the seasons, and when it comes to cleaning the pond, or inspecting them for diseases, you have to learn how to handle them, making sure they don't get too frazzled. So there was a lot of work for me to do, reorganizing the pond, extending it, putting in the water-fall, installing the necessary pumps and filters. Cost a fair amount, but I didn't mind. Audrey didn't either. She loved the fish as much as I did, at least to begin with she did. Torvill and Dean I called them, on account of that pale blue on their backs, and the way they moved together, twisting and turning, over and under, like partners in an endless underwater ballet. But it was time-consuming. What with keeping the car looking spick and span, and seeing to their needs, I didn't have much time for indoors and anyway Audrey and me hadn't been getting on that brilliantly, not after Carol had fucked off to London in search of her swagman. Far from bringing us together, Torvill and Dean quickly drove us apart. Audrey began to resent it, the hours I was out there, and I admit it, I did spend a lot of time, watching them swim in and out of each other, so constant, so true.

'Look at you,' she said, after I came back in an evening's carp-gazing. 'All dreamy-eyed watching love's wet dream. What about looking at me for a change, paying me some attention? They're fish, for Christ's sake. I'm a human being. I walk, I talk, I do your ironing.'

'Yes, but you can't slip and slide like they can, Audrey. Aesthetically, you're not up to their level. Anyway, it's not true. I do look at you. I'm looking at you now.'

'You're staring at me, Al. It's not the same thing. It's all you do these days, stare at me. God knows what you're thinking.'

God knew all right. Luckily no one else did. Or so I hoped.

As soon as I got there, I knew I had been right to be concerned. Torvill's head was poking out the water, her mouth open, her gills flared. Dean was up the island, looking up Aphrodite's fundament, doing the same. Oxygen, or rather the lack of it. I checked the pump. There was a blockage in the filter. The water wasn't being aerated enough. I washed it through, washed all the filters through, scrubbed out the filter box and switched the pump back on.

'Sorry, my beauties,' I said, and by way of an apology, threw in a small lettuce head, and watched them nudge it round the pond, nibbling at the edges.

When I got back Audrey was busy at the kitchen table, dabbing droplets of perfume onto the Major's bra. She had her gardening gloves on. She'd put bits of grass in the cups too. That's one thing I'll say about Audrey. When she does something, she gives it one hundred and one per cent.

'This'll put the cat among the pigeons,' she said smiling. 'Tina uses this perfume all the time.'

'How do you know?'

'I helped Ian choose it for her, when we were still on speaking terms.' She put the stopper back in the Ma Griffe bottle. 'It was a birthday present.'

'A birthday present. A very prescient touch, Audrey. Have you done the note?'

'I have. Just as we said.' She giggled. 'I made it look a bit like Dr Holiday's. That'll teach him to examine me with cold hands. See?'

I looked over her shoulder. It did look a bit like Jimmy Shooter's handwriting, all sloping backwards, like it was about to keel over. Jimmy used to be the police doctor, until he ran into the back of them one night, a trifle worse for wear. They didn't prosecute, but they didn't use him again. If anything it made him hit the brandy and ginger that little bit harder. He missed the camaraderie. Good laugh, Dr Jimmy. One of the old school. You want six fried eggs for breakfast? Crack 'em open. You smoke forty Rothmans a day? Light up, chum. Feeling a bit low? Pop down to your local, get stuck in. Take an aspirin, that was his motto.

Audrey stuffed the brassiere into a small jiffy bag, patting it affectionately, like she was sending a surprise gift to a treasured grandchild. Even though I was a mite nervous, I couldn't help but admire her, the commitment she showed. I put my hand on her shoulder, and she pressed her head against it. Spite always brought the best out of her.

'I'm not saying I don't approve of your tactics, Audrey, but don't you think there might be a fatal flaw in this enterprise. Not to put too fine a point on it, Tina wouldn't be able to wear a bra like that, would she? She can't . . .' I weighed the other hand.

'Fill it, you mean?'

'Precisely.'

'I know that. You know that. Ian probably knows it, but it doesn't matter. All it needs is for doubt to set in. He's a possessive little squirt. He'll be driving along, thinking about it all day, wondering where she is, what's she doing, despite her protests of innocence, because of them, probably. And who knows how we might be able to fuel his suspicions in the days following. Besides, women like Tina often pad themselves out, especially if they're looking for advancement. It's the sort of thing she might do for the sake of the business.'

'That's possible,' I agreed. 'When I first saw her in that uniform of theirs, I thought that there was something not quite natural about her deportment. Remember me saying that? Go on then, let's give it a try. What we got to lose?'

She slipped the letter in and pressed the flap down.

'There. Next time you're in Wareham, pop it in the post.'

'I can do better than Wareham. I'm driving over to Dorchester later on. I'll stick it in one of the backstreet post boxes. I'm taking Mrs Blackstock to have her . . .' My voice trailed off.

'Yes?'

'Her teeth done.' I tapped my pocket. It was still there. 'Right. I'm off to get breakfast. Coffee's in the pot.'

I stepped out to get the bread rolls. Lucky I didn't have the parcel with me. Ian Newdick's people-carrier was bouncing down the lane, headlights full on. I despise that in a man, driving in broad daylight with your headlights on. It's all Sweden's fault with their poxy Volvos on permanent beam. They might have to stumble about in the dark for half the year but, guess what, the rest of us CAN SEE WHERE WE'RE GOING. Write that on your Scandinavian forehead.

He turned into the drive, stamping on the brakes, sending the raked gravel spurting over Audrey's flower-bed. She wouldn't like that. I heard the handbrake ratchet as he threw open the door and jumped out the car. The uniform wasn't looking so smart these days. The trousers were a little too shiny around the knees and the jacket pockets beginning to sag. He was tall, Ian, tall like a beanpole is tall, thin and knobbly. He had big ears too. He was waving his little peaked cap in the air, like he was trying to fend off a wasp.

'Al. I want a word with you.'

Another one. All I am trying to do is to get on with my life, and yet everywhere I turn, I find confrontations.

'Everyone wants a word with me these days, Ian. What's yours?'

'I'll tell you what mine is. I've had a complaint.'

'Tina's driving, you mean? Don't say I didn't warn you.'

'Don't get funny with me. Major Fortingall. You picked him up from the station yesterday.'

'Helping you out if I remember, not that I got any thanks for doing so.'

'He says you've stolen his running bag.'

'I've done what?'

'He says he left this holdall of his in your car and that for some reason you're refusing to give it back. So he's rung up to complain. Half an hour on the phone. Says you were sarky with it, too. He's threatening to go to the police.'

'Let him. I don't care. Think they're interested in one poxy holdall?'

'Well I do. I have a reputation to consider, even if you haven't. I won't have you harming my business standing.'

He stood there breathing through his nose, spoiling for a fight. I thought of the package lying on the kitchen table. Following days? I could fuel his suspicions right now, before it had even dropped through his letter box.

'I was doing you a favour, Ian, that's all. If all I get is an earful, next time you come begging I mightn't be so amenable. Busy were you, the both of you?'

'Of course we were busy. I don't turn away regular trade like that in a hurry.'

'Only I thought I saw Tina's Hitachi on the back road that morning, backed up on the lay-by. Might not have been her, of course. But it looked like her car. I hooted as I went passed, but her head was down, like she was looking in the glove compartment, so I don't know for sure.'

That stopped him in his tracks. A regular venue for al fresco leg-over, that spot, though usually after the sun goes down, after the picnickers have left. Ian brushed the shoulders of his suit, like he'd discovered a fresh deposit of dandruff. I got to hand it to Audrey. She does have an encouragingly malignant little bonce on her.

'It couldn't have been Tina,' he said. 'She was over Winfrith way. Gone most of the morning.'

'Well, someone's got a car exactly like yours in the neighbourhood.' I made a conciliatory gesture. 'Look, Ian, I don't know if you know this Major Fortingbrass well, but he's an officious little bleeder. He was in a bad mood the moment I turned up, practically blamed me for his train running late. Didn't say nothing all journey. Left without a word of thanks. Now he's ringing up, telling all and sundry that he left his bag in my car, and I'm telling you he hasn't. I'm checking with the garage, just in case they took it out while they gave the inside the once-over, but other than that, it's nothing to do with me. If I find it, I'll call him. Tell him . . . tell him not to get his knickers in a twist. And I'll thank you to show me some consideration. I mean I ask you, what would I want with his poxy bag? Do I look like someone who wants to dress up in someone else's sweat-stained jockey shorts? Now, if you'll excuse me, I've got a business to run.'

He got back in and drove away, didn't say another word. Came here all pumped up, left all limp and deflated. That's a Newdick for you. Well, what else could he do? Search the house? Check the floorboards? Look under the bed? The bed! I'd forgotten what was still lying under there. I hadn't had a chance to move it, not with Audrey wandering around like the ghost of Christmas Pissed. Luckily she wasn't a great one for hoovering, certainly not in places where she had to bend down. She took a minimalist approach to all her domestic duties. When I bought her the dishwasher, the first thing she did was to chuck out everything you shouldn't put in it, copper-bottom saucepans, crystal glass, the bone-handled fish knives that had belonged to my mum. Out they went, the bloody lot of them. Polishing, cleaning, waxing the tiled hearth, it's all done under sufferance, save her precious doorstop, and all that's good for is tripping over. We got a blow-up colour photograph of Torvill and Dean over the fireplace, taken with an underwater camera that I bought off of Kim, and the number of times we've had words about the dust on the frame.

It was late by the time we finally sat down to it, but at least we were back to the usual regarding the menu. Fresh rolls, Irish butter and cherry jam for me, muesli and skimmed milk for her. She was dressed in her usual clothes too, brown with frills, what I call the Laura Gulag look. Ian Newdick's little package lay in the middle of the table like a vase of flowers, only heavier scented. I moved to touch it but she slapped my hand away.

'Not until you got your driver's gloves on, Al,' she said. 'No point in taking chances.'

I told her about what I said to Ian. She beamed with approval.

'What we want now is for you to get someone he doesn't know to ring in and book a taxi with them and insist on it being Tina. Not yet, though. In about a week's time. Know anyone?'

I thought for a moment. Wacko Jacko would do it for the right money. He'd enjoy it too. He'd have come across Ian at the base, but Ian wouldn't have spoken to him at any length. He'd have been how he always is once inside that uniform, stuck up.

'Yes, I do as a matter of fact.'

'Trustworthy?'

'Like a crab with one claw. But he'd keep his mouth shut if I told him what we were trying to do. It would appeal.'

Audrey grinned. To be honest, I was beginning to have second thoughts about it all. I had enough uncertainties to deal with without unclaimed underwear floating around. Better if I just pretended that I'd posted it, but slipped it back into the holdall. Besides, the Major had some explaining to do.

The gravel span again. Not Ian again. Audrey looked out the window.

'They're here,' she said.

'Who?'

'Who do you think?' She grabbed a tea towel, and picking up the parcel, shoved it into the top cupboard where I keep the fish food, before going to the front door.

'Remember what we agreed, all right?' I reminded her.

If she heard me she gave no reply. I heard the front door open, polite murmuring, feet being wiped.

'The police are here, dear,' she called out. I took a last swig of coffee and walked into the front room. I was pleased in a way. I wanted them to find Miranda safe and sound, take the weight off my shoulders. I didn't want her lying at the bottom of the cliff, her blood on my hands. There were two of them, PC Corn-Plaster, otherwise known as Police Constable Dave Stone, and DI Rump. I'd seen Rump a couple of times in the Spread Eagle, having

dinner with the wife. Waste of money in my opinion.
I mean you have dinner with the wife every evening. If
you're going to make an occasion of eating out, have it
with someone different for a change, someone you can
talk to.

'Adam Rump,' he said, pleasantly, holding out his
hand. 'Pleased to meet you.'

And you too, chum. He looked like a Rump, fleshy, big
round eyes on a big round head, feet planted on the floor
as if he had four of them. He wouldn't knock over in a
hurry. Audrey patted a cushion on the settee and turned
her Sunday smile on him. She'd smeared some lipstick
on too. Looked like she'd just sunk her teeth into a fresh
young virgin.

'Would you like some coffee, Inspector? I've some in
the pot, freshly brewed.' *I'd* got some in the pot freshly
brewed, she meant, but I let it go.

'That would be lovely, Mrs Greenwood. Two sugars if
you don't mind.'

Audrey rubbed her hands like she'd just won the
church raffle. I motioned him down. Corn-Plaster could
sit where he bloody liked. As Rump sat down he arranged
himself with his right hand. Funny how some men can
do that in public without batting an eyelid. What, they
think we can't see? Audrey returned with the lacquered
tray, two cups and saucers, and a plate of Peak Freans.
If I'd been him, I would have arrested her on the spot.

'You're fond of fish, then?' he said. She wasn't expecting small talk.

'I'm sorry?'

'I couldn't help noticing, the photograph on the wall,

the design on these cushions, the glass ornament on the sideboard. You must like them, to have something that size.'

'It was part of a pair,' I butted in, 'but Audrey dropped the other one. It's solid glass. How they got all the different colours in beats me.'

'It must weigh a bit.'

'The one that landed on my foot did. I bought them in Tenby. They were like compliments to the real-life specimens outdoors.'

He leant forward.

'You're a Koi man?'

'You bet I am.'

'What you got?'

'Two Asagi out the back. Torvill and Dean I call them, on account of their colour.'

'On account he's a bit touched,' Audrey added. DI Rump threw her a smile straight out the Klondike.

'I go for Kohaku mainly. Look.'

He dug out a picture from his wallet. There were two of them, in a net half out the water, red splotches dancing up their backs.

'I show those two. Lovely specimens. Look at that lovely patterned four-step. The one on the left won Bronze Koi of Dorset and Hampshire, last summer.'

I was a bit taken aback. Here was my girl missing, God knows what had happened to her, and here he was, going on about his fish. Still, I couldn't blame him in a way. They were gorgeous-looking, graceful and elegant yet somehow strong and dominant at the same time. What a combination. It made me a mite jealous. I handed the photo back. 'Brilliant,' I said. 'But you haven't come here to talk about fish.'

'More's the pity.' He slipped the picture back in his wallet. 'You probably know why we're here. Miranda Grogan? She hasn't been seen since Sunday afternoon, nor has she got in touch with anyone. She's not answering her mobile either. Understandably her parents are getting worried.'

'And you?'

'Frankly, I'm not that bothered. If I had an extra carp for every young woman who flies off without a moment's notice only to return a couple of days later, I'd have to build myself a new rock pool. Still it isn't like her, they say. Not to get in contact.'

'She's a very lively girl.' Audrey pressed her hands together, looking him straight in the eyes. We all knew what she meant. It wasn't right, her slagging Miranda off like that, when she wasn't here to defend herself. DI Rump took out a pencil and notepad, then plunged back in.

'She worked at the NAAFI, I understand.'

'That's right.'

'As you do, Mrs Greenwood.' Audrey screwed up her face. It's not something she likes to be reminded about.

'Just the weekends. I only do it really to help out. It's important for the village that we support the camp.'

'And this weekend?'

'I was there Saturday lunchtime.' He nodded, his eyes slipping over to the photograph above the mantelpiece. I'd mounted it in one of those classy frames, all gold and ornate, like a proper painting, with a spotlight shining down, Torvill and Dean staring out at you with their mouths open, like they were singing at the top of their voices.

'Is that a recent picture?' he asked.

'Eighteen months ago. They were well settled by then.'

'They take some time to acclimatize, don't they? Heated pond?'

'I wouldn't like to keep them in an unheated one.'

'It's surprising the number who do. Now, Miss Grogan. At the canteen, Mrs Greenwood, did she have any special friends there? Ones that her parents mightn't know of?'

'I don't think so, but I wouldn't know even if she did. She's regular staff. We volunteers don't mix socially.'

'Though she worked with you, Mr Greenwood, for a time, I understand. For about a year.' He tapped his pencil against the notepad. He was going through the motions, that's all.

'Seven months. Seven months and five days, to be exact.'

'What, she didn't suit?'

'No, she loved it here, the driving, the customers. Like feeding the fish too. Every Friday she'd feed them, when she come to pick up her money.'

'Well. It's a special time, isn't it. What do you feed them on?'

'Usual stuff. Paste, pellets. They like a lettuce.'

He nodded. 'Ever tried an orange?'

'An orange.'

'Yeah. Cut it in half so they can suck out the flesh.' Suck out the flesh. Sounded good to me. Audrey coughed. I got back on track.

'No, the job was fine. It was hours that didn't suit.

There's more things a young woman wants to do on a Friday night than ferry piss-heads back from Mr Singh's Curry House.'

'No trouble, then, while she was working here? No one showing an unhealthy interest in her? No one stalking her?'

'Not that I know of. I'm exaggerating the piss-heads, Inspector. What I meant was . . .'

'I know what you meant, Mr Greenwood. Just trying to get a clear picture of her, that's all, what sort of person she is, where she might have gone. Have you any ideas?'

'Hard to say. As my wife said, she's full of spirit. If she'd had a row with Ted, she might have buggered off to Dorchester or Wareham. She has any number of friends in Wareham, old school chums and that. And there's the health club. She worked there for a time, after she left school, the one that Pat Fowler manages. You must know it, Judes.'

'Judes? Oh yes, I know Judes. My wife's a member.'

I tried not to look disappointed. Sometimes I wonder if there's anyone under the age of thirty-five who isn't a member of a health club these days. What is it about this fetish for exercise? What's wrong with just a couple of hours' decent screwing every now and again?

'Yeah. Pat gives her special rates, I believe. He's known her since she was a kid, like all of us.'

'Are they particularly friendly?'

'Not that you'd notice. Miranda, she was friendly with everyone, know what I mean. That was her nature, bright and bubbly.'

'Was?'

'Is. I mean is. Why did I say that?'

'It's a common enough thing, Mr Greenwood. But you think it's unusual, for her to go off like this?'

'Yes, I do. She might fall out with her dad, but as you said, what daughter doesn't. She's a considerate girl. She wouldn't want to worry him. It's not in her nature.'

'So, you what – you think something's happened?'

'Stands to reason *something*'s happened.'

He nodded. Audrey prodded the biscuits at him.

'Have you managed to trace any of her movements, Inspector?'

Rump took a biscuit and broke it in half. He nibbled at the edges, a bit like Dean and the lettuce. He'd look better in the water, I thought, more at home.

'The cleaner at the Spread Eagle thought she might have seen her down by the bus shelter opposite, at around four thirty. She saw a yellow raincoat anyway, and we know that's what Miss Grogan was wearing. The bus had gone fifteen minutes earlier, so she might have been simply sheltering from the rain. Of course it might not have been her, though she thinks it was a woman, despite the poor visibility. So it's important we find who it was, to eliminate them from our inquiries.'

Eliminate them from our inquiries. I looked across at Audrey but she was nodding away like she was listening to Martin Luther Ghandi. 'I couldn't help noticing a yellow raincoat in the hall, Mrs Greenwood. You weren't out at all that afternoon, by any chance? You didn't see anything unusual?'

## T.J. Middleton

'Me? Goodness no. Al and I stayed in all day.'

I couldn't believe it! After what we'd agreed. She just kept on smiling.

'All day?'

'Absolutely. You'd have had to be mad to go out in that weather. Mad or in a mood. I did pop across to Gaynor's, though, to borrow some cooking provisions.' She put a hand on my knee. It felt like a branding iron. 'That was last Sunday, wasn't it, Al?'

I nodded. I felt queasy, like I'd just done six rounds on the Ferris wheel.

'Gaynor?' Rump questioned.

'Mrs Stokie next door.'

'Everything seemed OK there?'

'Well, she keeps a very tidy house, despite him being a fisherman.'

'Now, her parents have told us that Miranda is an acquaintance of *Mr* Stokie. Is that right?'

'Yes.' She brushed her knees again. 'They've been close for a number of years.'

'No point creeping around it, Audrey,' I put in. 'They've been seeing each other off and on for the last three years. Driving everyone mad with their carry-on. That's what Ted said the argument was about. She told him they were getting back together. He lost his rag. She walked out.'

'Exactly. Was his wife aware of this impending arrangement, do you know?'

'Gaynor?'

'Yes. Did she say anything to you about it, that afternoon?'

72

Audrey sniffed. 'Oh no. We're neighbours, but not friends. Her mental condition makes it difficult. Such a shame.'

Rump pursed his lips, nodding in acknowledgement. PC Corn-Plaster had obviously filled him in concerning the niceties of the Stokie household.

'Is she aware at all of her husband's relationship, would you say?'

'Everybody else is. I'm sure someone's found it incumbent on themselves to tell her.'

'And Miss Grogan. Is she a regular visitor there?'

'To their house? I don't think she's ever been inside. Kim and Miranda met outside you understand, him being married indoors. It wasn't a menagerie.' I tried not to laugh.

'What about when she was working with you, Mr Greenwood? Were you witness to any nearby assignations?'

'Not at all. She was very professional.'

'Even though she was seeing him then?'

'She might not have been. I think that was one of the times when it was off.'

'Was there someone else?'

'Well if there was, she didn't tell me. Anyway, she's not like that.' Audrey snorted.

'You must have got to know her pretty well, when she worked for you.'

'Well, we had different cars of course, so much of the time we were different ends of the county, but yes, we had the odd chat, waiting around for the next call.'

'And those late-night wedding parties,' Audrey put in

helpfully. 'Sometimes they didn't get back until two, three in the morning.'

'Did she confide in you at all? Things she might not have told her parents.'

'Nothing,' I lied. 'She wasn't like that. She's an open sort of girl. She doesn't have secrets.'

'Everybody has secrets, Mr Greenwood. Especially young women where their parents are concerned. Now last Sunday. You didn't do any business at all that day.'

I shook my head.

'Are Sundays always that quiet?'

'For the past few years, yes. I got competition, see. The Newdicks. There's two of them, they can cover more ground. You should ask them. They might have seen something. Anyway, I like taking Sunday off. It's the only time I get Audrey all to myself.'

'And last Sunday. Did you see Mr Stokie at all that day?'

'Not that I can remember. Have you questioned him at all?'

'We have.'

'And what does he say?'

Adam Rump looked at me as if I'd asked an impertinent question. Audrey stuck her oar in again.

'Oh, you mustn't mind my husband, Inspector. Where Miranda's concerned, he's very protective. He's her godfather.'

'Unofficially,' I added. 'We were all quite close at one time, us and the Grogans.'

DI Rump put his pad away. 'Well, I think that's all for

now. She'll probably turn up tomorrow a little worse for wear. Thank you for the tea, Mrs Greenwood.'

'Coffee.'

'Of course.' He got up, his eyes lingering on the photo. 'I don't suppose I could take a look at them? I've never seen Asagi in their natural surroundings.' Audrey looked put out.

'It would be my pleasure,' I said.

I led him outside, down the side path and round the back. It was a nice approach to the pond, the path lined with all the shells and driftwood that I'd brought back from the beach. It had that artistic look. We stood and looked. I was proud of the pond, the ferns and rocks and little waterfall. If you closed your eyes you could be in Shangri-la.

'I like your waterfall. It looks natural.'

'Took me a month to get it to fall right. First time it looked like someone was pissing in it.'

'The figurine's a nice touch too. Back to nature and all that. Pity about her kneecap.'

'I tried to stick a new one on with a bit of cement, but it made her look paraplegic. It's not what you want, is it, on a nymph.'

We gazed down. Torvill and Dean were doing the dip and dive. They'd heard us coming. He was mesmerized, the way they moved. Most people fill their pond with too many carp, don't give them enough room. Here, they had it all to themselves. We must have stood there a full five minutes, not saying a word. Then he straightened up, tapping his mouth with his forefinger.

'Do you belong to any club at all, Mr Greenwood?'

'No. I get enough socializing behind the wheel all day. Peace and quiet is what I crave. These two are all I need.'

'Still, a club can be quite useful, you know. Special rates on food, pond ware. I belong to the Carp Crusaders based in Poole and we can negotiate really good discounts. We've over forty members.'

'I didn't think of that.'

'And we all try and help each other out, in times of trouble. And there will be times of trouble, believe me, however hard you try. Look at me. Out of the blue, for no reason at all, one of my Goromo has developed dropsy.'

'Dropsy?'

'I'm pretty sure it's dropsy. It has all the early signs, swollen body, protruding eyes.'

Sounded like Audrey after a bottle and a half of Merlot.

'What do you do for that?'

'Not a lot you can do. It's usually fatal. Still, these look healthy enough.'

'Oh, they're tip-top. All day in the gym, see.'

He laughed. 'You should start showing them. Club level.'

'Really?'

'Absolutely. They're good enough. And you don't often see Asagi on show these days. Look, why not come round one time, see for yourself. Every last Wednesday of the month. Be my guest.'

He gave me a card. He was the club secretary.

'Thanks. I might take you up on that.' I shook his hand, carp man to carp man, and walked him to the drive.

*

When I got back, Audrey had fished out Ian's surprise. I showed her the card.

'What an A1 pillock,' she said, handing it back. 'No wonder the streets aren't safe, if all he thinks about is fish.'

'He was just doing his job, Audrey. I thought he was all right, for a copper.'

'God, the fish man cometh. I suppose you're going to join his stupid club.'

'I might. There's advantages in it. Special rates for food and pond ware. Anyway, fuck that. What about this "we were in all day" bollocks? I thought we'd agreed.'

'You agreed. I didn't. Why get involved when it's got nothing to do with us?'

'Because Mrs Poke Nose or someone very like her will have seen you striding about through the village and will tell them. And then they'll be back, wanting to know why you said we were in all day. And why did you keep on smiling at him like that?'

'Nothing wrong with smiling.'

'You never stopped. It was like you'd been embalmed.'

That's the trouble with murder, you see. It's so final. You can't undo it, and whatever loose ends lie there, they lie there still. You can't tidy them up, simply point people in the right direction. Why couldn't she have stuck to our story? Someone went up that bloody pimple. Why couldn't it have been her? Audrey. She never listens.

'You're complaining about what *I* said,' she was saying. 'I don't know how you've got the nerve. Thanks to you and your precious fish, we'll probably never see the back of him. Sometimes, Al, I don't think you've got the brains you were born with.'

The mobile rang. Audrey picked it up. She liked to check up on me every now and again.

'Yes,' she said. 'Yes. I'll tell him.'

'That was Mrs Blackstock,' she said. 'She doesn't want to hassle you, but you're five minutes late.'

'Doesn't want to hassle me? Old Poke Nose said that?'

'Her very words. And I wish you wouldn't call her that. One day you'll say it in front of her, and then where would you be?'

'Paradise,' I said, and went out and started the car.

# Six

Mrs Poke Nose lived in the only two-storey house on the lane. Dancing Days, she'd called it. Used to be plain number 32 before she came waltzing in. Dancing Days. I ask you.

No one of us knew much about Mrs Poke Nose. She'd come over from Dorchester way four years back, after burying errant hubby number two who was something in the music business. The moment she came she started sticking her fingers into things, parking rights, litter collections, punters coming out the Spread Eagle too late and too happy. She was always calling on you with some petition or other, button-holing you as you walked the street on account of the dog doo or the lack of lighting or the state of the donkey farm down the road. It was a big house for one person, Dancing Days, bigger than most people in our lane had for four. Audrey was invited inside once and said it was poor and posh at the same time, like she'd run out of money: nice furniture on bare floorboards, a baby grand, with one leg propped up on the *Guinness Book of Records*, a huge cracked mirror in the hall, like you'd find at Blenheim Palace. Her living room she said was upstairs, and ran the length of the house. Made no sense that, a sixty-five-year-old woman having to climb those stairs all day just to sit down and have a cup of tea all comfortable – that is until you got to know her better. She could see it all, couldn't she, from upstairs, back, front, even the rear of the Spread Eagle on the road below and the little village green beyond.

I'd had a number of run-ins with her over the years. She didn't approve of the carp for a start, said it was cruel keeping them in such a confined space, but when I showed her, and she saw how healthy they looked, she sort of relented. Not completely, but she could see I was treating them as best I could. That was the funny thing about Alice. Most of the time she was like a ferret on two legs, wouldn't let go, but despite it, there was something about her that I couldn't help liking. She had principles. She was always busy doing things, unwarrantable things, irritating Poke Nose things. She tried to get the kiddies' Guy Fawkes' night banned. Celebrating torture, she said it was. In summer she used to patrol the day-tripper car parks, looking for dogs with their tongues hanging out. If she found one, she'd take out this little geological hammer and smash a window open. Got hauled up in front of the bench for it more than once, but she didn't care. She was a vegetarian, of course, and used to complain to the council about Kim boiling up the live lobsters out the back of his yard. She had a point. Twenty in the pot and you could really hear them screaming, like fingers down a blackboard. Gave her nightmares, she claimed, but they took no notice. Well, where do you think they got their lobsters from? He caught a really big one once, must have been twenty, thirty years old, huge he was, and showed him off for a couple of days, sat on a slab of marble like old Father Neptune, proboscis waving about, out of his element, looking lost, yet graceful in his age. We all felt kind of sorry for the old boy, having got this far, only to end up as some tosser's Thermidor, but only Alice said it wasn't right and tried to buy him, so that she could take him down to the cove and set him free. But Kim wouldn't sell him to her, however much she pleaded, however much she offered. Wanted to see what an old one tasted like, he told her, a leer in his voice. Uncalled for, I thought. Disrespectful. So, you know what I did? *I* bought it. Told Kim I was going to barbecue it, have half the village round, but instead, drove Alice down to the beach and together we watched the old fella tiptoe back into the sea. Like an aged ballet dancer he was, bulbous in tights. She never used anyone else to drive her around after that. She'd even change appointment dates if I couldn't do it. Good customer relations, Audrey called it, saying that I should apply the same standard to all my customers, but it was nothing to do with that. I didn't do it for business reasons. I did it because I liked the spirit in her, that and the dignity she felt living in that fellow creature. She was an old-timer too, and I could relate to that. Kim, Kim didn't talk to me for over a month.

I rang the doorbell. The door sprang open. She must have been standing right behind it. She had a weird smile on her, like it had been borrowed from someone else.

She was wearing one of those embroidered Tibetan caps with a Mao Tse Tung type jacket and a shawl tossed over one shoulder. She had long black trousers on, silky cotton, and on her feet little black slippers. It wasn't her usual type of outfit. She looked, what, relaxed, but kind of springy. She took a deep breath.

'Time is a jet plane,' she said.

'I'm sorry?'

'A jet plane.' She tapped her wristwatch. 'It moves too fast.'

I didn't know what she was on about. Looking at her, I wondered if she knew herself. She didn't seem quite there.

'Sorry to keep you waiting, Mrs Blackstock. I had the police in.'

'I saw. What you done this time? Eaten it?'

She was referring to my altercation with Wool's only traffic warden a year back, when I was fined for jumping up and down on his peaked cap. I'd only been two minutes, picking Audrey up from the chiropodist, and there he was, slapping a ticket on the windscreen. Two minutes! Made the papers that. Made me a bit of a hero too.

'No more prosecutions for me, Mrs Blackstock. I've learnt my lesson. Needless aggression towards synthetic fabrics never accomplishes anything. No, if you must know, Miranda Grogan's gone missing. He was asking around.'

'The police have been called in?' See, she already knew.

'Well, it's hardly an investigation. She hasn't been gone that long. Er, the door, Mrs Blackstock. Shouldn't you be locking it?'

'What?' She'd wandered out, looking at the sky and the trees, leaving the front door wide open. She was moving funny too, as if some of the nuts and bolts inside her had been loosened. She waved her hand in the air, like she couldn't give a monkey's.

'Pull the bugger to,' she said. 'Let's get this show on the road.'

I escorted her to the car. Usually she sat in the front, but that day she went for the back. She had a bit of difficulty with the handle. When she got in, instead of settling herself in a corner like most people, she sat cross-legged plumb in the middle, her feet tucked underneath her like a little wizened Buddha. Feet on the seat. I couldn't say anything. She saw me looking at her.

'I'm just trying to keep calm. I'm not looking forward to this.'

I stuck it in gear and off we set. Up where the lane joins the main road up out the village, DI Rump was standing by the police house, talking to the bunion. As we slowed down, Mrs Blackstock flipped the window switch.

'Ahoy there,' she shouted. 'Master Rumpy-pumpy!'

He span round. I looked away. One thing I learnt in my youth, it's not a good idea to call policemen names. She stuck her head out the window.

'How do you measure the circumference of a circle? Come on, quick now.'

His face broke out into a broad grin.

'You run round it with a tape measure, Mrs Black-stock.'

'Attaboy.' She gave him the thumbs up and sank back, giggling. We turned into the main road.

'You know him, then?' I said, adjusting the mirror.

'Adam Rump? I used to give him maths coaching, for his O-levels.'

'Well, I never.'

'A good seventeen years ago it must be. When I lived

in West Knighton. He used to play with himself under the table.'

I felt the wheel twitch under my hand.

'These budding policemen,' I said. 'I bet you put a stop to that.'

'Why should I? It's perfectly natural, a boy to play with himself. Perfectly natural for either sex. We should all play with ourselves every once in a while.'

I looked in the mirror. She had her Tibetan hat off and was running her fingers through her hair. Her eyes were glassy and the air coming from the back smelled unnaturally sweet. Then it struck me. Alice Poke Nose had been at the weed.

'Are you all right there, Mrs Blackstock? Only, you don't seem your usual self.'

She breathed deeply.

'I've taken a little something, to calm my nerves. Can't stand injections.'

'What you in for, then? A filling?'

'Root canal. The works.' She leant forward. I thought she was going to tip over onto the floor. 'You won't leave me, will you? You'll be there for me in the waiting room, just in case. If you hear me screaming I want you to stop them. Use force if you have to. Just get me out of there.'

She sank back, twisting the fringes of her shawl round her bony fingers. We sped along, up the hill and past the camp, the Centurion tank sitting on its plinth like a squashed bug. Dad had been stationed here for six months back in 1950. It was how he and Mum first met, right on this very same road, him coming up the hill from the boozer with his pals, her coming down from the farm where she worked. I often thought about that, where it was, the exact spot where the bastard started it all. And I'm the result, a part of him, the part I wish I wasn't.

'Bring back gas, that's what I say,' she announced.

'What?'

'When I was a girl we had gas, laughing gas they called it. They just slipped this mask over you and whoosh, off you went, floating on cloud nine for twenty minutes. Fantastic. Now they stick needles in your mouth.' She shuddered. 'The damage done.'

'The damage done?'

'You're too young,' she said. 'What's the time now?'

I looked at the dial. It's lovely and clear on the Vanden Plas. Always made me think of driving on the Continent, old style, with a map on your knee and hamper in the back and a pretty young girl in a flowered dress by your side, going you didn't know where, but which you knew would be good, just because. When I was growing up, fourteen, fifteen, my mum and me had plans, that she'd buy a little car, one of them old Morris Travellers or something, and go touring all round England and Scotland and Wales, me behind the wheel and her sitting next to me, safe and close, full of smiles. She couldn't drive, see, and me, I knew I'd pass first time round. But it didn't happen like that. She hadn't got the money and me, when the time came I didn't bother with things like driving tests. I didn't bother with much, tell the truth. I just borrowed cars as I saw fit, and drove them. Never got caught neither. Not once. Shame really, that we never did that. But things don't, do they, happen how you want them to.

'Just gone twelve.'

'Pull over.'

We were passing the Red Lion. I didn't go there much. It was out of town and besides, it was where the Newdicks drank. A bouncy castle out the back and bouncy maids at the front, one of those blackboard menus that try and fool you it was written up fresh every day, and one of those flat plasma screens so that they can show football Mondays Tuesdays Wednesdays Thursdays and Fridays, and if you're lucky, Saturday and Sunday too. A crap pub, in other words. She marched up to the bar and plonked her little leather handbag on the bar.

'Double Absolut,' she ordered. 'Straight up. No ice.'

She'd said that before.

'Is this wise, Mrs Blackstock? Just before an anaesthetic?'

'The less one knows the better,' she said. 'Like the first time you . . .' She let out a long stream of troubled air. She wasn't coping well. The barman looked at me. I shrugged my shoulders.

'Just a tonic for me.'

We sat by a table near the open window. Her hands were shaking. She had that cold, clammy look you see in doorways.

'I've been awake since four,' she said, 'thinking about it.'

'Perhaps you should cancel.'

'I don't want to talk about it.' She tore a beer mat in two, then laid them back side by side. She took a deep breath and looked up, her face unnaturally bright. 'Tell me, how are your fish? One day I'm going to slip in under cover of darkness and liberate them. Like we did Methuselah.'

'Of course you are. Just don't put them in the sea, that's all. They wouldn't last two minutes. And I know who to go to too, who'll hunt you down to the four corners of the Earth. Your Mr Rump. Did you know, he's a carp-fancier too. Got quite a collection, by his own account.'

'Doesn't surprise me. He was mad on goldfish as a boy. Carried one around in a polythene bag in his satchel. He was a bugger to teach.'

'Did you do a lot of maths coaching, then?'

'Maths and geography. French at a push.'

'A regular little college, your place. A nice little earner too.'

'It wasn't the money. I liked children, not having any of my own.'

'Don't do any now?'

'I'm not up to speed.'

She said it with regret, like she missed it, missed doing something positive. I could see it too, a younger Mrs Poke Nose, firm, energetic, willing them to learn. If I'd had a Mrs Poke Nose standing over me, I might have come out all different. Then it came to me in a flash.

'How about it, if you taught me?' I said.

'You? What do you want with maths?'

'Not maths. French. I've always wanted to learn.'

It was forming before my very eyes. That's what I would do. Get rid of Audrey, sell the business and go live in France. French rolls for breakfast, good coffee and a nice little cafe somewhere for the evening for a glass of vino. I could go into property development, drive taxis. I could do anything I wanted. Have to take Torvill and Dean with me, of course, but that shouldn't be a problem, though they wouldn't like travelling. France, that was the answer, somewhere in Normandy or a bit further down, Bergerac. Maybe inland. I'd had enough of the sea.

'Well, what about it? A couple of hours a week.'

'Oh, I don't know. It's been years.'

'Go on, Mrs Blackstock. What you got to lose? Tell you what. You give me French lessons and you can have free rides in the taxi, any time you want.'

She laughed and tossed the drink back. In one. Barely touching the sides.

'All right. You're on. Come on, then. Let's get the torture over with.'

She didn't want to go in. I had to give her one of my cigarettes outside, and she stood up against the bonnet, smoking it between her fingers. She smoked it quickly, with energy, like a young woman might, with skill and a touch of edge. Age was slipping off her by the minute. I could see by the way she stood, the little gestures of impatience, the way she rested her rear on the slope of the hood, how she must have been once, how she must have looked, slim and self-assured, Alice somebody else, not Mrs Blackstock, not old Poke Nose at all.

Once in, she didn't have to hang about. They must have known that it wasn't a good idea. I sat in the waiting room and leafed through a couple of women's magazines. Useless. Nothing in them about France at all. I read a kiddie's book after that, about a cat and a broomstick. It was quite good. Some old biddy kept looking at me like I was hogging the swings in a children's playground, but a story's a story isn't it, whatever age they're meant for. They're all kids' stuff really, all made up. Forty minutes later she reappeared, pale, smiling thinly.

'Time to go home, Al. Time to go home.'

She wobbled down the hallway. I tried to take her elbow, but she shook me off.

'I'm OK. Anyway, even if I fell down, I wouldn't feel a thing. Three injections she pumped into me. Unusual tolerance, she claimed. My past catching up with me.'

She opened the rear door and started to climb in like a large dog would, head forward, both hands on the seat, one knee coming up. I grabbed her by the waist.

'Here. Let me.'

I tightened my grip and span her round. There was nothing to her, but underneath, despite the skin and bone, there was a kind of litheness to her. She sank back and closed her eyes. We started back. An amiable town, Dorchester, creaking with history, hanging judges and old forts and smock-coated shepherds herding their baa-baas to market. They had a writer here too, a bit of an old misery guts by all accounts; took a bleak view of what is known as human endeavour. One slip of the foot, one wrong turn, and as far as he was concerned, that was it mate, you'd had it. I was beginning to know what he was talking about. Still, he didn't do badly out of it, apparently, all that grief.

Going down one of the roads leading out we passed one of those ancient letter boxes, stuck on legs, peeking out the hedgerow. Looked like an old-age pensioner waiting to cross the road. It reminded me. I'd forgotten to retrieve Audrey's parcel. I didn't want that hanging round unattended. And there was still the Major's holdall to deal with. Once out of the speed limit, I put my foot down.

'How about a smoke?' Old Poke Nose had come to.

'A cigarette? I don't know, Mrs Blackstock. My customers . . .'

'Not a cigarette. A proper spliff.' She tapped her bag. 'It's in here, ready and waiting. We could park somewhere, light up. It's good stuff.'

'This is illegal talk, Mrs Blackstock. I've got my licence to consider. Besides what would Adam Rump say, his favourite maths teacher trying to corrupt a knight of the road?'

'Who cares? Who cares what anybody says? Who cares anything about anybody? Does anyone care about you, Al? Truly care?' She was slurring her words and speaking out the side of her mouth.

'Probably not.'

'See? Me neither. And poor Miranda, does anyone care about her?'

'Her mum and dad do.'

'Apart from them.'

'That's enough, isn't it.'

'Not usually. What's the theory, then, about her going?'

'I don't think there is one.'

'Well, I've got one. She wanted out. Simple as that. Didn't you at that age? I know I did.' She started to sing, not any song I knew, something about leaving this town for another one, repeating the same line over and over, like you do when you can't remember the words properly.

The tune was out the window too, that is if there was one there in the first place. It was hard to tell, her swaying about like she was on a bad Channel crossing, bringing it all up half digested. Then she grabbed one of the straps and, straightening up, swallowed it down. 'How long she been gone?' she said gulping, burping something horrible and sweet at the end.

'Sunday, afternoon. It was raining remember, chucking it down. She was wearing a yellow oilskin.'

'She was?' She leant forward, her eyes suddenly bright. 'I saw her! Out of my window.'

'Oh?' I didn't like the sound of that, Poke Nose on Busybody Alert.

'Going up towards the Beacon. A yellow sou'wester! I wasn't paying much attention because my clothes line had come down, and my washing was being blown all over the garden. Half four it must have been, thereabouts.'

She sat there, looking triumphant. This was a tricky one. What should I say? No, it wasn't, yes it was? Perhaps Audrey had been right all along. I found myself echoing her words.

'Well, it might not have been her. Half the village wear those yellow oilskins. You couldn't say definitely it was Miranda, could you?'

'I couldn't say definitely it wasn't either. If they're looking for someone wearing a yellow oilskin.' She put her hand to her mouth. 'God, the cliff. You don't think . . .' She started swaying again.

'Now, now, Mrs Blackstock, I think we might be jumping the gun here. As you say, Miranda's probably done a bunk, upped sticks to London, or caught the ferry from

Poole, having fun with a Frenchman. There's no telling where she is.'

'But the police should know what I saw, shouldn't they.'

'Hard to say. They'll want a whole picture, something definite. They don't want to go chasing after maybes. Did you see anything definite that afternoon?'

'Yes I did.'

'What?'

She leant forward, tapped me on the shoulder. 'I saw you.'

I felt cold then, cold but very calm. Water was swirling round my feet, strings of history floating underneath.

'Me. Saw me when?'

'That same afternoon, in the rain. You were hurrying over the back path, crouching down, like you were hiding.'

'I'd pulled a muscle that Saturday, lifting stones.' I rubbed the small of my back. 'Still giving me gyp.'

'Didn't stop you from jumping your fence though, did it?'

I looked in the mirror. She was sat bolt upright, her head to one side, like a dog, mischief on her mouth. Old Mrs Poke Nose. On first glance looks like a puff of wind. I laughed.

'Where were you, Mrs Blackstock? I don't remember seeing you.'

'Up a tree. I told you, the clothes line had come down. Half my knickers were up there.' She giggled. 'I was just trying to pull them down when I saw you, slinking along. Like Geronimo you were, after a scalp.'

'Trouble was there were no white men out that afternoon, Mrs Blackstock. A waste of good warpaint.'

'Well, you were up to something.'

Jesus. This wasn't good.

'I was looking for Audrey, Mrs Blackstock.'

As soon as I said it I knew it had been the wrong thing to say. But it was embedded in my head, that we'd both been out, Audrey in a yellow oilskin, me in a mood. It's what we'd both agreed. If she hadn't changed our story at the last minute, it would have been the right thing to say, *exactly* the right thing. Poke Nose leapt on it like a terrier with a rat.

'In the hedgerows?'

'We'd had a bit of a barney. She'd gone out in a huff. Been out for some time. I went out looking for her. Thought she might have slipped in a ditch. I wasn't hiding.'

She snorted, like she didn't quite believe me. I didn't blame her. I didn't quite believe me either. This was bad, and getting worse.

I drove on, the soft springs of the car making her sleepy again. It does that, the Vanden Plas, relaxes you even when you're all wound up. The drink and the mary-jane helped too. By the time I parked up opposite her gate, her head was lolling against the back seat like a rag doll. She hadn't passed out exactly, but she wasn't far off.

'We're here, Mrs Blackstock. Home sweet home.'

'What?'

'Dancing Days.'

'Dancing Days? Dancing Days!' She started to sing again, dribble coming out of her mouth, where her lips wouldn't quite work. 'Dancing Days are here again. Dancing Days are here again.' More giggles.

'Would you like me to help you in, Mrs Blackstock, just to make sure you're safe and sound?'

I lifted her out the car. I led her up the garden path. I took the front-door key out of her little bag and un-locked the door. The mirror looked back at me, in my suit and my tinted glasses and my brown leather gloves. I could see thoughts spiralling out of my head. If only we could walk through the crack of it, into another world.

I hung the bag over the balustrade and closed the door behind me.

'Where to now, Mrs Blackstock?' My voice echoed down the hall, as if the house had been empty for years. I suppose it had in a way.

She jerked her head up.

'The living room,' she said. 'I need to lie down.'

She took my arm this time and we climbed upstairs, slowly, her weight on my left arm. It was a nice feeling. I like old ladies, their strength, the things they've seen. There were posters on the wall, old rock concerts and pop festivals, and pictures of a bald-headed man with trophies and gold discs in his hand. Hubby number two, I reckoned. At the top of the stairs a little corridor ran off to the left. I could see a couple of doors and a bathroom at the end. Otherwise it just opened up into this big room, with bare floorboards and sofas, a huge collection of LPs all down one wall and the baby grand, all shiny mahog-any, stuck in the middle. There was the *Guinness Book of Records*, holding up the back leg. We walked across to the big sofa by the window. On the piano there must have been twenty framed photographs of this young girl, gorgeous-looking, kaftans and lacy tops, lots of leg, not bad up top either. Regular party-goer.

'Your daughter's having a good time.' That pulled her up.

'Daughter? I told you. I never had a daughter.' She began tapping them one by one. 'That's Mark Bolan, that's Aynsley Dunbar, that's Noel Redding.'

'You're not telling me that's you with them?'

'Correct.' She beamed. I looked again. That's what age does, of course, takes all that away from you, not simply that you'd done it, but that you could have ever done it. It makes you look like you could have never been that person, that that was someone else, long gone. I thought of Audrey, when I first met her. Was she like this? Was she legs and lacy tops? Was she fun? Was I? I couldn't remember. There must have been a bit of that mustn't there? There must have been *something*.

Alice Blackstock was showing me another photo. She was stretched out, lying in the arms of four lads all in need of a hairbrush. She had a cowboy hat on and a fringe dress that stopped way above the knees. God, she looked the part.

'Recognize them?'

'Can't say I do.'

'Led Zeppelin! Robert Plant, Jimmy Page, John Bonham, John Paul Jones.' She waved her arms about. I had to hold her, just to keep her from toppling over. 'They were it. Best rock band in the world. I followed them everywhere. Flew in their private plane hundreds of times. All over. Christ, the games we got up to.'

It was said with feeling.

'I'd never have guessed, Mrs Blackstock.'

'No? I wasn't always sixty-three. I was twenty once, just like you were, just like Miranda was. I knew what I wanted. Best time of my life, even though I paid the price. I was in my mid-twenties by the time they came along. I named this house after one of their songs, their fifth album, the one with the girls on the cover, *Houses of the Holy*. Remember?'

'Not right away.'

'You must remember. March '73 it came out. They were touring all that year. Sheffield they started, right after the New Year, then Liverpool, and all the big towns, then Europe. By May they were in the States. I couldn't go out until July. Followed them all over, Chicago, Indianapolis, Detroit. What a time that was. Bet you weren't doing anything as fantastic as that.'

I bet I wasn't. I was here on my sixteenth birthday, like we always did, July 15th, pretending everything was hunky dory, walking down to the kiosk to buy a bag of peaches and then up over to the pebble beach, Mum sitting on the little ledge, staring out to sea, smoking fag after fag, me diving in the waves, feeling the cold wash the anger away, that it had to be like this. I did what I always did in those days, made sure I enjoyed my birthday, whatever the weather, whatever the circumstance, 'cause it meant so much to her. So I ducked and dived and shouted to her off shore. Later she splashed out, double cornets on the way back and, later, steak and chips in the restaurant looking out over the Cove, before telling me, her hand on mine, that she wasn't very well, that the doctors were going to have to take the old carving knife to her, cut bits off her, my mum. No, she wasn't very well, but it took her another three years to bow out, didn't it. Some birthday present that, eh?

She'd put the photo down and plumped herself down on the sofa by the back window, head back, eyes closed. I took a quick look around. One door was locked, a key in the door, but I couldn't get it to work. The other had her bed in it, a single bed with no pillow, a nightdress folded on the sheet, and a bedside table; nothing more, save a brass chest in the corner, and a sort of linen cupboard where her dresses hung. More like a monastery cell than a bedroom. It's what you do, isn't it after burning the candle, wear the hair shirt?

In the bathroom I felt the need. I raised the lid, had a pee, lowered it back down. I wasn't going to make that mistake. My footsteps sounded heavy coming back.

'Duncan, is that you?'

She was sitting there, cradling the phone.

'It's me, Mrs Blackstock. Al Greenwood.'

'Al. Of course.' She looked down at the phone. 'I suppose I better call Adam now, tell him what I saw.'

'Not today,' I told her. 'Do it tomorrow, when your head is clearer.'

'No, I should do it now. He needs to know right away.'

'Tomorrow, Mrs Blackstock.'

I took the phone from her. She looked up at me. I don't know what it was, the way I'd said it, the way I was standing over her, but as she looked up at me, I saw her eyes change, a different sort of light go on in them, like deep down she knew what I was thinking, that something here couldn't be left alone, but she couldn't quite work out what it was, what had gone wrong.

'Tomorrow? What does tomorrow know?' She struggled to get up. 'I haven't paid you yet. I must pay you.'

'That's all right, Mrs Blackstock. You can pay me tomorrow, after you've called the police.'

'We could start those French lessons if you like. Would you like that, tomorrow?'

'That would be very nice.'

'I'll pay you double too, for all the trouble I've caused. Where's my bag?'

'You left it in the hall.'

'I'll go and get it.'

'There's no need, Mrs Blackstock.'

'No, no I insist. See you to the door.'

She stumbled to her feet. I followed. I didn't want to do anything, believe me I didn't. I had nothing against her really, but she'd seen me, hadn't she? She wouldn't keep a thing like that to herself, not from her old pupil still jerking himself off under the table. She reached the head of the stairs. I was right behind her. The sun was streaming in through that big window. She looked like a little old angel, with a halo round her head, ready to fly off to the stars. Jimmy Page. Robert Plant. You'll go down like a lead zeppelin. That's what Keith Moon said about them, that's how they got their name.

'Stairway to Heaven,' I said.

'What?'

'Stairway to Heaven. That was theirs, wasn't it?'

'Oh yes. Fourth album, fourth track.'

She put her right foot out. I did what I used to do on

the football pitch. I put my left out too. I'd done with pushing for a while. She went over, clawing the air, her head bouncing down the stairs like a rubber ball, somersaulting over and over till she lay all crumpled and twisted at the bottom. I ran down. Her eyes were wide open, but there was nothing behind them.

'Silly old Poke Nose,' I said. 'I should have let you have that smoke.'

I lifted the tobacco tin out the bag. She made a decent joint, Alice Blackstock, nice little cardboard filter, neat little twisted dove-tail at the end. I walked out. It was not yet three o'clock. I had two hours to kill before I met up with Iss in the caravan. I wondered how long it would take someone to find her. Two days? A week? I let the brake off and let the car roll down the last fifty yards. Gaynor was back at the sink. More kittens for the chop. Kim was out in the yard, dropping lobsters into the pot. Somewhere in the bungalow, Audrey was waiting for me to come home. Everyone was killing something that day.

Oooh, makes me wonder

# *Seven*

Solitude. It's what a man needs sometimes, and yet it seems the most difficult thing to find these days. When I was young, we had tons of solitude, my mum and me, rainy days in the bungalow, she in the front room reading one of her historicals, me at the back, looking out for Indians coming through the long grass, or just lying back on my bed staring up at what might be. Even on the beach, we chose the out-of-the-way places, where solitude just washed up back and forth on the pebbles, and she'd sit there, looking at it floating on the water, while I swam out of my depth in it, or walked over to the rock pools and lifted stones looking for it, or simply sat on the few patches of sand, making plans for when I could wrap it round us like a shell and let no one in. That's how it was between us. Some days we'd hardly talk to each other, while others it was like we'd left the tap running, the words just pouring out. And there was a kind of solitude in that too, with just me and her and the way we said things. But then when she went, she took solitude with her. I couldn't find it anywhere. All that was left was noise and blather, whizz and lager, skirt and cock, knuckle-fuls of fists. I'm not my old man's son for nothing. And where's it got me? Here, in this poxy bungalow, driving my poxy fares, living this poxy life. I should have seen the light earlier on, sought solitude out, sailed round the world solo or better still gone back in time and been a cowboy out in the old west, like the man with no name, or Shane. Shane has solitude sewn into his buckskins. He looks solitude, he acts solitude, even his voice sounds as if he hasn't talked to anyone since the Grand Canyon dried up. 'Where are you heading?' he's asked. 'Somewhere I've never been,' he replies. That's where I want to go, somewhere I've never been, or rather, somewhere I glimpsed once as a kid, and want to find again. That's what this was all about, to find old mother solitude again, fit that bit of space around me. I wanted it permanent.

I parked the car, slipped the tobacco tin in my pocket and gathered myself together, trying not to think of poor Mrs Poke Nose lying all crumpled at the foot of her stairs. It hadn't been me really, not really. Just a foot, no, not even that, just an inch of leather-soled suede held at an angle of forty-five degrees. I couldn't have had her blabbing on about me being outside, I just couldn't. Up a tree for pity's sake, in that weather. Asking for trouble.

Audrey was in the conservatory, feet up on the bamboo two-seater. She'd been at the face paint again, her lips like those barriers workmen erect round a manhole. It gave me the collywobbles just to look at them.

'How was she?' she asked, flicking through some periodical.

A good question. Time to lay the groundwork.

'Not great. They gave her Christ knows how many injections. Could hardly walk straight, getting back to the car.'

'I hope you made sure she was all right when she got home.'

'Course. Walked her up her stairs and plonked her down on the sofa. Even offered to make her a cup of tea, but she wouldn't have it.'

There was no telling if that had registered or not, so busy was she with her reading matter. I mean what's the point of having alibis and sowing seeds if no one takes a blind bit of notice?

'Audrey. I thought I might go and . . .'

'Feed the fish. Yes I know.'

Flick, flick. She didn't even bother to look up. I went into the kitchen. I was happy to feed the fish, but that wasn't what I was really after. I had to dispose of Audrey's parcel, put that bra back in the Major's hold-all, put a stop to all that nonsense. A distraction like that I did not need. I opened the cupboard door. One packet of fish fodder. No parcel.

'Audrey,' I called out, casual as possible. 'What have you done with the Newdicks' special?'

'What did you think I've done with it? I've posted it.'

'In the village! Are you out of your mind?' I stormed back in, the carton rattling in my hand. She was sitting there with one of her I've-got-one-over-on-you smirks on her face. I could have stuffed the packet down her throat. 'Why didn't you go the whole hog and deliver it by hand? They got a brand-new CCTV camera outside their drive-way. I could have rung up, made sure they had enough film loaded.'

'All right. Keep your hair on, Al. I got the bus to Wareham.'

'What the hell for?'

'To make sure you didn't get cold feet and only pretend to send it. Besides, I needed to pick up a few things.'

'What, like a criminal record.'

'Holiday brochures.' She patted a great mound of them piled up against her left thigh, full of carefree couples cavorting under the sun. What do they know? Tenerife, Marbella, the Isle of Capri, we've had some of our worst moments together wearing sunglasses. She never learns.

'Audrey, I thought we agreed, we weren't having a holiday this year. Tightening our belts and all that.'

'Yes and I could drop down dead tomorrow or fall off a cliff.'

'Sorry?'

'Fall off a cliff, get run over by a bus, choke on a pretzel. Fat lot of good tightening my belt would have done then. So we're having one, a proper one, somewhere different. What about the Nile?'

'What about the Nile?'

'Do you fancy it? A boat trip, floating past the pyramids?'

'What if you fell in? You know I'm not a good swimmer.'

'Oh, go fuck a fish, Al.'

I took myself down to the pond, Alice's tin in my pocket. I hadn't touched the weed in a long time, but seeing it there, set out like a rolled napkin, how could I resist? I sat across from the nymph and blew smoke at her one good kneecap, the sudden sweetness filling me all of a rush. Torvill and Dean swam restless below. They could tell I was unsettled. They're sensitive that way.

'I got blood on my hands,' I told them, 'not the middle-aged variety I was hoping for, but young blood, old blood, blood I wasn't suppose to have. But it's on me now, see?'

I held them out, but they couldn't see, and after a while, I couldn't neither. The smoke drifted up long and slow. I felt a bit elongated myself, as if I was heavier and lighter, slower and quicker, all at the same time. It didn't seem to have anything to do with me, what was going on. I rolled another. Alice was in Wonderland, Audrey was making eyes at Ramses the Second, and me, I was still in the same place, twisting and turning like my friends under the water trying to find a way out. She had a point, Mrs Poke Nose. It was a prison, the pond, how-ever nice I tarted it up, like the bungalow with its two en-suite bathrooms was a prison, like the village with its wishing well and its thatched cottages was a prison, like the Alcatraz of my whole fucked-up world.

I went back inside to get the car keys. Audrey was on bundle two.

'Don't tell me,' she said. 'You've got a customer.'

I could have said yes, but something inside me told me not to, that the truth would serve as well as anything.

'No. I'm off to see Iss. She's in a bad way.'

She nodded, surprised at what I'd said, pleased too, though she didn't want to show it. Perhaps that's what I should have done years ago, told her the truth, what I was feeling, what I was missing. If I had, maybe we wouldn't be where we were now.

'OK. Tell her . . . tell her I ran off once, as a teenager, didn't come home for a whole week.'

'You never told me that.'

'Didn't I? Perhaps I should have done. Perhaps I should run off from you too, sail down the Nile alone, just me and the pharaohs. Perhaps then you wouldn't think me such a waste of space.'

'Audrey.' I moved towards her. She waved a brochure at me. Spring in the Swiss Alps.

'Go on, Al. Before you say something nice.'

There were tears in her eyes I swear, but she wouldn't let me get any closer. Driving up towards the caravan site, that brochure got me thinking. Switzerland. Interlaken. The Jungfrau. Snow like a plumped-up pillow. That sounded a lot better than sailing down some river the colour of your auntie's diarrhoea. Anyway, didn't the Sphinx have his nose missing? Why would I want to sail down the Nile just to gawp at someone with half his face blown off? I'd already got a nymph without a kneecap and that was one disfigurement too many. I don't get it, all this fuss over ruins – it's just rubble under a different name. Switzerland, now that was more like it, everything clean and tidy and in good working order; music-box chalets, cows with bells on, walks along flower-strewn meadows and scenic mountain paths.

Now there was a thought.

Iss hadn't arrived when I got there. I unlocked the caravan door and opened up the large window at the front. Any trace of Miranda's perfume should have long gone, but I wasn't taking any chances. I checked for any other signs too, fag ends with the smudge of her lipstick on the filter, one of those celebrity mags she sometimes brought with her, moustaches drawn on anyone she didn't like, things like that, but the place was as clean as the inside of the Vanden Plas. It's how I like things to be, the caravan, the car, everything neat and trim. It's how I'd like the bungalow to be, but with Audrey stuck in it I'd have more success in sticking a sail on the roof and sailing it over to Cherbourg. She won't even bother to put the right towels in the right bathroom, the pink towels in the pink bathroom, and the blue towels in the blue. 'What does it matter?' she says, whenever I complain. 'They're towels, aren't they? You'll be asking me to piss in the right colour next.' Colour coordination. Never her strong point, unless it's brown.

Iss appeared almost straight away, her little Fiat bouncing along the track like a sack of potatoes. She slewed it to a halt and hurried over. Though she'd kept herself trim over the years, with her dark bobbed hair and her eyes tucked in and her waist not much different from twenty years back, coming up the steps she looked as if all the things she'd kept in check over the years, the gossip, the rift with Ted, the empty drink-filled days, were busting out. There was a weight on her shoulders and a pasty grey to her skin, her eyes all sunken red, but despite it all there was a determination there too, to see it through, whatever the cost. You could tell by the way she flung open the door.

'Iss,' I said, as she came through, 'is this wise, meeting here?'

'Never mind that,' she said. 'Out with it.'

'With what?'

'The twitch at the wheel. I know your little ways, Al, how you drive. You do it when you're unsettled. It's what you did when I told you I was pregnant. That's when I knew I was right to jack it in. And you did it yesterday, when Ted mentioned the yellow oilskin Mimi was wearing. So, what is it? Did you see her?'

I mean how unfair was that? I thought I had everything covered; the wife, the accident, the safe route back home and twenty-four hours later I'm like Crippen on the SS *Montrose*, everyone staring at me and nowhere to go.

'Nothing like that, Iss. It's just Audrey has an oilskin like that.'

'So?'

I took a deep breath. I had to get this absolutely right.

'She went out in it that afternoon. Very briefly. To Kim's.'

'To Kim's? Whatever for?'

'Cooking materials.'

'From Kim Stokie?'

'From Gaynor, actually.'

'The one woman in the road who won't let anyone in? Sounds a bit desperate.'

'That's it exactly. Look, it wasn't cooking stuff she was after. It was drink. Whisky.'

'Whisky?'

'Whisky. She hasn't been good lately, Audrey, alcohol-wise.'

'And that was it? Her going out to cadge some booze? That was the twitch?'

'I've been worried about her, Iss. We've not been getting on.'

Iss laughed, bitter dregs in the glass.

'Al Greenwood, worried about his wife. Well, you have turned over a new leaf. So, she went to get this whisky and then what?'

'She came back.'

'How long was she out for?'

'Iss, I wasn't paying attention. I was having a kip.'

'So you *think* she just nipped across the path, but she could have been out longer?'

'Yes. No! Iss what is this?'

'It's the twitch, that's what this is. What she want the whisky for, anyway?'

'I told you. She's been hitting the bottle lately.'

'What, you don't have any drink in the house? She couldn't go down to the off-licence and buy a whole bottle? She'd lost her credit cards, run out of money?'

'It was Sunday afternoon, Iss. There's no off-licence open.'

'So, what did she say, I think I'll just nip across and borrow some whisky from the Stokies, the most inhospitable family in our street?'

Funnily enough, I'd never thought of that. Why did she go there? Walking back from the Beacon she could have called in to lots of places. But of course she didn't go to the Beacon, did she? She went somewhere else. And yet she called in on the Stokies. It was almost as if she was in a hurry to get it, before I got back. *Like she'd come back early, found me gone.*

'I told you. I was asleep. It was a surprise, for when I woke up. She made us a couple of hot toddies.'

Iss put her fingers to her forehead.

'I'm just trying to get this picture clear in my head. There you are, Sunday afternoon and it's chucking it down. You're asleep in the armchair, snoring your head off if memory serves, and Audrey's looking outside, wondering what to do next. Suddenly she thinks, "I know what. I'll pop across to next door, borrow some whisky that I don't know they have, and make a nice hot toddy for when my loving husband wakes up?" Why do I find that scenario peculiar?'

For the same reason as I did. It was complete bollocks. Or rather part of it was. I mean, Audrey did make me a hot toddy. Had it ready and waiting for when I got back from pushing her off the cliff. Why, I don't know, but there it was, all hot and steamy in the fireplace. Like Audrey herself.

I tried to convince her.

'But that's the whole point, Iss. That's why I'm worried about her. She's not acting rational. It hasn't been easy for us, since the Newdicks set up. Custom drying up, money worries, me moping round the house all day.'

Iss scratched her fingers through her hair, like her brain was hurting.

'I don't know, Al. First you tell me she went out because she got a drink problem, then you tell it was to make things up. Which is it?'

'It's a bit of both, Iss. Not everything is cut and dried in this world.'

She got up and started to pace about, the old floor giving with every tread. They're sensitive that way, caravans. In our prime, careering around stark bullock-naked, Ted in his little hut in the cliff top, Audrey out looking

109

after her old man, we nearly knocked the thing off its perch most Thursday afternoons. What did we care? It was better like that somehow, all cramped and furious, like we were prisoners of ourselves, and this was our punishment, to go at it like we were breaking rocks. It could have rolled down the field and over the edge and we wouldn't have stopped. We lived for it, every waking minute. It was hard to think of now.

'And so you drank it, did you, this hot toddy?'

'Of course.'

'It was there waiting for you, when you woke up.'

'Not on the hob, so to speak. I woke up and she said, would you like a hot toddy?'

'And you said, "Yes, Audrey, what a good idea." To your wife, the budding alcoholic.'

'She's not an alcoholic, Iss. She's just drinking too much.'

'So why didn't you tell us all this, when you were in the car?'

'I didn't want to confuse the issue. I mean half the village have got those things, haven't they? I didn't think it important, Audrey nipping down the road.'

'Not important! Her going round to Kim Stokie's, the one house in the village that might have something to do with it? She might have seen something. Have you asked her?'

'Of course I've asked her. So have the police. She didn't see anything.'

'You believe her?'

'Why shouldn't I believe her? There's no reason for her to lie about something like that, is there?'

'Isn't there?'

She looked at me, history in her eyes, hers and mine, and all the mess in between. 'She knows, Al. She's always known. She's never liked Miranda. Even when she was in her pram, she looked at her as if she was something out of *Rosemary's Baby*. She hates her.'

'I wouldn't say hate.'

'What would you say, then? Oh God, Al. Our Miranda. What's happened to her?'

She started crying, great heaving sobs. Our Miranda. The first time she ever called her that. Like knives it was, cutting into my heart. And you know what? I wanted to tell her, tell her what had happened, what I thought I might have done, wanted to tell her the reasons and how I never meant it to be this way, that I would never hurt Miranda, never. But here I was, a man and the things he's done, standing before her. I wanted it to break all over me, feel the caravan shake again, teetering on the edge of doom. And if she'd wanted it I'd have kicked the blocks away myself and taken us all over the edge, her, me and Miranda, so that we could meet up all mashed up at the bottom. Old misery guts would have approved of that, wouldn't he? She was Miranda's mum, but I was her dad, God help me. I was her dad.

But I said nothing. I just put my arm around her, sat her back down. She didn't throw me off like I expected, just wiped her eyes and stared out the window. I made us some tea, laced hers with plenty of sugar. Iss always had a sweet tooth. Miranda too. We drank looking out across the sloping field, and the sea beyond. Was she really out there, carried God knows where like some piece of driftwood, my beautiful Miranda nothing more than a bit of flotsam? And this hand that held this cup, had it truly done this to her? If only I'd checked, looked at her legs or something, her height, her hands. But that yellow oilskin, it was all I saw, all I needed to see. I'd known who was in it, hadn't I?

Iss wiped her eyes, pulled back, pressing her knuckles down on the foam covers.

'You're right. We shouldn't have met here. It's not a nice place this, full of deceit and deception. Do you still bring women here?'

'Iss.'

'So that's a yes, then. Jesus. Anyone I know?'

'Iss. I don't go in for that sort of carry-on any more.'

'No? So why are you so nervous? If you'd been driving, we'd be in Dorchester A&E by now. What is it, then? Something mystery woman has left behind?'

She caught my eye. I was looking at the cups hanging from the hooks above the cooker. Miranda, she hangs them up any old how, but me, I put them all facing the same way, like they were soldiers on parade. That's what Miranda had said to me once, watching me put them away. 'You should join the army, Al, everything up for inspection. Look, even the biscuits look like they're passing out,' and she laughed that throaty laugh that came from every inch of her and popped one in her mouth. The cups were all in order here, save the last two at the end. They were facing the wrong way. Typical Miranda. But then I remembered the last time we were here, her doing the washing-up, me standing beside her, joking about Brazil and all the women I wouldn't see. *I'd* hung the cups up, not Miranda. There's no way I would have hung them up like that. No way. Which meant . . .

'What is it, Al? There's something you're not telling me. I know it.'

'Iss. There's nothing.' I tried not to think of it. The outside was all dazzle and light. It hurt my eyes with its brightness.

'I should get back,' I said. 'I don't like to leave Audrey alone too long.'

'No, we mustn't upset Audrey.' She took hold of me, her eyes suddenly gone soft. 'You would tell me, wouldn't you, if you knew something. She must mean something to you.'

'Something? She's the main reason I stay here.'

'Is she?' She pulled back, her body suddenly limp, shoulders slumped, the life running out of her. I'd been wrong. It wasn't determination that kept her going, it had been hope, and I'd just knocked it out from under her.

'I know I shouldn't say this, Al,' she said, 'but part of me thinks I'll never see her again. I know I should be positive, but I can't help it. She's gone, Al, in my bones I know it. I don't know why, and I don't know how, but she's gone. And there's nothing you can say to change my mind, is there?'

I stood by the door, watched her drive off, then went back inside, took them down. *Two cups.* Not just Miranda, but Miranda and someone else. Kim? Did she meet Kim here on the sly, on the afternoons when she knew I was working, or in the evenings, all dark and secretive, ready for action, primed as a pump. God, I knew how great that felt. Was that why she'd been so friendly towards me, 'cause she wanted the use of this place? I remembered when I suggested she had a key too, how her face barely moved a muscle, like she'd been waiting for it, but didn't want it to show. I'd put it down to the feeling of *us* she was having, but couldn't quite explain. 'I could have the tea ready,' she'd said, but she never did, not once. I was always the first to arrive.

I gave the caravan another search, a bit more rigorous this time; under the bench seats, the drinks cabinet, the little bedroom at the back. There was nothing there, but then I went back to where we'd been sitting, lifted the cushions, pulled back the seating covers. She'd stuffed one of her mags down there, Posh on the front cover with half her teeth blacked out and a patch over her left eye. I looked at the date. A week back. Miranda had been here, no more than six days ago, without my knowing. It seemed all wrong, her coming here behind my back, using it like I once used it, taking me for a mug. For the first time I thought about getting rid of it. Since she'd been coming here, it had gained a sort of innocence, the caravan, like a fresh coat of paint. Now all that had gone. I couldn't wait to get out.

But it wasn't that simple. I knew I couldn't go back to Audrey straight away. There was somewhere else I had to visit. As I locked the caravan door, I could feel it pulling at the back of my neck, like it was watching me, the Beacon, the gorse bush, and that little dip, all lying not half a mile away, still and quiet, with no sign of what had gone on before. But maybe there was something there, something that I'd overlooked, a shred of cloth, a button hidden in the grass, a clue to who I'd pushed off. It was crazy, but I had to go, to stand where I stood, see it again.

I cut across the field to the path. There were a few fresh-air herberts about ready to tip their bobble hats in comradely greeting, there always are littering this stretch of coastline, with their field maps and walking boots and knapsacks full of Kendal mint cake – but one look from me soon had them hurrying past. It didn't take me long, up the broad slope, Farmer Sparrow's fields to the left of me, Portland Bill a silver strip shining on the sea. Used to be a Borstal out on the Bill when I was a kid, a tough one with a working quarry and screws as hard as the stone they had those lads sweating on. Dad always said that's why he had to use the belt on me, 'cause if he didn't it was where I'd end up. As if he gave a fuck either way. It was just an excuse to get to Mum, that was all. It's why I learnt to smile, smile when he was doling it out, smile afterwards so she wouldn't see nothing on my face. Trouble was smiling only made him work the belt that bit harder, so I had to smile even stronger. Talk about a vicious circle. When he died, I had this special wreath made up. Everyone was a bit surprised really 'cause they knew we weren't the best of pals, but no, I insisted, family's family and he was my dad after all. So on it went, this wreath of mine, on top of his coffin, the best money could buy. All over Acton it was paraded, along the High Street, down by the garage where he worked, up to the crematorium. Guess what it had in the middle, made out of chrysanths? A fucking great smile, that's what. A fucking great smile, like it was me grinning on top of his coffin, happy that the cunt was dead. Funeral march? I could hardly walk for laughing.

Then I was on it. I'd forgotten how quick you come on it from the farm end. There it was, all in front of me, like the set of a stage, empty save for me, the burial mound, the gorse bush below, and in front, that flat dip. There was no one else about. No one. A late summer's afternoon by the village beauty spot and I was the only one present. It didn't seem natural. I looked up half expecting to see Audrey perched up on the pimple, glass of whisky in her hand, but that was empty too. This was a solo performance, and me both actor and audience.

I stood there, letting it all run over me. The grass was smooth, cropped like a golfer's tee, but everything seemed to roll down towards that edge. I stepped in, skirting round to the back of the gorse bush, and the little hollow entrance where I'd stood and waited. I knew it well, that gorse bush. There was room enough for two inside, and if you remembered not to rear up in moments of extremis, very accommodating it could be too. Not as wild as the caravan but still single-minded, what with the thorns and fingernails digging into your backside and the prospect of uninvited anoraks dropping in for tea. I crouched down behind it, like I had that Sunday afternoon, trying to remember it all, how she stood, what she looked like, how tall she had been, how broad, how her head sat on her shoulders. I tried to picture her, striding up the path, bursting in upon the scene, turning into the wind and rain, moving out towards the edge.

The edge.

I raised my head up and looked at it full on. I could

see the sea far away, glittering like a nabob's jewel case, and I could see the line of green where the cliff dropped away, but between them there was a kind of flat area, sort of solid, sort of nothing, like a trapdoor hanging in space. I took a step forward, moved out to where she had stood. No, not quite. I was too far away. I took a step forward, then another one. That was more like it. I was near the drop now, nearer than I had ever been in my life. I could hear the suck of the sea below, feel its breath racing up the cliff face. I closed my eyes, trying to think of what I had seen, what I had heard. It was like something dug up from the grave, that cry, full of dread, like it had been torn out of her soul. If I'd listened to it properly then, I would have known it couldn't have been Audrey. Audrey might have been angry with me, but nothing she couldn't handle, nothing she hadn't handled before. It took a lot more to get Audrey howling like that, Carol losing her leg off the Great Australian Barrier Reef for instance, or me backing over our dog. And as for Miranda, it didn't seem likely either. She'd had a bust-up with her dad, that was all. No reason for her to be wailing up here like the walls of Jericho were falling about her ears. She was getting back with Kim, wasn't she? Wasn't that what she'd told him? She would have been happy, not sad. Maybe it hadn't been Miranda. For the first time a little ray of hope was peeking through my clouds.

I opened my eyes. There was nothing for it now. I had to look. She could still be there, for all I knew. I took a pace forward, the tip of my shoes on the brink of oblivion, the wind rushing to my face. I could see over the edge, but not down to the bottom. My eyes were racing down to where I couldn't see, where it was white and blank, all whirling round my head like a snowstorm, with nothing for me to hold on to, nothing to fix on. I had to see beyond that, to where it all stopped, the cliff base and the rocks and the sea. So I did what I shouldn't. I leant out. You can do that when there's an offshore wind blowing in. It holds you up see, so you can lean out further than you should, further than your natural balance can cope with. It's a common trait found in the teenage holiday-maker. Makes them look a bit of a daredevil, like they know how the sea and the wind work. Look at me, Ma! Top of the world! Then the wind drops and they discover they're not daredevils at all. They're fully paid-up pillocks, on the way out. Goodbye, Mum, cheerio, Dad, it was nice knowing me. Ted Grogan gets to fetch a body back up that way once a year, regular as clockwork. And there I was, pillock-brained as the best of them, daring it to pull the rug under me too.

But it did the trick. I could see where I had to now, in all its spotless glory, the wind buffeting my body, the chalk shining smooth like it had been freshly polished, like it was a runway hurtling down to where it all kicked off, the point of impact, the spread of the cliff and the glisten of the rocks and the deep minty sea washing in and out, like it was lulling them to sleep. There was a roar in my ears, the world spinning about me, yet down there was a kind of calm, like nothing could move it, not the sea, not the wind, not even a body falling out the sky. I screwed my eyes, searching for a tear of yellow, a hank of brown, even a streak of red where her head might have cracked open, but it was all scrubbed clean, starched and folded. There was nothing there, nothing. And staring down at the emptiness of it, it came to me then, what I'd done. I'd pushed someone off, right here, not two days back. There was no sign of her now, not down there, not up here, but she'd been here, standing on this same bit of grass, just as she'd been down there, her body smacking up against those rocks. I'd run up and had pushed her off, someone who hadn't done me a whisker of harm, someone I didn't know, someone who didn't know me. Maybe she was going to jump anyway. Maybe she wasn't. Maybe she'd sprouted wings and was going to fly across to Bayeux and piss on their tapestry. Who knows? The point was, it should have been her decision, hers, not mine. I'd ended a life. And I had to find out whose.

It was time to go. I was going to move back, but you know what, I found going back more difficult than moving forward. When you put one of your feet back, all your weight rests on the foot in front. Under normal circumstances you don't give it much thought, but when the foot in question is hanging over a two-hundred-foot drop, there raises the tricky question of weight distribution. Can that little patch of earth take it all? Which is the best foot to move, the right or the left? Is that a hint of instability creeping up your leg or urine running down? I froze, not knowing what to do, wondering perhaps if I should fall back on my arse and drag myself back by my elbows. And then I saw it, wafting in and out between the rocks. At first I thought it was a seal, but seals don't bang their heads up against rocks, unless they feel a bit mental. It was a boot, not wafting about exactly, caught somehow in a hidden cleft. Whether green or black I couldn't tell, but it was a boot, a Wellington boot. Did Miranda wear wellies? Yes she did, green ones, with little straps round the top. I remembered her taking them off in the caravan once, the long yellow-and-red-striped socks she'd worn underneath. She'd had her name written on the inside of them too, for when she left them in the canteen's changing room. If I could get Kim to get his boat close in . . .

The shock propelled me back. I was out of breath like I'd been running the hundred metres.

'Are you all right, Mr Greenwood?'

Adam Rump was standing there smack in the middle of the green. He put an arm out, beckoning me in.

'You're standing very near the edge, Mr Greenwood. I'd be very much more comfortable if you came well away from it. The wind can be quite dangerous at times. They should really fence this area off.'

I stepped back, annoyed that I should be caught like this.

'Out for a walk?' he asked.

'Something like that.'

'My wife and I used to come here all the time when we started going out. It's a very popular spot with young couples.'

I thought of the gorse bush. He didn't seem the type.

'Audrey's always trying to get me to do more exercise. Bad for my posture she says, sitting behind a wheel all day.'

'Worse if you fell down there,' he said. He moved round, putting himself between me and the edge. I tried to make light of it.

'It was stupid, I know. But sometimes it's hard to resist, looking into the abyss.'

'Well, try, that's my advice . . .' His voice trailed off. He was looking all the way round, the pimple, the flat dip, the gorse bush. What the fuck was he doing up here?

'You taking the air too, finished with your inquiries, then?' I asked.

'Not exactly. The woman at the car-park kiosk thought she saw someone walk up this way on Sunday afternoon, as she was closing up for the day. In a yellow oilskin, too. Thought I might come up here, take a look around. Is she a walker, would you say, Miranda Grogan?'

'Not that you'd notice. And in that weather? Why would she want to? Why would anyone want to?'

'To look into the abyss?'

He moved forward, tried to peer down. He didn't like going near the edge any more than I did.

'Did you see anything?' he asked.

'Just rocks. No yellow macs, if that's what you're thinking. She's not a jumper, Inspector.'

'People don't always fall off of their own accord, Mr Greenwood. People have accidents, or worse.' He smiled, his eyes straying back to the gorse bush. 'Well, don't let me keep you. I'll just nose around here for a couple of minutes.'

I got back to the car, drove out as fast as the suspension allowed, my feet still on the edge of that abyss. When I got back, Audrey was out by the pond, talking to Torvill and Dean. She was so engrossed she didn't notice me. I watched her from the little gate. She was standing over them, pointing her finger at them, like she was telling them off. I didn't like Audrey talking to my fish. They were my fish. I talked to them, knew the tone to take. A couple of raised decibels and she could put them right off. I had to put an end to it.

'Just like him,' she was saying. 'Just like him.'

'What's just like me?'

She looked up, annoyed she hadn't heard me coming.

'Popping up out of the blue when you're not wanted.' She straightened up, put away her finger. Dean I noticed was at the far end of the pond, sheltering under a frond. He had his head screwed on, that fish. 'How's she taking it?'

'Better than I thought, actually.'

'Any news?'

'Not that she told me.'

'Must be tough on her, not knowing.'

'Careful, Audrey. Your sympathy is showing.'

'I'm a mother too, Al. I know what it's like. Whatever I thought of her I wouldn't wish this on anyone.'

She stood up, patted her hair. It was hard, like a helmet. She'd been spraying it again. She had a frilly blouse on and a pair of tapered trousers I hadn't seen before, belted up high on her waist. All she needed was a horse and she'd be a candidate for the Battle of Naseby.

'You've changed, I see.'

'That's because you're taking me to Mr Singh's. I fancy a curry.'

Now, if there's one thing that Audrey and I have in common, it's we both like a good hot curry. When we were first going out we had a competition to see whose throat had better fire insurance, hers or mine. We'd sit opposite each other, shovelling it in, chilli massalas, fish jalfrezis, plates of industrial-strength vindaloos, necks bulging, cheeks puffed with pleasure, long tall Sallies of ice-cold Kingfishers by our sides. We never liked each other that much, but a session at the curry table seemed to iron out the creases, all that heat coming off. I liked the smell of her afterwards too, laid out on the back seat, her pores all open and sweaty, her skin reeking off the stuff. It's still a matter of principle to us, a decent curry. Whenever someone next to us orders a lamb pasanda or that dansak pap we just sit back and laugh. 'We got pussies in the pantry,' I'll say, 'hit me quick,' and she'll take a knife full of Mr Singh's double-strength lime pickle and spread it on a plain naan, like it was strawberry jam, and stick it in my mouth, then take a chomp herself, both of us grinning from ear to ear. It puts them right off their poppadoms.

I was suddenly hungry, ravenous in fact. A curry. A thick fat juicy curry. It was just what I needed.

'Do you know what, Audrey?' I said. 'It's the best idea you've had all week. Just let me get out of this clobber and freshen up and we'll tootle over. Have you booked?'

'Seven,' she said. 'Use the spare bathroom. There're clean towels in there.'

I did as I was told, pleasantly surprised. Blue towels in the blue en-suite. I stuck in some bath salts, wriggled my toes and had a good soak, trying not to think of poor old Poke Nose, stiffening up at the bottom of her stairs. I'd have to do something about that, if no one found her. I mean fair's fair. The least I could do was make sure she got buried in a decent space of time. We'd had an influx of rats that summer, what with global warming and Kim Stokie's dustbins, and I didn't like the idea of them scuttling along the corridor to nibble at her face. And once she was out the way I could concentrate on what really mattered. The Wellington boot, where Audrey went, and what had happened to Miranda. Not to mention the Major's holdall.

All in all, I had a busy day ahead of me.

# *Eight*

The meal was not a success. It was like scratching away at an itchy scab. Whatever was put in front of me just didn't hit the spot. Audrey felt the same, even went so far as to question Mr Singh as to the strength of the lime pickle. Several megatons short, she complained. Singh just shook his head, told her that it was the same as always. She leant back on her chair, her forehead shining with the wasted effort. The heat had rendered the frilly blouse half transparent. She had her best crimson half-cup on. She was in an argumentative mood.

'Are you saying it's me,' she said, 'that I've changed, that I'm getting immune to it, like I am with penicillin?' Singh put out a placatory hand. He had the neatest fingers I'd ever seen on a man, thin and delicate, skin crinkly like old parchment, white in the creases.

'Less pickle, Mrs Greenwood, I implore you. Between penicillin and my lime pickle, remember, my pickle kills more germs,' and he walked away, shaking his head with laughter. Audrey glared after him.

'I never knew you were immune to penicillin, dearest,' I said. Audrey gulped back her Cobra and chucked her napkin on the table.

'There are any number of things you don't know about me, Al. Ten per cent of them are between me and my hair stylist, the rest reside in my bosom alone. Shall we go?'

Getting back in the car I thought Audrey wasn't far off the truth. She had changed, Audrey, we both had, like in some science-fiction film. My body had felt strange ever since I'd found her in front of that fire, like it wasn't really mine any more, like Audrey's wasn't Audrey's, like after that moment on the cliff I'd been going through the motions of being me without being me, and Audrey was doing the same. I remembered after the break, how she'd looked down at what we were doing with a kind of horrid fascination, as if she couldn't quite believe what she was seeing.

'How do you feel, Al?' she'd said, her lips all slow and heavy, as if the words had little weights attached to them. They'd felt weird to me too, like they were growing in my mouth, awkward to get out.

'I'm not sure exactly. Kind of odd, if the truth be told.'

'Like it isn't you doing this, you mean?'

'No. Like it isn't you.'

She'd grabbed me round the neck, her face all twisted, not with pleasure, but not with pain neither. Something else, something bang on the edge.

'Perhaps it isn't. Had you thought of that?'

'Isn't what?'

'Isn't me, Al. Perhaps it isn't!'

Driving back I kept looking at her from out the corner of my eye, that voice of hers buzzing in my head. What if it wasn't her any more? What if I had pushed her off after all, and this was something else? What if I'd gone down with her and we were both dead, in some sort of hell, me for killing her and her for whatever she'd done. Or perhaps this was my hell but her heaven, there to torment me until the trumpet called. Don't get me wrong. I didn't really think I was dead. I didn't really think I was in hell, but I was somewhere I didn't know, somewhere in the brimstone.

'God, I'm burning up,' Audrey was saying. It was getting to her too.

'And there you were, complaining about the pickle.'

'Not the food, Al. There's a storm coming. Can't you feel it, sticking to your skin?' She pulled at the frills on her blouse, like she was on fire. 'You shouldn't have drunk all that lager.'

'There aren't any police around this time of night. It's too early.'

'I wasn't thinking about the police.' She undid a button. 'Why don't you pull into the lay-by?'

'Audrey! It's been a long day.'

'The lay-by, Al.'

So the lay-by it was. The only car there, surprise surprise. I parked up opposite the old milestone that marked where the old road once ran, where it looks out along the coast, not that you could see much, the sky coming down the way it was, black and full of menace. You could feel it though, closing in on you, ready to pop your socks. The back of my neck began to sweat, my hands all clammy on the wheel. It started to rain, a trickle at first, and then a great solid gush of it, thick and hard, drumming on the roof and ground, relentless, warm and steamy, the Gods relieving themselves. My bladder started to swell. Audrey leant over, switched the headlights back on. Outside the rain was bouncing the earth up and down.

'What does it say?'

'What does what say?'

'On that stone. What does it say.'

'It's a milestone, Audrey. It doesn't say anything. Just tells you how far you've got to go.'

'How far?' She laughed, and then, 'Sometimes I think I can't take it any more, Al.'

'Take what?'

'This. Sometimes . . .'

Thunder broke over our heads, lightning slashing down through the trees, like it was trying to break in, a sudden wind stripping the leaves off the trees. Audrey shifted in her seat. I could smell the curry coming off her already. The car began to shake.

'Wouldn't like to be out in that tonight,' I said, flicking the wipers on, trying to keep it light. Liquid poured off, heavy and viscous. It didn't help.

'We are out in that tonight.'

'You know what I mean.'

Lightning flashed out. Across the valley we could see the firing range, new dummies set up like a line of monster ducks. We were closer to them than from the bungalow. They seemed real and yet unreal, close and yet far away, still and yet charged with a kind of static motion.

'We used to go there,' Audrey said, 'you and me.'

'I remember.'

'Do all sorts of things.'

She was staring into the dark.

'Do you ever have bad thoughts, Al?'

'What?'

'Bad thoughts. Do you have them, really bad ones. I do.'

'You do?'

'All the time. All the lifelong time.'

'And are you having them now, these bad thoughts?'

'Yes.'

'What about?'

'Everything. Global warming. Man's extinction. You.'

'Me? Like what me?'

'Like what a person like you could get up to on a night like this. What you could do to someone else, right here, with no one to hear their cries for help.'

'What kind of thing?'

'Bad things. Bad for them, bad for you. Our world is made for bad things, isn't it? Look at our village, our little bungalow, Kim, the Newdicks, Miranda, it's all gone to bad.' She put her hand on my leg. 'That's why I wanted to go out tonight, like we did when Dad was alive. You always brought me here after a curry, didn't you. You liked it, after a curry. Your service charge, you called it.'

'It's not the same now,' I said.

'Why not?'

'Because. Because any number of things. Your dad's dead. We're married. Besides, that was twenty years ago. We're not the age for that sort of carry-on any more.'

'What are we the age for, Al? My golf? Your fish?'

'You haven't played golf in a while.'

'I'm playing tomorrow as a matter of fact. With Tina, if

the weather clears up. I rang her when I got back from Wareham. She was pleased. We always got on, before the bust-up.'

I didn't know what to say. I could feel things slipping out of my grasp again.

'Don't look so shocked, Al. It's called playing one against the other.' She paused. 'It's bad out there.'

Whether she was referring to the weather or the free-market economy I couldn't tell. I didn't ask. She reached under for the lever, and pushed her seat back.

'Why don't you kiss me?' she said.

'What?'

'You heard. Kiss me like you always do, cold-blooded, like you don't mean it, like you wish I was dead. Finish what you started.'

'What I started?'

'That Sunday. There was a storm then, out and in. There's a storm now. Finish me off, Al. I wish I was dead too.'

She twisted up and fell upon me, a jag of lightning spilling onto her. Her face was torn up, her mouth was broken, half smile half snarl, her blouse hanging open. Her breasts looked like they'd been dipped in blood. I shrank back.

'What's the matter, Al?' she said. 'Bitten off more than you can chew? The corpse biting back?' Thunder rolled.

'I need to go,' I said, and pushed open the door. The rain was streaming down, splashing up from the ground, the roar of it drowning out the sound of her laughter. I ran over to where the trees stood and unzipped. I was soaked through just getting there, but I didn't care. It was such a relief to be out there, pissing with the Gods, away from the danger. Suddenly the ground sprang to life. Audrey had flicked on the headlights. The engine started up.

'Audrey,' I shouted. 'What the fuck?'

She laughed again, and my door slammed. Lights began to swirl in a circle as she threw the car into reverse.

'Audrey! Cut that out!'

The wheels span on the dirt, the arc of light sweeping round, catching me standing there like a schoolboy caught with his trousers down. Then there was just the dark and the walk home and the rain filling my shoes.

I was up an hour past dawn, pulling on my waterproofs. Kim had already left but I knew if I hurried I'd catch him on the tide. I was right. He was standing by his rowing boat, loading up the bait. It was another calm-after-the-storm day, no sign of the night before at all. It's all wrong, the way the weather's going, downpours one minute, Mediterranean sun the next. Everybody knows it. Remember snow? What happened to that?

'You two not getting on?' he said, a smirk on his face.

'Sorry?'

'The spare bedroom,' he announced. 'The light were on late.'

'Curry,' I said.

Kim chuckled. A satisfactory explanation, even though not strictly accurate. I hadn't seen Audrey since she'd driven away. It had been a long walk back, but the truth was I was strangely glad of it. My best jacket ruined, my tan loafers stained, it didn't seem to matter any more. The words she'd said kept ringing in my ears, the way she had said them, fierce in the dark, the rain pounding like a regimental drummer calling his boys to war. There'd been blood in her voice, blood and battle, and yes, a longing for it too. So she wished me dead as well, not just gone, but dead, someone to stand and blow the bugle over. 'Finish me off,' she'd said. 'Finish me off!', almost a taunt, like she was throwing it in my face. Did she know? Was that what Sunday by the fire was all about? Were her insides churning like mine? No wonder we couldn't stop. But she couldn't have known, could she? Unless, unless she had come back early, and seen me sneak out, followed me, seen me do it, knowing what was in my heart. Was that possible? I tried to imagine it. She'd have run back helter-skelter, heart banging like a pinball, alarm bells ringing, her whole tilted world lit up with fear. Fear and something else. Knowledge. Power. Then what? A breathless pant next door, half a bottle of borrowed whisky, dashing back, stripping off, the kettle, the bottle of champagne, listening for that back door to open, ready to watch my reaction, my face, every inch of it. 'Stretch out,' she had said. 'Make yourself comfortable.' And then sucked into that timeless black hole, not knowing where I was or who I was, or whether I'd ever be able to climb out of it again. Could she have carried it through, all that night and in the morning too, worked her way through me, knowing all that. Could she? Course she could. She was Audrey.

And then, walking back, water up to my ankles, it had struck me. I didn't want her dead any more. There was sudden light in the sky, the moon shining down on the slick of the road, flood in the fields around me. It was like I was walking through a parted sea to another place, another set of rules. I could hear cries of the old country behind me, faces and memories looming up on either side, faces and memories I didn't need. There was only Audrey and Miranda and the woman I pushed off. In the worst-placed scenario two people, in the best, three. If I could fish that boot out, maybe I'd find out which number it was. I didn't need Audrey dead any more. I didn't want Audrey dead any more. I was beginning to like this Audrey, this Audrey by the fire, this Audrey of the Newdick parcel, this Audrey who laughed and left me in the lurch. It was a better, more interesting, more arresting Audrey. Sparks were flying, metal against metal. We were breaking into something new. If I could find out where she went that afternoon, I might even tell her where I went, what I'd tried to do. I could watch then, to see if she had known all along. If she had, that would explain it. And if she hadn't, I had the feeling that she'd be glad I'd told her, that she'd go for this new me the same way I was leaning to the new her. It was flesh what counted with us, not in the sex way, but in the blood and sweat, the muscle and mouth way. We didn't have time for starry-eyed love-guff. We needed something to grab hold of, something solid, the meat and potatoes. Sex was just the salt and pepper. I'd had any amount of salt and pepper in my time, but sprinkled on convenience food, burgers and takeaways and boil-in-the-bags. For meat and potatoes, there was no one like Audrey. No one.

When I got back that night I felt quite invigorated. An hour and forty minutes it had taken me, the bungalow all wrapped up in dark, save the blue light in the spare bedroom. Fair enough. We both needed a bit of breathing space. Before I went to bed I wrote her a note and left it on the kitchen table.

> *If I don't see you beforehand tell Tina that we're getting a new Merc for the business and I'm taking you down the Nile this winter. Two weeks. Watch her slice herself all over the course.*

> *PS You were good and hard last night. I liked it. I liked it a lot.*

Kim loaded up the last bucket of bait and we rowed out to his fishing boat. It was a cramped, smelly little craft, bullet-shaped like its owner. It started up well enough this time. Off we chugged, out the cove and into the open sea. On a fine day, it looks the same, the sea, in the cove or out of it, but it isn't. The wind tells you that much, the taste on your lips, the colour of the water too. It's so much bigger than you, so much bigger than anyone, the biggest thing on this planet. And it knows it.

I'll come clean. I don't like the sea. Looking at it, dipping my toes in it, even pushing people off a cliff into it, I can handle, but stuck out on top of millions of cubic feet of it, I don't think so, not even when it's flat as a millpond. In fact flat as a millpond is one of the most scary things a sea can be. It's like that fairy story my mum used to read me, with the little Jack and the giant snoring by the fire in his seven-league boots, the smell of blood in his nostrils, like my dad spark out in his chair and the two of us waiting for him to wake up, peace and quiet on the surface, mayhem below. It's like that with the sea. I'm always waiting for it to wake up, belt the crap out of me. Still, if you have to be on it, if you're going to make a living on it, lobster-potting is one of the easier options. It's a straightforward affair. Up the pots come, out comes the catch, in goes the new bait and down the pots go again. They look good then, freshly caught, the lobsters, kind of handsome in that metallic blue, that shimmering shine. It's the way they walk, the way their feelers twitch about, like they can hear and see things that we can't, like they have an intelligence we know nothing about. Bollocks I'm sure, but I can't help feeling it, every time I see them hauled up from the deep, dripping with what they've left behind. There was a film I saw of them once, walking along the ocean floor in single file, feeler to tail, like they had a destination, a mission, a plan. Like the old fellow on the marble slab. He *knew* he was going to be put back, I'm sure of it. He was just waiting for me and Mrs Poke Nose to turn up. The sea's full of things like that, unsettling inexplicable things, all dark and hidden. We don't know the half of it.

We tootled along, me helping Kim swing the pots up on deck and fish the buggers out. The sun had come up, but there wasn't any heat in it yet, just bare light and the chill of the night breeze, and the water, hardly woken. It's a lonely place to be in the morning, the sea. Kim had three sets of pots, all strung out about half a mile from the cliffs, the furthest almost underneath the pimple. The first two didn't give up much, which was a shame for I wanted him in a good mood. At the third we got to the buoy markers and started to haul them up. Audrey Falls was right above us. It made me dizzy just to look at it. God, the distance that woman had to fall. I thought it would have been over in a second, but Jesus, it must have taken her hours. And I put Miranda through that? Seeing it from this end, the sharp end, it looked so different. Up top, it was just a ledge of nothing. Down here it was everything, body tumbling, legs flailing, stuff, terrible stuff coming out of her lungs. Even Audrey hadn't deserved that. My mouth went dry all of a sudden. I could feel my heart banging like it was trying to break a door down. It didn't feel good, being here. For a moment I thought the craziest thing, that I'd been brought here by the lobsters to see it happen all over again, only I'd see it from down here this time, see Miranda pushed off, hear her screaming and falling, watch her drop, right in front of me, bounce on the rocks, smack into the sea. My own daughter. Did she scream? I couldn't remember hearing anything. She must have screamed, mustn't she? Wouldn't you?

I had to get a grip. I had to get closer.

'Audrey was up there a couple of weeks ago,' I offered, as calmly as I could, pointing upwards. I was thinking of the boot.

He took no notice. There were three lobsters in the first pot, all a decent size. We tipped them out and started hauling up the rest. Each pot we brought up was better than the last. It was turning out to be a good catch.

'Lost a hat, would you believe. Perhaps, when we've done, we could go in, see if it's still there by any chance.'

He looked at me. 'Have you gone soft in the head.'

'It might have got caught on the rocks. She was fond of that hat. I'd get lots of Brownie points if I'd found it.

You can never get too many Brownie points where Audrey's concerned, if you know what I mean.'

He raised his eyes to heaven, and started stuffing the bait in the pots, little lumps of meat.

'What's this, then? Chicken scrams?'

'Some old pig off of Alan Sparrow. Died of something nasty.'

We tossed the pots over the side, watched them drift down. If only I could have gone down with them, see who it was lying on the bottom there. Those lobsters we'd caught, they'd know. They might have walked all over her, taken little nips out of her legs and face. Crawled inside her yellow oilskin. I shuddered. It didn't bear thinking about.

'You want to go in now? Take a look?'

We puttered in. We could feel the swell of the sea as it came up against the cliff. The sleeping giant, boots tucked under the table. But I couldn't see any sign of a body, or the Wellington boot. I was disappointed and relieved at the same time.

'Can't we go in any closer?'

'Not in this, you can't. You can take the dinghy if you want.'

I didn't but I had no choice. He held it close while I clambered in. I've done it often enough, but each time's like the first, standing up in a rowing boat. It's like trying to stand on a horse, you have to be born to it to be any good. Kim was born to it. Kim can stand up in a rowing boat. He can stand up and pull a jersey on, stroll up and down it like he's on a Brighton pier. He can stand up and row. He can stand up and row backwards or forwards, whichever takes his fancy. Forwards is trickier, but it doesn't look that way when he's doing it. He can do it with a fag dangling on the end of his mouth and he can do it with his mobile clamped to his ear, while he negotiates the price for his catch with Le Cassoulet over in Dorchester. All I do is wobble, wobble and then sit down with a bump. I wobbled. I sat down with a bump. The boat lunged from side to side.

'Mind what you're doing,' Kim called out. 'You'll capsize if you're not careful.'

I grabbed the oars and started in. I could feel the sneer on his face every time one of the blades skimmed the water, or an oar slipped out of the rowlocks. The rocks drew near. Up top they'd seemed to merge into one. Now I could see there were four of them, jagged things, strung out in an uneven line from the face. I rowed cautiously, half-expecting to bump into her, floating face down like an unexploded mine. That's what I thought would happen if I found her. I'd explode, right there and then, ker-boom, all over the sea. My hands were shaking, the oars rattling in their sockets. If I remembered rightly, the boot had been stuck in the two nearest the cliff. I manoeuvred the boat round to the right, to look at them broadside on. A couple of seagulls swooped down to see what I was doing.

'Careful,' Kim warned. 'If you hole her, you're swimming back.' He laughed but he meant it.

There was nothing there. How could there be after last night. Though what was that, in amongst the seaweed? I steered the boat, stern forward, a little closer. A tow was pulling me right to left, dragging me towards them. I had to swing round again, to try and keep it stationary.

It wasn't a boot. It was some rubber casing, from a fuel pipe perhaps. A sudden swell seemed to lurch from nowhere, one long heave of it, like a shaken blanket.

'Pull away!' Kim shouted. 'You're too close.'

I leant in, dipping the oars in as hard as I could, too hard, too deep, the boat sluicing round like a toy boat in a bath. We rode up, carried towards the nearside rock, not fast, but inevitable. It didn't seem much, despite Kim shouting the odds, so I put my hand out to push the boat away. Only I couldn't keep it straight out, because by the time we got there, the top half of the boat was higher than the rock, so I had to reach down and push. That was my mistake, 'cause the boat didn't take any notice, the rock neither, they just smacked together, mashing my hand between them. Then the boat fell away, scraping down the side, and I managed to twist, pushing with my good left hand, tucking the oar underneath my arm, shoving away as hard as I could. I slapped the oar back in, pulled swift and hard, the blade taking its time, the pull of the current compensating for the drag of the strokes. Then I had to stop altogether. The pain had bitten in.

Christ it hurt. I tried to pick up the right oar, to get back to Kim, but I couldn't. My fingers were all seized up, my hand curled around the hurt. I'd forgotten how much hands can hurt. Everything's so close in the hand, the flesh, the bone, the nerves. I hardly noticed Kim leaning out with a boat hook and dragging me alongside.

'Get in before you do any more damage,' he said. I did as I was told, though it wasn't easy. I stood on the deck, sucking on my fingers, while he tied up.

'Dad once got hold of my left and slammed the car

door on it, just 'cause I sarked him over his sideboards. Were no good for a month. Couldn't even wipe my arse with it. Dip it in the ice bucket. That'll stop the swelling.'

He turned the boat out to sea. Pushed the throttle forward.

'Not finished yet?'

He nodded his head out to some fixed point I couldn't see. 'Thought I might lay a net down, near the sandbank there. See what we get.'

It's funny how long it takes to get close to the shore, how quickly it is to put yourself at a distance from it. In no time at all we were way out. Looking back it was like you had gone to the back of the theatre, you could see it all, the sea and the cliffs and the fields beyond, little figures scurrying about, little cars, little houses, little lives. There was the pimple and the smear where the holly bush stood. There was the cluster of trees marking Sparrow's farm.

'You still got that caravan?' I turned round. Kim was looking in the same direction.

'Yes. Why?'

'No reason,' he smirked, going back to his net.

So, Miranda *had* taken him there.

'Use it much, do you?' he said, the smile still in his voice. I sluiced my hand with more ice, trying to keep my voice steady, trying to get the picture out of my mind, Miranda in my caravan, doing what I used to do with her mother, with him, right under my very nose. I was fuming. She'd put one over on me; he had too. I could hear them, laughing at me behind my back, like me and Iss used to do, behind her dad's, behind Ted and Audrey's.

This was a side to Miranda I didn't appreciate, a cocky, stuff-you side. If only she'd told me what she wanted it for. If only she'd told me.

'What's it to you, Kim, what I do with it?'

'Nothing. Seems a bit daft, though, having a caravan not a stone's throw away from where you live. Surprised you haven't got rid of it.'

There was a bang, and the engine seemed to splutter.

'What's that?'

'Danged if I know. This old tart.'

He lifted the hatch, clambered down, started banging about. We started to drift out. Now, I think I mentioned before, but there's this band of water lying a ways out called the Race. It runs from St Alban's Head to Chesil Beach. On a clear day you can see it from the top, a lighter shade than the rest, snaking across. It's fast too. When I was a kid, the paddle steamer that came from Weymouth once got into trouble because of it, had to get the navy boys out to pull her free. Not something you want to get caught in, the Race, especially when it's flat as a mill-pond. Its reach is all the greater. And there we were, moving slowly out, with a boat full of disgruntled lobsters. Kim poked his head up.

'Something's dropped off inside,' he said, 'damned if I know what. She'll go,' he said. 'But slow and not much pull. Fuck the trawl. We'd best get home, best way we can.'

It took us an hour and a half, the engine coughing her guts out. On the way we made the catch serviceable, dividing up the crabs and lobsters, slipping rubber bands round their claws. They were climbing all over one another, waving their pincers about, poking at each other. They might be very touchy-feely full fathoms five, but up there, it's every lobster for himself.

'I'll buy it off you,' Kim said suddenly. 'The caravan. Cash. Just name your price.'

He stared at me hard. He meant it.

'I thought you just said you didn't see the point having somewhere so close to home.'

'My home's different from most folks.'

'It wouldn't be because of what I heard, then?'

'What's that?'

'That you and Miranda were getting back again. If you were, a place like that could come in handy, to meet up on the quiet.'

He didn't move a muscle.

'And who'd you hear that from?'

'Can't recall offhand. Ted, I think.'

'Well, Ted don't know dick, do he?'

'So, what? You weren't getting back together?'

'Not that it's any of your business, but no, we weren't. Quite the opposite. She jacked me in.' He grabbed hold of a lobster and wrenched one of its claws off. You could see its eyes swivel with the pain.

'Jesus, Kim. Go easy. I don't understand. She told Ted that you two were getting back together again. Permanent. That's what he said their argument was about.'

'If she told him that, she told him a lie. She told me it was over. There was someone else.'

'Someone else?'

I felt like I'd been punched in the stomach, and yet I knew it, knew it the moment I saw those cups and that mag stuffed down the back. Jesus, Miranda, all that guff you'd told me about Kim being the only one! You'd been lying to me, lying with a knowing smile on your face, as if I was part of the secret while all the while . . .

'Did she say who?'

He shook his head.

'How long had this been going on?'

'She wouldn't say. Started while she was still seeing me, I'm sure of it. Six, seven months by my reckoning. Maybe more.'

'When did all this come out?'

'Couple of weeks back. I went up to the camp one weekday, caught her coming off her shift. She'd been blowing hot and cold for I don't know how long. I wanted to know why.'

'And she told you.'

'Said she was glad not having to lie to me any more. Not that she was truthful then. Said it was serious.'

'And you've no idea who?'

'I didn't say that. I said she wouldn't say. I've got my suspicions.'

'Who? Someone in the village. The camp?'

'Pat Fowler. He's always had an eye for her. We used to laugh about it. Whenever she went to the gym, he'd always be there, hovering about.'

'Well, he is part owner. That doesn't mean . . .'

'No? He has money too. She's fond of money.' There was fury in his words, powerless fury, like a boxer in a ring with nothing to hit.

'Oh, come on, Kim. She's never seemed a gold digger to me.'

'She doesn't seem a lot of things, a lot of things she is. Fooled the lot of us, that girl.'

He fished out the three smallest and tossed them overboard. Maybe they'd never see a lobster pot ever again. The ones that got away.

'Well, I'm sorry, Kim.'

'You're sorry?' He tossed another one back. 'What you got to be sorry about?'

'You had something going, we all know that.'

He wiped his hands on the back of his trousers.

'I loved her, Al, loved her true. Everyone thinks I got Portland stone in me instead of a heart, but I loved her. If Gaynor had been half mended, things could have been different. But I couldn't leave her, not in the state she's in. So I did the best I could. Weren't enough. Well, she's gone now.'

'Gone?'

'Pissed off with her man, whoever he is.'

'Is this what you told the police?'

'What else would I tell them?'

'Poor old Pat, eh? You don't really think he's got anything to do with it, do you? Him of the baldy head and bulging eyes. Miranda wouldn't go for him, even I know that. You just wanted to give him a hard time.'

The engine burped, thick black smoke reeking out the hold.

'He touched her once, she said, pretended it was an accident like. Do him no harm to have the police crawling over him for a few hours. Besides who knows what they might find. There's something not right about men like him, in the gym all day, sniffing other people's body odours.'

'I'm with you there, Kim. Tell me, with the police, did you mention the caravan at all?'

'Caravan?'

'My caravan. I mean, you wanting to buy it off me. It's not really for you, is it? It's so she can't use it again, like you used it with her. You did use it, didn't you, the two of you?'

He straightened up, twisted the rubber band round his fingers and snapped it round a big four-pounder.

'So what if we did. It's your fault as much as anybody's. You gave her a key. You told her she could use it whenever she wanted. It wasn't like we was breaking in. Thing is, when we stopped, I used to see her sometimes, walking up through the fields just like she used to, on her way to meet me. I thought she was taking a short-cut home. I know different now, don't I?'

He turned back to his haul. Didn't say anything the rest of the journey. Just as well. He'd left me pretty speechless too. Kim in love, Kim two-timed, Kim doing the decent thing by his wife. And Miranda. A little harder than I'd thought possible, a touch deceitful. A little less like her mother, a little more like me.

I left Kim stacking his catch onto his pick-up. Normally I'd have helped him, take a drop of his whisky afterwards outside the fisherman's cabin, getting a bit of warmth back, but I wanted to see Ted Grogan right away. I still didn't get it, Miranda telling Kim one thing, Ted another.

They couldn't both be right. It was funny. Here I was trying to find out what happened to her, while all along it might end with the finger pointed at me. But I had to know, not just about that, but about everything else, who she was seeing, what she was doing, what part I played. First there was Audrey trying to pull a fast one, and now there was Miranda. That's the trouble with being alive. There's no one you can trust.

The cove is shaped like a crab, its claws the two heads that guard the narrow entrance. The coastguard hut stands at the head of the right-hand claw. I didn't expect him to be there considering, but I could see Ted's bike chained up to the railing at the bottom of the stone steps. His back must have mended quick, but then, when you've worries bigger than your own, a body can forget its own troubles for a while. Like my hand. It wasn't hurting so much, me thinking about Miranda's mystery man, remembering her voice all soft and sugary every time we met, and me lapping up every word. I climbed up, tonight's supper swinging in a Tesco's bag. He'd managed to poke his one good claw through. Looking for the other, no doubt.

I knocked on the door and stepped in. Ted was looking out through a pair of binoculars in his hand, radio chatter coming through the receiver on the table in front of him. Perched up there, sea all around, you could almost imagine you were in charge of it.

'How's it going?' I asked. 'Any news?'

He shook his head. Like Iss, all the colour had gone out of him.

'I've just been out with Kim.'

'So I saw.' He tapped his logbook. 'That boat of his should be sold for scrap.'

'Wouldn't get anything for it, Ted. That's why he's waiting until it sinks under him. Then by God, you'll see an improvement in its condition.'

'Did he say anything?'

'Yes, as a matter of fact. That's why I'm here.'

'Oh?' He put his binoculars down. 'What?'

'Before we go into that, tell me, tell me exactly, what Miranda said to you on Sunday.'

'I've already told you.'

'You've told me what you *thought* she said. Tell me exactly what you heard. Word for word if you can.'

Ted brushed the logbook with his fingers and gave a cough. He's a methodical little man. How he and someone like Iss ever got together in the first place is mud to me.

'I was in the kitchen, making dinner. I was going to make something a bit special, 'cause I hadn't seen her for a few days and I always like feeding her up when she's been away for a while. It's the dad in me still. She'd been staying with one of her friends in Dorchester. But when she came in, it was clear she wasn't staying. You can always tell. She had something else on, but didn't want me to see how much of a hurry she was in to get away again. I was annoyed. She was late anyway, and she knew, lateness, it's something I don't like. Everybody can be on time, if they try.'

'Try telling Audrey that,' I said, without thinking, even though I knew that Audrey in fact was quite the opposite, unless she was trying to make a point. Then it struck me.

Putting Audrey down was what I did, what I had always done, ever since Carol was a toddler. It just came natural, like lighting up a fag or leaning up at the bar and ordering up a pint. It was part of my routine. I enjoyed it. And yet . . . 'Go on.'

'There was something about her, she was almost lit up, Al. Happiness, I don't know. "Good time?" I said. "Great time," she said and put her hands on my shoulders, fixing me with that deep look of hers. "I've got something to tell you," she said. "First, about me and Kim."'

'About me and Kim, that's what she said?'

'Her very words. "You're not to worry, Dad," she said. "It's permanent this time." And I looked in her eyes, and they were smiling, full of that happiness, and I thought, she's been with him, that's what that look's about. She's been with him. And it made me . . .'

He stopped, choking on his words.

'I shouldn't be on duty you know. I keep . . .' He wiped his eyes. 'I can hardly see when I get going.'

'It's a clear day, Ted, never mind that. What happened next?'

'I lost control, blew my top. Told her she was ruining her life. She started screaming at me. "Listen, Dad. Listen! You never listen!"'

'And you said?'

'I said, "I don't have to bloody listen. I've heard it all before." I said . . .' He ran his fingers through his hair. 'I said, "I'd rather you left home right now than stick around with that waster."'

'And then she walked out?'

'Ran out, ran up the stairs, grabbed something from

her bedroom and then was out the door before I could stop her, God forgive me.'

He got up and fished a handkerchief out of his jacket hanging on the back of the door. He was feeling all sorry for himself. I couldn't believe it.

'God might forgive you, Ted, but I won't. You know why? She was right. You never listen. She was leaving him, you pollock. She'd come to tell you that it was all over, that she wasn't going to see him again. *It was permanent this time*, remember. You drove her out, you fucking moron.'

I lashed out, caught him on the side of the head. The pain doubled me up like a soggy cardboard box. I'd forgotten about the hand. Ted staggered back.

'Jesus, Al, what you do that for?'

''Cause it's all your fault. My girl, you drove her out into the fucking rain. If you'd listened, she'd be with us now.'

'What do you mean, your girl?'

'Oh, you're listening now, are you? Why didn't you then, when it mattered? I've got some things to tell you, she said. First about me and Kim. She was going to tell you something else, Ted. Know what? About some other bloke she'd fallen for.'

'What other bloke?'

'The other bloke she told Kim about, the one he told the police about. She was seeing someone else. That weekend? Do you know who she was staying with?'

'One of the girls at the gym, we thought. She's long gone eighteen, Al. We had an agreement, that I didn't enquire, when she wanted to be away. It was only right.

But we haven't been able to find out who. Us or the police.'

'Well, I bet there was no girl friend that weekend. Full of happiness, you say? Full of happiness and probably something else as well. Serious, she told Kim. And if you'd given her half a chance, she'd have told you too. She wouldn't have run out in the rain. And I wouldn't have . . .'

I stopped.

'And you wouldn't what?'

'I wouldn't have gone a bit bandy and bruised my bad hand.'

'My girl,' he repeated. 'You said my girl.' He had such open, honest eyes. I could hardly bear it.

'It just came out like that, Ted. I've always felt close to her, you know how. I've seen her grow up, from that funny little scrap into someone really special, not just on the outside, but what she is. I'll tell you the truth if you must know. I like her better than my own. Better than my own daughter. That doesn't sit easy on a man, Ted.'

He nodded, as if it was the most natural thing in the world.

'The police never told us about some other bloke.'

'They never tell you everything, you should know that. All they know is that you and she had a quarrel. As far as they're concerned, you might have something to do with all this. Didn't you ever think there might be another bloke?'

'Not for a moment. Kim, he'd had such a hold on her. Still does, if you ask me. I mean, this confession of hers, we've only his word for it.'

'There's that, though I must say, he acted the part.' I caught Ted's questioning look. 'Of a man given the push.'

'That would be reason enough, wouldn't it, reason enough for a man like him to . . . ?' He couldn't finish the sentence. Miranda was still alive, wasn't she. I tried to reassure him.

'But then he wouldn't tell me about it, would he? He'd make out they were both still lovey-dovey. Look, I don't know what happened, do I? I just thought you ought to know what Kim told me, that's all.'

'Yes, thanks, Al.' He touched my shoulder, all grateful like. He seemed to have forgotten all about the punch. 'I must tell Iris about what Kim said. You never know, she might think of something.'

I left him, took the car to the garage to fill up for the day ahead. I needed to get one or two things straight. I was no nearer finding out whether it was Miranda or not I'd pushed off. Maybe she'd run off with this new bloke of hers. And if she had a new bloke, she wouldn't have been standing on top of a cliff crying her heart out, would she? On the other hand, maybe it wasn't despair I'd heard, just sheer exasperation. Perhaps she'd just run out the house, up to the Beacon, raging at her cloth-eared dad. When I got home, Audrey was getting ready, dressed in her golfing tweeds and a Tyrolean cap. There's always a breeze out on the course; besides, she looks intimidating in green and orange check.

'Look,' I said, holding up Kim's offering. He was waving his arm about. 'Don't you think he looks like that weather man on the telly?'

'The one with the glasses?'

'No, the one who waves his arm about.'

'Not a lot, no.'

'No matter. I'm going to stab him in the back of the head anyway and stick him on the barbecue. Bottle of Riesling in it if you keep that hat on.' She smiled and then frowned.

'What happened to your hand?'

'Kim's boat, that's what.'

She went to the bathroom, came back with a roll of bandage.

'Give it here.'

I held out my hand. She held it by the wrist and began winding the crêpe round, all gentle and tender. It was strange, the quiet of it, me standing there, my hand in hers, both of us saying nothing, thinking thoughts.

'I read your note,' she said, not taking her eyes off it.

'Did you?'

'Yes.' She raised her eyes up to mine then back down again. 'I liked it.'

'Did you?'

'Yes.' She squeezed my hand, very gently, enough for it to hurt a little. 'I liked it a lot.'

'I must write you more.'

'I must give you more to write about.' She tore the end of the bandage into two, tying the strips round my wrist.

'There. Can you drive?'

'Mostly.'

'I could help if you want. You could sit in the passenger seat, make sure I was doing it right.'

My mouth must have dropped open, for she stepped up and put a finger on my lips.

'If the Newdicks can, why can't we?'

There was a hoot on a horn. Tina was outside, behind the wheel of her suppository. She looked in better nick than Ian. She smiled and waved. I waved back. Audrey stroked the feather in her hat and pecked me on the cheek.

'Think about it,' she said.

I thought about it. I thought about it while checking on my client list for the day, and I thought about it while driving to Wareham and Winfrith and Osmington Mills. In between thinking about it I thought about Miranda and the new boyfriend and in between that I thought about poor old Alice Blackstock, still lying at the foot of her stairs, her house all shrouded in death. I was uneasy, no one yet clocking on to the fact that she wasn't about any more. I wanted her out the way. All it needed was someone to peer through the letter box and see her feet sticking up, but that was the trouble with people like Mrs Poke Nose. No one *wants* to miss them. You're pleased when you haven't seen them for a while. You don't go looking for them.

Richard the postman called, stuffed a couple of letters through, but that was that. Mrs Poke Nose left to ripen for another day. Had it happened in days gone by she'd have been discovered in no time. The milk bottles on the doorstep would have seen to that, but we don't get a milkman any more. We buy it from the supermarket, like everyone else. When I was a kid, the local farmer used to trundle by on this little three-wheeled motorized cart he had, red it was, like a kiddie's tricycle, handles like one too, only with smaller wheels and a loadful of gold top rattling up behind. Lovely on a bowl of cornflakes, that gold top. We all used to wait for him, me, Kim's dad, the rest of us kids, running after him, jumping on the metal plate, doing his delivering for him. It was fun, see, nothing else but, just the cart and the milk bottles and us bare knees bouncing along without a care in the world. I suppose the farmer might have had his share, but that's not how I remember him. I remember him all weather-faced, brown and wrinkled, happy that we were there, content that he was the centre of something so simple, something that fed every part of us.

I got back from my last run about half two. Audrey was round the back, whacking golf balls into the field. She had her hat on still.

'How did it go?' I shouted. She settled on her feet and drove it high into the air before answering.

'I won,' she said, grinning.

'I knew you would. Those tweeds and your power drives. They're a fearsome combination.' She shook her head.

'It was a close game. She's a good swing on her, Tina, a good centre of gravity. Gail Fowler was there, Pat's wife. Very thick those two. It's the gym, you know. They all go.'

'Tina goes to the gym too?'

'Three times a week. She's in great shape.' She swung again. 'It was good getting out again, seeing all these women having fun, enjoying each other's company. I thought I might sign up to the gym myself. Join in.'

'Don't take this wrong, Audrey, but would you fit in? They're a lot younger than you.'

'Gail isn't. She's a month older, though you wouldn't think it to look at her. She keeps fit, that's all. Yoga classes too, apparently. We could afford it, couldn't we, the gym?'

'Course. If you want.'

'I think I do want. Like that trip down the Nile. It's time to spread our wings, Al. Live a little. Tina and Gail are doing a sponsored bungee jump next month. Can you imagine it, a fifty-three-year-old woman, plummeting hundreds of feet with nothing but an elastic band tied round her ankle.'

'You mean down she goes, and then back she comes up again? Funnily enough I can.'

'Asked me if I wanted to join in.'

'And?'

'I said I'd think about it.'

'Audrey. Taking up golf, taking a turn on the exercise bike is one thing, but bungee jumping.'

'That sounds as if you care, Al.'

'Well, of course I care. Walk before you run, Audrey. Walk before you run. A jolt like that, you don't know what it might do to your insides.'

'Oh, my insides can take all sorts of punishment. You should know that.' She took another whack, the ball sailing over the fence into the field. It was fairly long, the grass.

'Isn't that rather reckless, banging them out over there? How are you going to get them back?'

'You're going to look for them.'

'I am?'

'You are. You like doing things for me, remember?'

I laughed. This was what I meant. It was getting fun again.

'Learn anything else, apart from the gym?'

'Oh, once we were out on the course she couldn't stop herself. She and Ian aren't getting along.'

'The post have anything to do with it?'

'I didn't ask. He's lazy, she says. Won't wash his feet before he gets into bed. He lets her do all the work, then accuses her of playing around when she comes back late.'

'Did she ask about us?'

She nodded. 'I said we were getting on famously, that you were thinking of upgrading to a Merc.'

'And?'

'She said, "Great!" like she was pleased. She's not a bad sort, Tina. It's Ian who's the prick. I wish I hadn't sent it now. They had a blazing row over it this morning, about her seeing other men.'

'What did she say?'

'Told him where to get off.' She put another ball down on the tee. 'You know what I used to think of, when driving off. That this was your head. But I didn't today.'

'Whose head was it then?'

'No one's. It was just a golf ball. Riesling, you say, if I keep the hat on.'

'Depends.'

'On what?'

'On the mood underneath.'

She smiled and walked over.

'Let's feed the fish,' she said.

I went and fetched the feed. We stood there and sprinkled it on the surface. They came up, kissing each other. They were happy to see us, the two of them, the two of us, Torvill and Dean, Al and Audrey. I did the same to her. A peck on the cheek. It felt quite nice.

'Al!' she said. 'In broad daylight and without the aid of alcohol.'

'I know,' I said. 'But I've been thinking about what you said. With the hand being as it is. We could give it a try. Not on short journeys. Short journeys I'm OK. But I've got a long one on, in a couple of days' time, Salisbury and back. See how you take to it. What do you say?'

'I say, you're on. And I also say, you can tell me what I'm doing wrong and I won't mind. As long as you do the other thing.'

'Which is?'

'Tell me when I'm doing right. That way, I'll listen to you.'

'It's a deal. Listen. Talking of listening, Kim told me a funny thing this morning.'

She looked at me, not wholly at ease. There was still the matter of where she had been that afternoon. I hadn't forgotten. Neither had she, presumably.

'Which was?'

'That Miranda was seeing someone else, that she'd chucked Kim permanent. She wasn't going back to him at all. Ted had heard it all wrong.'

'Who someone else?'

'No one knows. I don't suppose there was any gossip, up at the NAAFI.'

'Not that I heard. Though she didn't mind men looking at her, you could tell that. What about her yoga classes? They're well attended, Tina said, men and women. There might be something there. All those legs in funny positions.'

'Classes?'

'Yes, didn't I say? Miranda gives yoga classes, every Friday at the gym. Tina, Gail, they all go to them religiously. If I did join, I think I'd give them a miss. Life lessons from Miranda? I don't think I'm quite prepared for that one, do you?'

'Probably not.'

'That is, if she's coming back at all. Do you think she's coming back, Al?'

'Why not? It's a hard place to leave, don't you think. People just bounce back. We got elastic bands tied round our ankles too, Audrey. Only we just can't see them, that's all.'


I left her in a good mood, polishing the doorstop. I had a five o'clock. Wool station to Gallows Hill. It wasn't on my way, but on my way back, I called in at Judes, once a pumping station, now the home for Wareham's fitness freaks. It's an ugly-looking building, slightly outside of town, squat and square and made uglier by the procession of smug, tracksuited herberts going in and out. I parked the car and walked in. The stink was like running into a glass wall. You couldn't see it, but Christ it didn't half set you back once through the door. There was a girl behind the counter. There nearly always is. She was wearing a blue T-shirt and a white smile. She'd drunk enough perfume to give her a protective shield with a radius of about two feet.

'Pat Fowler in?' I asked.

'I believe so.'

'Could I have a word?'

She eased herself out and walked the shield up the stairs. If there were any advantages in joining, looking at her gyroscopic arse would be one of them. To my right a pair of swing doors led to the downstairs gym. I could hear the whirring of bikes and rowing machines, and those contraptions that pretend they're three feet of road. They're not, for unlike normal roads, they do the running for you. You just put your feet down. It's a basic flaw in the design, but it doesn't seem to worry the punters. They make them go up, they make it go down. They leave happy. Look at me, Ma. Top of the A31! I mean if you want to run on a road, then run on a bleeding road. Inconsistent I know with my previous statement concerning joggers, but then that's what we humans are, aren't we? At variance with our internal emotions.

I peeked in. There they all were, pulling and pedalling and panting away with mad staring eyes. It's the panting that does it, the panting that shows you what the gym is really all about, that panting without a partner. It's the new wanking, the gym, only wanking in public, wanking by machine. Some of the women there had retained some sense of decency, reading magazines while doing their thirty-minute cycle through the Black Forest, chatting to one another, but the men. Locked up, every single one of them, given a severe talking to: T-shirts riding up on slugs of fat, wispy-haired bellies, sweat-soaked, grunting like they were screwing their neighbour's underage daughter, and shorts that the Lord Chamberlain wouldn't even have allowed Nureyev to wear. A close-cropped hunk of love, a white towel slung over a slab of shoulder, strutted about on his hind legs like an overweight cockerel, joshing and joking with everyone. Pleased with himself? You could imagine him sticking his head out the window and crowing every time he had a decent shit. He caught me looking at him. Yeah you, you prime cut of prat.

I let the door swing to, took in the noticeboard on the wall. Rowing competition, quiz night, free towel with every fifth go in the suspension tank. Then my heart gave a little bang. There she was, smiling at me in full colour, Miranda, sitting cross-legged on the gym floor in a white kaftan, and underneath a form for those who wanted to join her autumn intermediate yoga class. A number had already signed up: R. Vandenberg, Mary Collier, Tina Newdick, G. Barret, Audrey Rainbird, Gail Fowler.

'Can I help you?'

Pat Fowler was stood behind me, a black tracksuit with a silver stripe down the leg and his smarmed hair shining like an oil slick. Ponging like one too. There's not many things Pat Fowler lacks, healthy business, loving wife, top of the range C-class convertible, but one of them is a neck. His head squats on his shoulders like a toad on a bollard.

'Al!' He stepped forward. 'Well, this is a surprise. Don't tell me you're going to join, after all the aggro I used to get from you down the Spread.'

He shook my hand, cold and clammy. Looked like a toad, felt like a toad. Talked like a toad too, all deep and croaky. There was no way Miranda would have gone for him. At least Kim looked human. At least he had a neck to bite.

'No such luck, Pat. It's Audrey who's got the bug since talking to Tina. Your wife, too. I thought I might take out a year's membership for her, as a surprise.'

'You sure?' He glanced over to where the girl was settling her arse back on her stool. 'I only say that because some people have been known to take it the wrong way, gift memberships. It's like saying, you're an unfit, flabby tub of lard and I don't like the look of you any more.' He stared at me. We'd never got on.

'No, no. It's something she's been thinking about. Do you do special rates?'

'We do an early morning commuters rate, and a pregnant mothers rate, but a help-me-out-with-the-wife rate? Sorry.' He blinked, dead pan. Greedy little cunt.

'No? How about a neighbour-who-used-to-drive-your-mum-to-the-bingo-every-Tuesday-afternoon-for-nothing rate? Got one of those in your bottom drawer?'

When Mum got really bad, and we came down here to see the last few months out, it was old Mrs Fowler who called in every day, lent a helping hand, cooking and feeding and doing the things Mum was embarrassed for her son to do. Never forgot that. She was a good sort, Katherine, an old-fashioned countrywoman, flowery patterned dresses, big capable hands. So I did her favours in return, gave her a bit of leg up when life got a bit grim. Unlike son number one standing in front of me.

He smiled, a hard, empty thing, flashed with gold. Raking it in, he was, even then. Why he hadn't moved, I couldn't work out.

'I could do ten per cent, I suppose,' he said, tapping his foot.

'How about twenty?'

'Fifteen. Take it or leave it. That's three hundred and forty quid. Do you want to do it now? Karen, have you got a membership form handy?'

We did it then, Audrey Massingham Greenwood, born April 3rd 1955. Occupation: housewife and part-time nourishment operative. And still alive.

'You heard about Miranda, then?' I said, handing over the plastic.

His eyes gave a little swivel.

'The police were round yesterday. DI Rump. His wife's a member here.'

'Is that right? She going to that class too?' I pointed to the noticeboard, wondering who had taken the picture, and when. Dark it was outside. After hours maybe.

'She went to the beginners', so yes, probably, though it's not starting up for a bit. Miranda will be running the beginners' again, if Audrey's interested.'

'She won't be running anything if she don't turn up.'

'She'll turn up.' He franked the little membership card, green and gold, and handed it to me. Audrey M. Greenwood. Member No. 28764.

'Yeah? You sound very sure.'

'She can take care of herself, Miranda. You should see her in the women's defence class. She's gone off with a bloke, that's all.'

'I wish Ted was as sure as you.' I wished I was too. 'She's a regular here herself, then?'

'Every day. It was her idea, the yoga class, in exchange

for free use. She got the better deal, but that's our Miranda.' Our Miranda. I didn't like that. He rubbed his hands. He wanted to get this over. Guilty memories of his mum, no doubt.

'There was no one giving her a hard time?'

'The police asked me that. There was no one. No one dared.'

'And when she took her last class, she was OK?'

'She was right as rain, completely better.'

'Better?'

'She had to cancel the week before. She had a bad wisdom tooth. Had to have it out. Really took the sails out of her.'

I sat in the car trembling. I could feel it, still in my pocket. How could it be hers? I remembered the clothes tumbling out the bag, the skirts and the bras and the stockings and the frilly blouse which had reminded me of one that she had worn. Jesus Christ the bra! What if they took it to the police? It was bound to have something of us on it, the gloves, the grass, Audrey drooling with anticipation. If forensics ever got hold of it ... Maybe it wasn't Miranda's. Maybe it was just a coincidence.

I pulled the handkerchief out, unfolded it fully this time. I hadn't noticed it then, but I saw it now all right, the monogram in the corner, the $\mathcal{M}$ all twirly, like I'd paid for. This was Miranda's all right, one of the lace handkerchiefs I'd bought for her eighteenth birthday, made up special by some old trout in Dorchester, hand-stitched, in a little presentation box, six of them. Miranda's tooth, Miranda's clothes, Miranda's bag.

My head was reeling. Miranda and the Major. The Major and Miranda? She'd dumped Kim for him? I folded the handkerchief back up, and slipped it back into my pocket. In the back of my mind was the thought that maybe this was the last bit of Miranda I would ever see, ever touch. If I did kill her, accidental like, then at least I'd have a little bit of her left to remember her by. I could make it into a pendant or put it in a locket or something, wear it round my neck, close to my heart.

Back home, Audrey was in the kitchen, peeling potatoes. She still had the hat on.

'I've got the barbecue out,' she trilled. 'It needed a bit of a scrub-up.'

I went into the bedroom and hauled the Major's bag from out under the bed.

'I've got to go out,' I said, standing in the doorway, bag in hand.

'What's that?'

'It's Major Fortingall's, remember, the one you wrote the card for. He left it in the car. He needs it.'

'Can't it wait?'

'No it can't.'

'When will you be back?' I raised my eyebrows.

'I don't know, Audrey, when I'm back, all right? Inquisition over?'

Her arms dropped to the side.

'Didn't last very long, did it?'

'What?'

'The new Al. The one I was growing to like.'

I felt it go out of me, like a tyre.

'Sorry.' I laid the membership card on the table. 'Look.

The old Al would have said, "See that? You're an unfit, flabby tub of lard and I don't like the look of you any more." The new Al says, "See that? You're a one-time power house, whose batteries are charging up again. Keep that hat on and tonight I'll search for your golf balls on my hands and knees by the light coming off you. Together we'll bungee jump down the Nile."'

It was bigger than all the rest of the houses in Chevening Road, number thirty-two, a little add-on to the right-hand side, with a separate door and a brass plate set into the wall. I stepped over to take a look. Major Fortingall, RCDS. Well, that explained the tooth.

I rang the doorbell. A voice called out. Nothing happened. I rang again. The door opened.

'Yes?'

She was older than the Major, Mrs Fortingall, flecks of grey in her short-cropped hair. She had a nice-shaped head, like a deer's, a trim figure with careful movements, and a mouth just a fraction too big for the face. She wasn't wearing any shoes.

'Al Greenwood, Mrs Fortingall. We spoke earlier on the phone.' I jiggled the bag in my hand. 'Is your husband in by any chance? I was passing and I thought . . .'

'Yes, yes. Come in, do.'

She stepped back, checking over her shoulder how presentable the place might be.

'Neil,' she shouted. 'You've got a visitor.'

I wiped my feet and stepped into the hall. Usual stuff. Little ornate mirror, little table with a little plant. A hall on the way to nowhere. We hovered. I could smell the antiseptic. I suppose they bring it home all the time, dentists. She looked like she could have been a bit of a dentist herself, calm, practical, a touch suggestive with all that stern efficiency. I noticed, her toenails were painted blue on one foot, red on the other. Not quite the straight arrow as she made out, then.

'Been running lately, Mrs Fortingall?'

'What? Oh.' She smiled, remembering our conversation. 'Not as much as I'd like.'

'We never do enough of the things we like doing, that's my belief, Mrs Fortingall. Life seems to get in the way. You must know that, having the surgery right on your doorstep.'

She nodded, nervous, unsure of where the conversation was going. She turned again. 'Neil, did you hear me?' She turned back. 'Is that the bag?'

'I hope it is, otherwise I've come here for nothing.' I looked right onto her mouth when I said that. She knew what I was really looking at. 'Ah, speak of the devil.'

Footsteps came clattering down the stairway, followed by pale legs and spotted boxer shorts. Major Neil Fortingall. When he saw me he stopped, his hand gripping the rail.

'Ah, Major Fortingall. Al Greenwood here. You remember, your taxi driver from the other day? I think I might have found your holdall.'

I gave it a friendly shake. He looked at it like there was somebody's head in it. Of course, in a kind of way, there had been.

'Since when have you taken up running?' Mrs Fortingall put a hand on her hip, tension in her voice.

'I was going to surprise you,' he said. I'll say.

He hovered. It was time to help him out.

'What's the matter, Major? You don't look pleased to see it. Don't tell me this isn't it.'

He came down into the hallway proper.

'But it isn't. I don't know where you got that from, but it wasn't from me.'

He said it well, I must admit, not too strong, not too weak, just like he was a mite irritated, having his evening messed up. I shook my head, tut-tutted myself. I always was a good actor. Funny, charming, a little bit lovable, I could do them all, a sliver of ice stuck in my heart.

'I must have picked up the wrong one. The boys down the garage told me they'd taken it out the car and put it in the locker for safe-keeping. Maybe they'd said *on* the locker. If you want to check the contents . . .'

He stepped up quickly, putting himself between his wife and me, his mouth setting suddenly hard out of her vision, his voice staying the same.

'There's no need for that. I'm absolutely positive. Mine's army issue.'

'Army issue, right. This must be one of the mechanics'. I am so very sorry, Major. You were going away, you said.' I moved to the side, so that she could see the two of us again. Keep him on his toes. She picked up on that right away.

'Going away? We're not going anywhere.'

'I'm on leave. I might have said I was going away, just to hurry you up. You know how it is.'

'Indeed I do, Major. No need to apologize. I understand. Tell you what I'll do. I drop it by tomorrow, or leave it at the base.'

'At the base would be best.'

'At the base it is, then. Let me give you my mobile number, so you can call me when you'll be there next. I want to give it to you personally, make sure it doesn't go jogging all by itself again. Toodle pip, Mrs Fortingall. Keep those endomorphs happy.'

I hadn't gone half a mile when the mobile rang. He was out in the garden. I could hear a blackbird singing.

'What do you think you're playing at?'

'I'm driving while on the mobile, Major. An endorsable offence in these modern times. Now what's on your mind?'

'You know quite well. What the devil did you mean by it?'

'I was just trying to return this holdall, Major Fortingall, like you asked me to. It is yours, isn't it?'

'You know perfectly well it is.'

'I'm not so sure about that. I think it might belong to Miranda Grogan.'

There was a silence.

'Did you hear me, Major, or have you gone through a tunnel?'

'I heard you. What do you want?'

'I'm not sure, to be honest. First, though, I'd like to know what you are doing with Miranda Grogan's clothes and Miranda Grogan's underwear. Not to mention her tooth.'

'I'll tell you. Tonight. All right. You know the Red Lion, on the main road?'

'I know it.'

'Give me an hour.'

I parked up by the lay-by, went through that bag with a fine-tooth comb. Yes, these were Miranda's all right. I should have known by the cut of them, the way they flaunted themselves at you. Even without her body inside them, you could tell the sort of woman they belonged to, the sort of woman Miranda was. I sat there, leafing through them like they were photographs, trying to remember if I'd seen her wearing this or that, up at the caravan, down in the pub, or just walking along the street. Thought of them strewn about the caravan too, the Major's fingers scrabbling in amongst them, a button here, a clasp there. It was doing my head in, Miranda and the Major, using my caravan for that sort of carry-on. Every time she spent the afternoon there with me she'd have been thinking about the next afternoon she was going to spend with him, or worse still, thinking of the last time, patting the seats, rearranging the cushions, eating my biscuits, remembering it all. And I hadn't twigged at all, thought it was our own company she liked, mine and hers, our chats, our laughs, our special place, and all the time it was theirs. And he thought he was going to walk away from this, scot-free? Ask me another.

I zipped the bag up, chucked it in the back.

'Mr Greenwood?'

I looked up. PC Corn-Plaster was at the window.

'Dave.'

'Everything all right?' he said, peering in.

'Everything's fine. Just about to have a quiet smoke. Audrey doesn't like it in the house.'

'No worries, only just to warn you, we've had a number of reports from people coming here, courting couples and the like. Peeping toms. Dog watchers.'

'Dog watchers?'

'You know, people at it.'

'It's a bit early for that, isn't it? It's not even dark.'

'I know that, but if they happened to come along right now, they might get the wrong idea about you, all on your own. Those squaddies, when their blood is up . . .'

'Point taken, Dave, point taken. A smoke in the garden, much better idea. I'll be moving on.'

'That's the ticket.'

I watched the blue bulb on his police car disappear down the road, before turning round. It was going to be a nice evening. What wind there was had gone inland. There was the calm about the place that only that strip between the sea and the land can give, like everything has been pushed aside for it to lie just so. Audrey would be in the conservatory, leafing through her brochures, or outside, whacking another clutch of golf balls, maybe with my head on, maybe not. When I got to the Red Lion, Major Fortingall was already there, sitting at an empty table, drumming his fingers against the chipped varnish. He was worried.

I sat down. He leant forward, his face all ready for some furious whispering.

'Now. What exactly do you want?'

I smiled, rubbed my hands. 'Thank you. I'll have a Löwenbräu since you're offering and maybe a plate of nibbles. I haven't eaten all day.'

I watched him walk to the bar. He had his money in a little pouch, notes in one side, coins in the other. There was a composure about him, a neatness, which reminded me of Ted. No, it couldn't be that simple.

He returned, lager for me, vodka for him. Wife wouldn't smell a vodka.

'I got some olives,' he said.

'Very nice. I like a good olive.' I popped one in my mouth. Sump oil. 'So, it is Miranda's bag, isn't it?'

He took a deep breath. 'Yes. Can I see it?'

'No. Let's keep it in the boot, away from prying eyes. Tell me about it.'

'It's a long story.'

'Don't worry. When these olives run out, you can get some cashew nuts. You two are . . . I crossed my fingers.'

'Yes.'

'Serious?'

'More serious than we thought.' He drained his drink in one, stuck the glass back on the table. He was one for the theatrics, Major Fortingall.

'I need another.'

He went back to the bar. A double this time.

'When did it start?' I asked.

'About a year ago. She came for an interview. There was a job going, trainee dental assistant. We got talking, really talking. It was as if we'd known each other for years. It went on for over an hour, and then we kind of came to our senses and she flustered and I flustered and

I asked her back for a second interview, a week later. A week. I was at the camp that week. I kept seeing her. We could hardly look at each other.'

'And?'

'The second interview was terrible. The room was filled with static. I couldn't think of anything to say, neither could she. We knew it wasn't about the interview, even then. After about twenty minutes of me faffing around, she said, "You're not going to give me this job, are you?" I said, "No." She said, "What are you going to give me, then? You got to give me something. Look at me. I haven't got dressed up like this for nothing."'

I couldn't help smiling. That sounded like Miranda.

'And then?'

'I kissed her.'

'And then.'

'Then it started. It wasn't easy, her on her shifts, me with my duties, working from home half the week, up at the camp the other.'

'Where did you meet? Don't tell me. In a caravan.'

'How did you know?'

'I know, that's all. Since when?'

'Since about eight months ago.'

'Afternoons, evenings?'

'Afternoons mainly, though there were times . . .' His voice trailed off. 'Anyway, what's this got to do with you?'

'Never you mind what it's got to do with me. Eight months you say.'

'Yes, eight wonderful months. Only it wasn't enough. We wanted more. We wanted it all.'

'You know she's missing, I suppose. That this bag of yours . . .'

'Course I know she's missing. I was waiting for her.'

'Waiting?'

'My wife had been away for the weekend. I sneaked her into the house on Friday evening. We'd already decided to do it, make the break, quick, sudden, no questions asked, nothing held back. I was on call on Saturday, but my leave started on Sunday. Jumping the wall, she called it. I was going to leave a letter for Audrey.'

'Audrey?'

'My wife.'

I started to laugh.

'What's so funny?'

'Nothing. Go on.'

'Miranda left on Sunday morning, around lunchtime. She left her bag with me. She was going to go back to tell her mum and dad, about us, then meet me at the station, on Sunday evening. We were going to Paris for a week, take it from there. I'd bought tickets.'

'Only . . .'

'She never turned up. I thought she must have had cold feet.'

'Did you try calling her?'

'Her mobile wasn't on. Still isn't. I thought I'd try and see her that Monday. There was an emergency. The CO had cracked a tooth. The other dentist was over at Salisbury. I offered to go in, took the bag with me, before Audrey got back. I could have left it at the base, if nothing else. But I thought she'd be there, back on her shift.'

'Why didn't you drive?'

'Audrey had the car.'

'I see.' I shook my head. 'I wish she was called some-thing else.'

'What?'

'Your wife. I wish she was called something else. It doesn't sound very army of you, this running off.'

'So? The army was Audrey's idea. Her dad's army. Her brother's army. The whole bloody Rainbird family. It's a wonderful life, she said. I hate it. Bloody hate it.'

'And the tooth?'

'Two weeks back. Audrey was at the gym, Miranda was there, complaining about this pain, dentist couldn't see her until tomorrow morning. Audrey said, "Come over and let my husband take a look at it." It was a shock, seeing them drive up together.'

'And you took it out?'

'I extracted it, yes. It was a big one.'

'This it?'

I took it out my pocket, unfolded the handkerchief. We both looked at it.

'She was going to get it made into a pendant, so I could wear it.' He put his hand out. 'May I?'

'No. You may not.' I put it back in my pocket.

'What are you going to do with it, the bag?'

It was a good question. What was I going to do with it?

'I don't rightly know. I could drop you in it, that's for sure.'

'Perhaps you want money.'

See, he thought the worst of me. So I was happy to oblige.

'Perhaps, though your wife would be nicer. What do you say? That bag in exchange for your wife. She has a way with her that appeals. I mean, if you don't want her, why not? A shame to let an attractive woman like that go to waste. You could give me a few tips, what she likes and that, set me up.'

He looked at me unsure if this was a bargaining chip or a wind-up.

'You disgust me.'

'I can handle that. I mean it's better than money, isn't it? What do you care?'

'I care about my wife.'

'You're just saying that. Now, this gym she goes to. What time?'

'I don't know.'

'Yes you do. She's a regular. She'll go at a regular time. Now stop fucking about and tell me.'

'Ten thirty.'

'Every day?'

'Mondays, Wednesdays and Fridays.'

'And leaves?'

'An hour later.'

'And does she get changed there, or at home?'

'At home. Look, what is this?'

'You know what this is, Major. This is your passport, to peace, security and a shut mouth. But that aside, what have you got to lose? She may not go for me. You get the bag, I get nothing. The swap of the century. Think about it.'

I left him, drove the car round the back, and watched him climb into his Passat and drive off. Then I went back in, had a couple more pints. I didn't really want his wife. I just wanted to make him feel dirty. Dirty and unsure, dirty and worried, worried what might come out, worried enough to keep his mouth shut. If he started talking about Miranda and what they got up to, the caravan would pop up in no time, and I didn't want that.

It was late when I got back, later than I had hoped for, but when I parked the car it felt good, good to be back, good to be home. I rubbed my face to make sure I wasn't dreaming. Home with Audrey. Christ, I hadn't felt like that in years. I got out the car, unsteady on my feet, not through the drink, but what I was feeling. Audrey was standing by the back door, the barbecue apron tied around her waist. It was OK. The hat was still in place.

'Sorry I'm late. Is that the barbecue I can smell cooking?'

'Not cooking, exactly.' She handed me a glass of wine. 'You know you were asking about Mrs Blackstock?'

'Was I?'

'Yes. This morning. Said you hadn't seen her for a bit.' She was preparing me for a shock, bless her.

'Can't remember. God that smells good, Audrey.'

'Well, drink up. I've got a surprise for you.'

She led me through.

Mrs Poke Nose was sitting on the patio, tucking into my lobster. She had a whacking great bandage wrapped round her forehead, just like the one I needed for the crack opening up in my head.

'Al,' I heard Audrey calling out. 'Al, are you all right?'

# Nine

When I came round I was lying on the sun-lounger, Audrey standing over me, waving what was left of the lobster under my nose. I pulled back. It's not what one expects after a black-out.

'I didn't have smelling salts,' she offered, by way of explanation. 'What happened? You went all floppy.'

'I must have got out the car too fast,' I said. 'The blood just rushed from my head.' I lowered my voice. Mrs Poke Nose was sitting at the other end, tucking into a slice of Brie. 'What's she doing here?'

'Alice has had a fall,' Audrey announced loudly, using that kiddie, singsong voice she uses when talking to the waiters over at Mr Singh's. 'She lay there for a whole day, didn't you, Alice?'

'A whole night,' Mrs Poke Nose corrected. 'I fell down the stairs and lay there all night. When I came to, it was just getting light. I managed to crawl to the telephone and call the ambulance. They were there in fifteen minutes.' She patted her head.

'We never heard anything, did we, Al?'

I tried to shake my head, but it hurt too much. We wouldn't have, Audrey thanks to the litre of Shiraz she'd taken on board and me on account of smoking the remainder of Mrs Poke Nose's stash down by the pond.

'They wanted to keep me in overnight,' she was saying, 'but I wasn't having any of that, not with all those killer germs under the beds. Besides, I felt pretty good, considering I'd just spent a night on the tiles.' And she laughed. Quite a horrid laugh, actually.

'Very sensible, Alice,' Audrey agreed. 'Especially when you've got neighbours to look after you. What was it, just a giddy turn?'

Poke Nose shook her head. 'It was that trip to the dentist that did it. I'd taken some medication to calm my nerves, and what with that and all the injections they gave me, my balance was completely fucked. F.U.C.K., fucked.'

I winced, a stab of pain going through my left eye. It always unsettles me, that sort of language coming out of the Alice Blackstocks of this world. Not that she was totally in control. You could tell by the grin on her face while she said it that she still wasn't right.

'I suppose you had to help me up the stairs, Alan.'

'That's right, Mrs Blackstock. Set you down on your upstairs settee. You were a little woozy, I'll admit.'

Audrey wagged a finger at me. 'You should have stayed with her, Al. She could have been killed.'

Mrs Poke Nose brushed it aside. 'Don't apologize, Alan. I must have been quite a handful. Not that I can remember anything.'

And then she winked at me.

Now here's the thing. That wink. It got me thinking. Was she telling the truth? Couldn't she really remember, or was she telling me in her own queer way that she could remember *everything*, the ride back, the conversation, the foot.

'Nothing at all, Mrs Blackstock?'

'Nothing after the first injection. They said I was singing in the surgery. I probably inflicted the same punishment to you on the way back.'

'A little bit.'

'What was it? Neil Young? Leonard Cohen? Dylan?'

'Leonard Cohen?'

'Yes. I'm a great fan. "Suzanne". "Bird on the Wire",
"Songs of Love and Hate". All that darkness swirling
underneath.'

I tried not to show it, but it was horrible, hearing my
own thoughts coming back at me from someone like her.
Horrible. Leonard Cohen was private. She had no bloody
right to like him too. He was mine, not hers.

'No, I didn't think it was any of those, Mrs Blackstock.
Sounded more like the Monkees. "Last Train to Clarks-
ville".'

She shuddered. 'I don't know how you put up with it,
me wailing beside you while you were trying to drive me
home. Surprised you didn't chuck me out.'

Audrey seemed to find that funny. Laughed. Quite a
horrid laugh, actually. It seemed to be catching.

'You sat in the back, Mrs Blackstock.'

'Did I? See! I don't remember a thing! Good job I
had you to look after me. Goodness knows what might
have happened if I'd let a stranger take me home. Why,
he could have robbed me blind and thrown me down the
stairs and I wouldn't have been any the wiser. And call
me Alice, please.'

She folded her hands in her lap, and looked around,
like Audrey did in somebody else's house, inspecting

while not inspecting, marking it out of ten. Six, judging by her expression. Then her eyes fell on the set of baby-Jesus Titian blanket and cushions that Audrey had brought back from her coach trip to Lourdes. Four. Possibly three.

'Alice is going to stay with us a couple of days,' Audrey said. She patted a small suitcase that lay at my feet.

'You're joking!' Did I say that out loud? Audrey looked at me hard. My head was back on the golf tee again.

'It's all arranged. She can't manage two floors, can she, not in her condition. We've a spare bedroom, en-suite. Why not make proper use of it?' She turned to offer Poke Nose a confidence. 'We only use it when Al's drunk too much and starts snoring, but that's a thing of the past, isn't it, Al?'

'Yes. I'm a new man now, Mrs Blackstock. It's quite thrilling really.'

Alice clasped her hands in appreciation.

'Oh, you two. I don't want to be any trouble.' She cut another wedge of Brie, and bit into it, like it was a slice of cake. That was part of our packed lunch, for our run to Salisbury.

'Not any trouble at all, Alice,' Audrey reassured her. 'It's what neighbours are for. Now, is there anything else you'd like us to get?'

'My iPod perhaps, something to read. And, would you mind very much if I smoked?'

'Not at all. Al usually goes to the box room at around seven to have a private puff, but as long as we keep the windows open, you can smoke here in the conservatory any time you like. Just help yourself to Al's. He's always leaving them lying around.'

'Not any more. There's nothing I leave behind now, socks, cigarettes, subterfuge, all banished from the premises. You could say, once I've left a room, you wouldn't know I'd been there.'

Alice wagged her finger at us. She was enjoying it, this marital banter.

'Oh, I won't be smoking Al's. I prefer roll-ups. Sins of my youth. I've an old tobacco tin somewhere. It should be in my bag but I can't seem to find it. Perhaps if someone could have a dig around for me. Here, take the spare key.' She reached in her bag, fumbled about. 'It doesn't matter if you can't,' she said, handing it to Audrey. 'I've usually got an ounce or two tucked away somewhere.' She sat back, plumping up her cushion.

'Al will be happy to, won't you, Al?'

'Rather,' I said, getting up. 'Hand the key over, and I'll poke my nose around.'

I needed another drink. Not only had I failed to kill Audrey and Mrs Poke Nose, pushed the wrong woman off the cliff, now I had to replenish Mrs Poke Nose's dope tin with some credible replacement. It was unsettling. Every time I tried to bump someone off, up they popped in my front room. Bungee jumping wasn't in it.

Doc was in at his usual place on the stool in the corner, under the stuffed fox he'd shot from his surgery window. There are not many doctors who keep a shotgun under the examination couch. Wacko Jacko was at the other end with one of his mates. They looked like unwanted relatives at a cut-price wedding, horrible shiny jackets, horrible traffic-light ties, horrible groomed hair, plastered flat like on a cadaver. They were smiling too. Jacko raised a glass at me, a greeting or a warning I couldn't be sure. I pulled the stool out beside the reluctant medic.

'Doc. How's Dodge City?' He pushed his empty out, nodding to Paul the barman. Three already I'd have said, by the state of his eyes.

'Been spitting blood in my handkerchief all day,' he said.

I patted my pocket. 'Don't talk to me about handkerchiefs.' I caught his look. 'Never mind. How's business? Busy?'

'The usual holiday-maker troubles. Calor-gas burns. Cystitis. The obligatory smashed thumb. Tent pegs,' he said, by way of explanation. 'You locals are all leaving me for the new practice over at Wool. The waiting room's so empty I'm starting to read the magazines myself. And I've already read them. Something drastic is called for. I thought a couple of slot machines might do the trick.'

'What happened to the new partner, the one who was going to turn things around?'

He held up three fingers. 'Gone,' he said.

'What, weeks?'

'Days,' he admitted. 'One day moving in, one day getting to know me, one day writing to the BMW.'

He put his hand round his next drink. He had mottled hands, yellow fingers. The tremor was not just in his voice. It had settled in his whole body, like a disease. I could still remember when he first came, roaring up in his open-top MG. It wasn't that long ago.

'Don't you mean the BMA?'

'BMA, BMW, what's the difference?' He tossed the drink back. 'They're both driven by arseholes.'

He tried to make it sound funny, but he wasn't laughing. Bitter memories and a place at the bar, that's all he had left. Life had been plain sailing for him once; a jaunty cap, a rakish smile, a few rude jokes, that was Doc, a little bit fast, a little bit loose, a little bit risqué with his lady patients. Now he couldn't even smoke his pipe in public.

'Have you heard?' he said. 'They've found something down by the cove.'

My heart dropped, blood flooded my eyes. I had to hold on to the bar to keep the voice steady. I could hear every bad thing I had ever done accusing me. See what happens when you do wrong. It comes back, big time.

'What sort of something?'

He shrugged his shoulders. 'They never tell me anything these days. Saw our local flatfoot, though, scurrying down there as fast as his varicose-veined legs would carry him.'

'A body, was it?'

He shook his head. 'They'd fill the place up a bit more for a corpse. Forensics, dogs, the man with the rectal thermometer. I used to do that sort of thing for them once. Car crashes, gun accidents, the odd splat off the cliff. Makes a nice change, when they don't talk back.'

'Clothing, perhaps.'

'Clothing?'

'Yes. She was wearing a yellow oilskin.'

'Who was?'

'Miranda. Miranda Grogan.'

'What's she got to do with it?'

'You said they found something.'

'Down the cove, yes. I didn't say it was anything to do with Miranda.'

'What else would they be looking for?'

'How the hell should I know. Illegals? Drugs?'

That's it, see. Your viewpoint is different when you've crossed the line. You can't help showing it, however hard you try. It just bubbles up every time, like bad air. Doc didn't seem to notice, though. He just started banging on about the old days. Jacko slid over. His eyes were very bright.

'Jacko. You're all togged up tonight.'

'I'm meeting someone. Best to dress up, business or pleasure. So you found your way all right? To the administration block.'

'The other day? Yes. Nay bother.' He didn't rise to it, the fake Scots. They'd been told to be on their best behaviour down the local. It was quite fun, seeing how far you could needle them.

'Only I couldn't help noticing,' he said, his voice excessively polite, 'you didn't have any sat-nav in the Vanden Plas. I got a couple if you're interested, top of the range, very high quality, very nice turn of phrase on madam instructress.'

'Waste of money, Jacko. A map is all I need. You ken?' He tried to keep a straight face but there was a flicker under the left eye, and his hand tensed round his pint glass.

'A map? Did you hear that, Rodney? A map is all the man needs. I went on a course once, on Dartmoor, with a map. Orienteering. Know what happened?'

'No, what happened?'

'I got lost.' He started to laugh. 'Now, if I'd had a posh tart telling me where to get off . . .' He sipped his lager. 'Don't get me wrong. The Vanden Plas is a quality motor. All that walnut veneer, must be all of a millimetre thick. And those sprung seats. Why, they're very nearly leather, aren't they? All it needs is a quality sat-nav, and that Vanden Plas could grace the buttocks of someone even as prestigious as Lady Di.'

'And there's no better buttocks to grace than Lady Di's, dead or no,' Rodney added, shifting his weight onto his back foot.

'Not that there aren't some fine local buttocks to be had,' Jacko said, warming to the theme. 'It's all that salt in the air, that and the sea swimming. Plumps them up most vividly. Don't need a sat-nav to find your way round some of those.' Jacko turned. 'You know to my mind, Rodney, they missed a big opportunity there, with the sat-nav thing, getting the right person to do the voice-over. Some of them are no better than the speaking clock or that wee eunuch they got strapped to the microphone at Euston station. I mean imagine what they could have achieved if they'd got Lady Di to do it instead. There you are, driving down the A1 and suddenly Lady Di pops up and says, "Scotch Corner. Take the first left, you naughty boy." Imagine the sales potential in that.'

I looked from one to the other. They were holding their glasses in their arms and grinning horribly. Suddenly I could see it all, Jacko and the rest of them up in the NAAFI canteen, leering at her as she walked away. I put my pint down, faced them square on.

'You talking about Miranda, Jacko, Miranda Grogan?

Have you got something we should know about? You know she's missing, don't you.' The smile was wiped clean.

'Missing? No I did not. What, like vanished?'

'Last Sunday afternoon, when it was pissing down.'

'Sunday?' He scratched his head.

'Well?'

'No, I didn't know.' He sounded almost concerned. 'Sunday, you say?'

'Yes, I've already said Sunday. In the afternoon. Late.'

'And she hasn't been heard of since? I don't like the sound of that. Miss Grogan is not the sort of girl to go missing. Not with that head of hair, that spirit.'

'What do you mean? Sounds like you know her.'

'Of course I know her. Everybody in the camp knows her. There's no' many women at the end of a NAAFI serving spoon like Miranda Grogan. Whatever she's dishing out, the lads'll eat it, and come back for more. They can get away with some terrible concoctions as long as she's doling it out.' He supped his beer again. 'Missing,' he repeated. 'I do not like the sound of that.'

'No one likes the sound of it, Jacko. I'm surprised you haven't heard about it already. The police have been round, surely?'

I was staring at him hard. All those men, looking at her mouth, peering down her front, imagining it all, what they would like to do.

'Well, don't look at me, pal. I've got nothing to do with it. Fine Scottish name like that. Is that what the kerfuffle is all about?'

The zing seemed to have gone out of him. He looked deflated. Troubled even. Perhaps I'd got him down wrong.

'What kerfuffle?'

'Down by the cove. There may not be police up at the camp but they got plenty down at the cove at the moment, dogs and everything.' He put his glass down. 'And you thought to lay it at my door. That's not very nice, Mr Greenwood. One could take umbrage. The sort that's best aired outside. *You ken.*' I put my hand out.

'No offence meant, Jacko, on my life. As a matter of fact I was hoping you'd be here. I've a favour to ask.'

'A favour. Vanden Plas man wants a favour but no sat-nav.' The face became alert again, waiting for the chance. 'Drink up, Rodney, the next one's on him.'

'Yes.' I looked around. Doc was arguing with his fox. Under the circumstances it was worth a try. Anything to keep Mrs Poke Nose off my back. 'The thing is, I need some more . . .'

'Amphetamines?' Jacko didn't even bother to lower his voice. 'I've got some cracking stuff in at the moment. Like driving up the autobahn the wrong way.'

I shook my head again. Jacko looked disappointed. There was a time when I used to buy them off him, off and on. On mainly, work, play, the boring bits in between, that sort of thing. It's what I ran the dog over on. All I could hear above Audrey's screaming and the little dog bleating was the grinding of my teeth. That's when I stopped. If I hadn't batted out the drive like it was on fire, he wouldn't have had his insides squashed out like that. I liked that dog. Monty we called him on account of his stature and the way his tongue hung out of his mouth, like he was always thirsty. A desert rat.

'Well, spit it out,' Jacko said, swirling the last of his lager round. 'Are we moving into a more complicated territory here? Is it a gun you require? Or a grenade? I got some very handy grenades.'

'Jacko. What would I need a grenade for?'

'Fishing? Turf warfare? That Newdick fellow's cut you right out, hasn't he? That's why I was surprised to see you the other day. If you're thinking of moving on him, a sat-nav on your dashboard and a grenade in his could save you a lot of bother.'

'I'm not after anything military. Grass. Do you know where I might get some good-quality grass.'

'Not military, you say?' He laughed. 'What do you think the tank crews run on, diesel?' He looked down at me. 'Can't help you there. Too bulky, too easy to sniff out, too low a mark-up. We get ours from outside. Rodney knows someone who knows someone. Isn't that right, Rodney?'

Rodney made ready. But I wasn't listening any more. It had suddenly come to me what I must do, where I must go.

'What's today, Jacko? Wednesday? Thursday? It's Wednesday, isn't it?'

I left in a hurry, left without buying him that drink. Once outside I dug the card out of my wallet. Every last Wednesday of the month he'd said. And today was the 26th.

I gave the Vanden Plas some stick driving over,

worried that I might have missed them. I knew where it was, where they held their monthly meetings, some old village hall that had long been passed over for newer premises, made out of tin and corrugated iron. I'd driven past any number of times, seen it set back on a cracked plate of concrete, weeds growing through the gaps, the window panes all shrouded white like an abandoned shop, but it was only when I was standing inside on the bare floorboards, with the chairs in crooked rows and the little stage at the back, with the black curtain drawn across it, and the door to the side, where the little anteroom was, where they brewed the tea and brought out the biscuits, that it came back to me. It was where Mum and me used to come years ago, when I was still in shorts and she was in her prime. Every Thursday evening we went when we were on holiday, dancing, proper country dancing, run by Cecily somebody, tall like a silver birch, with strong brown arms and strong brown legs and a voice that cut through the chatter like the Shambles lightship foghorn. How old had she been then? Thirty-five? Sixty-five? There was no way a boy of seven could tell, but she was sturdy and lithe and never got tired. She spent all week doing the rounds, armed with her record player and her box of records, Mondays Langton Matravers, Tuesdays Winterborne Kingston, and in they'd come, spinsters in their long patterned dresses and shy smiles, couples glad of the chance of feeling another man's hand on their shoulder, another woman's arm round their waist, holidaymakers, most of them rubbish, clapping and stamping in that check-shirted hoe-down way that real dancers never do. But best of all were the farmers come down from the outlying farms, single men mostly, with their red-knuckled hands and their suet-pudding feet, and that awkward look in their eyes, faced with all that human cattle. But when they got on that dance floor, what! A kind of magic came over them when the music started up, like they'd been touched by a wand. The suet pudding turned to sponge cake, those red-knuckled hands went all light and delicate, those eyes began twinkling with such merriment you'd think they'd been on the cider. They'd dance the evening away, tea and orange squash and a biscuit halfway through, and then afterwards, the complicated stuff, when they could really show who's who. No better sight on the dance floor than a farmer who knows his steps. Mum was a good dancer too, and they knew it. They'd all murmur in approval when we turned up for the summer. We'd catch the quarter to six from the bus station and get there just as Cecily was setting up. I'd move the chairs to the sides while Mum helped with the refreshments, getting the cups and glasses ready. She loved those Thursday evenings. It was a kind of freedom for her, freedom to dance with men who would hold her respectful and have a bit of a chat, when she could feel the weight of another man's arms upon her, smell the scent of him, hear the study in his breath, and let it go at that. A kind of peace came onto her face those evenings, like a religion, like she'd found God, understood her place in the world. Then, when I was about thirteen, we stopped. I didn't want to go any more. Dancing was sissy, least I thought that sort was. So we didn't. She missed it, missed it something terrible. She'd ask me every now and again if I'd like to give it another try, but I'd sneer, turning my head away from her while doing it, so I wouldn't have to see her face, the disappointment she tried to hide. That's what I done to my mum with my selfishness, stopped her going, stopped it dead in the water, her little bit of pleasure in this world, when she could be just herself for an hour or two. She never asked for much and I stopped it. I feel bad about it even now.

I looked around. There were about twenty blokes, all standing about amongst the chairs, gabbing away in cardigans and brown shoes. A ginger-haired geezer at the back was packing up an old-fashioned slide projector, pushing his glasses back every time he bent down.

'Mr Greenwood! Alan! You found us all right, then?'

DI Adam Rump came striding up out of nowhere. 'You've just missed it,' he said, pumping my hand. 'Archie Warren has just given a very instructive talk on how to remove warts.' There was an excitement in his voice that seemed at odds with the subject. He had a little brooch stuck into his lapel. A pair of carps, kissing.

'That come with the membership?' I asked.

'Sign on the dotted line and you'll go home with one tonight. Come and meet the members. They'll be interested to hear about your Asagi. You have brought pictures, I take it.'

I had. I always had a couple on me. I liked having them around. They were family, Torvill and Dean. I was introduced, first one group, then another, knots of eager-beaver carp-lovers, sniffing around each other like pet terriers. They had a sort of crazy intensity about them, like it was a secret society. They talked in sharp bursts and every now and again two would go off for a hush-hush huddle, hands jabbing at the air like they were making a bomb or something. They were all interested in Torvill and Dean, though. It was quite a novelty for them, to meet someone who had a thing for such old-fashioned fish. I felt quite proud, and you know what, I thought Torvill and Dean would be proud of me too, the way I spoke about them. I kept my eye on Rump, though. The last thing I wanted was for him to bugger off before I'd have a chance to talk to him proper. I think he kept his eye on me too, for after about forty minutes we were back where we started, at the back of the hall, facing each other.

'Decent bunch, aren't they,' he said. 'Next month we're having one of Ireland's top judges over to give us a talk. We're each going to bring our prize specimen, to see what he says. Perhaps you'd like to bring one of yours along, or both if you're worried about separating them.'

Move Torvill and Dean? Slop them in a plastic bucket and have them banging about in the back of the car? The very idea.

'I'm not sure about that, Inspector. They're home-bodies, my fish.'

'Adam, please. No formality here. It's your decision, but if you're thinking of showing them at all, it's something you must get them used to, so they don't get too stressed when the time comes. It can quite ruin their chances, stress.' I nodded in agreement. Torvill did tend to go a bit blotchy when Dean got over-attentive.

'It's the curse of the modern age, isn't it, stress,' I said. 'I mean look at the village. Very tense, the atmosphere at the moment. No news, I suppose?'

'We're still trying to keep a lid on things, though poor

Freddy Lanchester has had to cull his whole stock. That's why he isn't here. An outbreak of herpes is just too risky.' He caught my look. 'Torvill and Dean would be quite safe, I assure you. We'll be taking all the necessary precautions. No chance of them going back with something they shouldn't.'

'No. You misunderstand me, Adam. It was more the worry in the village over Miranda Grogan I was referring to, you know the girl who's disappeared. There have been developments, I understand. Down by the cove.'

'On the path to the cove,' he corrected. 'I can't go into details, you understand.'

'Of course not. Good, bad?'

He shrugged his shoulders. 'We're not even certain if it has anything to do with her at all. Just an article of clothing. If nothing else turns up we'll have to let the matter rest. We are pretty sure she was meeting someone that day. My feeling is she did, and doesn't want to tell anyone.' He moved something in his fingers. A new lapel badge.

'Meeting someone?'

'Yes. Although he isn't very precise, her father thinks that one or two items of clothing have gone, though like most men he's not very good on women's wardrobes.' His nose twitched, then the right-hand corner of his bottom lip too. 'You know, we're a very unobservant genus, Alan, very unobservant, especially when it comes to our own kind. Why is that, I wonder? I mean, you can describe Torvill and Dean's markings, can't you? Of course you can, right down to the last detail. But quickly now. What colour are your wife's eyes?'

'Bloodshot.' It came out without thinking, the old Al speak. 'No, joking aside. Brown, I think. Bluey-brown, that's it, with a touch of grey.'

'See what I mean. You're not quite certain. It's like these sightings. They're all very nebulous, the yellow oilskin at the bus stop, the yellow oilskin on the path. The crying.'

'The crying?'

'Yes. Both at the bus stop and on the path. Both witnesses say they thought they heard the person crying.'

'You think they might be the same woman, then?'

He looked at me. I was showing too much interest, I knew, but I couldn't stop myself. Just couldn't.

'If it was the path and then the bus stop, I'd say quite possibly, but this way, I doubt it.'

'Oh?'

'It's the wrong way round, isn't it? Going for a walk and then walking up to wait at the bus stop is one thing. Waiting at the bus stop and then going for a walk is another. The first one's plausible, the second one isn't, even accounting for the upset emotions. And the timing of the sightings suggests the latter.'

'Unless she was just sheltering from the rain, before the walk.'

'What, sheltering until the weather got worse? And what makes you think they were both women?'

'Nothing, I just assumed . . . with the crying . . .'

'That's the trouble. Everyone assumes. Assumes the bus stop was a woman, assumes the cliff path was a woman, assumes one or both was Miranda Grogan, assumes there's something funny going on. We're not

sure who any of them were. Crying doesn't help. Men's
voices invariably rise a tone or two under such circumstances. The bus stop could have been a woman, but it
could have been a man. Likewise the path to the Beacon.
We could be dealing with two men or two women or one
man at the bus stop and one woman on the path, or a
woman at the bus stop and a man on the path, or the
same person, man or woman, each time. Do you see what
I mean? Six permutations of gender. They're not like our
fish, each one with particular markings.'

'Yes, they are, actually.'

'Well, yes they are, but they're not seen as such. Tall,
dark, short, fair, in my experience men and women tend
to blend into a sort of grey mass. Think how much better
it would be if we all had markings on our hands and
face, like your Asagi had, how much more interesting
we would be to look at, how much easier for identifica-
tion purposes. More rewarding too as regards to breeding.'

I looked at him. Audrey was right. The man was a
complete pillock, warbling on about his fish, when he
should have been out there, looking for her.

'So this find in the cove,' I persisted. 'You say it doesn't
point to anything specific, to do with Miranda?'

'It's too early to say. Of course, if it does prove to be
belonging to her, then it would point to the woman in the
yellow oilskin going up the path being her too.'

Please, don't say that. Please. Anything but that.

'Does that worry you, Mr Greenwood?' He was looking
at me, burrowing into my face.

'Worry me? Only in as much as I wish she was safe
at home with her feet up and had never gone out that

afternoon, specially not near the Beacon in that weather, that wind. Though she's a sensible girl. She wouldn't have stood near the edge of a cliff, not after what her father gets up to.'

'She's not like you, then?'

'Not at all,' I said, hoping it was true, knowing it wasn't. 'I'm a bloke. Only blokes do stupid things like that. You must see that all the time.'

'Every day of my life. We're not a very commendable species.'

'You prefer fish, I take it.'

'Don't you?' He looked around. 'Don't we all. Isn't that why you're here?'

He opened up his hand, question lines running across his forehead. The carp badge lay in his palm, fish lips kissing, just like Torvill and Dean do, barely touching, as if they're shy, kissing for the first time. I took out my chequebook and signed up, stood quite still as he stuck the little badge in the lapel of my jacket, the jacket with Miranda's tooth wrapped up safe in Miranda's handkerchief. It made me feel special that, her tooth and her handkerchief just a waft of worsted away from him and him knowing nothing about it. What did DI Rump know of men and women, up in caravans, in cars and lay-bys, in and out their yellow macs, tearing great lumps out of each other, bloody life in their hands? He saw it all, but what did he know? What would he ever know?

'Well, mustn't keep you, Adam. I expect you need to get back home.'

'Home.' He laughed, a bitter-tasting thing. 'The wife's left me, would you believe. Apparently I spend too much time with my underwater companions. I mean. I ask you, how can anyone spend too much time with their fish?'

He had a point.

'Audrey's the same,' I admitted. His head went up and down like a nodding dog.

'What is it, do you think, about women and fish? Jealousy, the fact that fish have got fins? I mean, it isn't as if women haven't got attributes of their own.'

I felt obliged to defend.

'It was Audrey's idea as a matter of fact, the carp.'

'Was it?' He seemed almost jealous. 'You're a lucky man, Al, a lucky man.'

He stood at the door watching as I drove away.

When I got back the bungalow was mostly in the dark, though I could see Audrey's bedside light shining through the curtains onto the lawn at the side. She likes a late-night read, Audrey, big clunky books that form a hole in the mattress, days of yore in the main, medieval monks, knights on chargers, the odd distressed virgin. Likes them bloody too, bloody battles and bloody murders, racks and red-hot pokers and that thing in the Spanish Inquisition they had, made out of ropes. She used to read the gory bits out to me in bed, and it made me laugh, the way her lips went dry, her voice all quiet with hearts ripped out and heads lopped off and little kiddies chucked on the bonfire. Medieval rumpy-pumpy she'd keep to herself, but I could always tell when she was reading it, because she'd suddenly shift herself, hold the book at an angle, so that I couldn't see the words, hear them ringing in her head. Some books seemed to have medieval rumpy-pumpy on every other page, for she'd be squirming about like that woman newsreader on breakfast telly, the short pert one who can't sit still, her hand hovering over the page, like she was back at school, hiding her work from prying eyes.

'What you got there, Audrey?' I'd say, giving her backside a prod. 'Come on, let's have a listen,' but she never would, just tell me to keep my hands to myself and carry on until it was safe for me to be in reading range once more.

There was a faint light coming from upstairs in Alice Blackstock's house too. Had that been on all the time she'd been away? I hadn't noticed it before. I took the tin out the dashboard compartment, walked up the path and slid in the key.

'Hello?' I said, opening the door. 'Anyone there?'

I could hear my voice going up the stairs, floating round the room above before coming back. It's funny how empty a house sounds when it's empty, not of things, but something living, how it doesn't care, how full of nothing it is. Just one person is all it takes, and it all sounds different, softer, less edge to it, like there's hope in the air. Dogs can do that too. Little Monty did that, despite his size. The bungalow never sounded empty when he was in it, but now when I walk in, sometimes it's like I've stepped into an abandoned submarine ready to send me to the bottom of the sea. Perhaps it's something as simple as body warmth that does it, absorbing the coldness, the indifference of the walls, I don't know. But as I stood there, listening, I knew, this was an empty house, light or

no light and I was glad of that. It was true what I'd said.
I had some poking around to do.

I'd asked Jacko for some, but that was more to get
myself out of a beating than anything else. I knew I didn't
have to go to him to get a refill for Poke Nose's tobacco
tin. All I had to do was to give her place the once-over,
look out for a few loose floorboards or depressions in
the carpet where furniture's been moved, scratches in the
woodwork, books out of kilter, anything that suggested
regular but concealed use and bingo. There it would be.
Her stash. She'd as good as admitted she had one. 'I've
usually got an ounce or two tucked away somewhere,'
she'd said, thinking that we both thought she was referring to tobacco. But I knew better. I knew there wasn't
any tobacco in her tin, not a whisper. Pure unadulterated
weed, that's what had lain underneath that little lid, good-
quality, home-grown, Wayne Fontana and the Mindben-
ders number one with a bullet. Skunk they call it now.
Not a name I approve of. Too alley-cat, too flop-house, too
altogether piss-in-the-corner low life. But weed or skunk,
that's what she had in that tin. But not the total sum of
it. The tin was just the amount she needed to carry about
in her bag while going for a walk, tripping down to
the shops, marching up Cliff Harris's drive to give him an
earful regarding the state of his donkeys. The tobacco tin
was like a sugar bowl, there for immediate use. The rest
was hidden away somewhere, somewhere not too difficult
to get at, somewhere discreet but handy. And I needed to
find it so that I could fill her tin up again, and while I was
at it, have another smoke myself, gratis. Of course I could

have told her I couldn't find the tin and still have had another smoke myself, but then that would have got Poke Nose doing what she likes best, raking over coals, thinking, about what had happened that day, and as far as I was concerned, until things had settled down and I'd worked out exactly what to do with her, filling Mrs Poke Nose's tobacco tin with the right stuff, filling it to the brim, filling it up like in that fairy tale so that it never got empty, was always there to get keep her all happy and smiling morning, noon and sodding night, quite unable to fix too well on the here and before, was somewhat of a priority.

'Fancy another smoke, Mrs Blackstock? Course you do. Don't mind us. Get stuck in, as the Doc would say.'

The downstairs was weird, stripped down, Spartan, not an ounce of comfort to be had anywhere. In one room there was nothing but floorboards and walls and a bamboo mat in the middle, with a white blind drawn over the window. In another stood a china sink and a wooden clothes horse and an old-fashioned mangle placed over a drain sunk in the floor. The kitchen was the same, bare-knuckle uncomfortable. One of them woks hung from a hook above a cheap Calor-gas stove, a black kettle standing on the hob. In front of the window overlooking the back garden was a chair and a small wooden table with a plate set in front of it, a pair of chopsticks by its side. At the back there was a big larder, but nothing in it except for those big sweet jars with screw-top lids, filled up with different veggie beans. Twelve of them I counted, twelve and a can of olive oil and a bowl of lemons. That was it. No fridge, no dishwasher, no Delia Smith cookbook, no multi-task food-processors, and definitely no crème brûlée blow-torch like Audrey made me buy her two Christmases ago and which she'd only used the once to wipe out the ants' nest. Just a drawer under the table with a set of wooden spoons and a packet of green tea. The whole downstairs was made for someone who wasn't there, even when she was.

I went upstairs. The light came from a standard lamp at the back of the sofa where I'd sat her down. I took in the other rooms at first, the ones I'd seen earlier. There was her bare bedroom and her bare bathroom, but I wasn't interested in those. I was interested in the locked door with the key in it, the door I couldn't open last time around. I jiggled it about, the key acting stubborn, like it didn't want to move, like it hadn't been used in a long time. A little patience did the trick, a little tender coaxing, a little down-on-the-bended-knee, close-up concentrating, working my fingers like feathers. Opens a lot of things, that kind of approach. Three minutes later and I was in. There wasn't a light switch, but a thick piece of rope dangling down, like a bell pull. I rang it.

It was a bigger room than her bedroom, bigger, closer, thicker; red wallpaper on the walls, dark like spilt blood, heavy brocade curtains hanging long at the window and, smack in the middle, like it was on show, a big double bed with a fancy carved headboard, naked dancers prancing about, all breasts and grapes, and below a quilt made out of rock-concert T-shirts, the Stones, the Floyd, the Dead, even one of the Fab Four at Shea Stadium, when no one heard a note they played for all the screams. At the foot of the bed, against the wall, was a chest of drawers, mahogany by the shine of it, the front curving in and out like a wave of sand, and on top, a photo of a man, the same one as I saw on the stairs, only he had Alice Blackstock in his arms this time, not a gold record, a younger Alice Blackstock, mid-forties, pearl-necklaced, smiling as if the sun came out for her alone every single day. Duncan, I supposed. The man who wasn't there. The house was full of them.

I pulled the drawers open, expecting clothes. Only they weren't hers, they were his, Paul Smith shirts and Aquascutum cashmeres, formal Turnbull and Asser stuff, gaudy Hawaiian rubbish, silk socks, gold cufflinks, silver tie pins, and in the bottom drawer a white linen suit with a yellow silk handkerchief tucked in the top pocket, the arms folded across like a corpse, everything wrapped in tissue paper, those little scented blocks of wood that Audrey has to keep the moths out in amongst them. Her man's best gear kept as fresh as the daisies he was now pushing up, next to the bed they'd made their own. No wonder she kept this room locked. No wonder she didn't go into it often. Go into a room like this and it would be hard to come out the same. I locked it behind me.

Now I'd been all over, it was easy to see how different the big room was to the rest of the place. It would be here, the stash, here in this big open room, here amongst the deep sofas, the scattered cushions, the ashtrays, the cut-glass whisky tumblers, the polished baby grand, the photos, the Morgan Short speakers standing like sentries on either side of the fireplace and opposite, along one whole wall, all those vinyl LPs. That's where her stash would be, I thought, behind a wedge of those, in a little recess, a cupboard.

There was a fridge in the room though, a big one, at the back, behind where the stairs came up, and I thought I should take a look at that first. No weed, but in the racks on the door stood bottles of vodka, Veda, Snow Leopard, Stolichnaya, some of that wicked Kremlyovskaya, and lo and behold, a bottle of Belvedere, which as it happened was my vodka of choice when I used to indulge. She knew her way around the distilled spirit, Alice Blackstock. Down the left-hand side was an ice dispenser, but I didn't bother with that, just unscrewed the top and took a belt. Unbelievable. I could practically hear it crunching through my nervous system like an icebreaker on its way to the magnetic North. The rest of the fridge was filled with chocolate, dark chocolate, bars and bars of it, Belgian, Swiss, German, that fancy stuff from France that I'd bought for Miranda one birthday a couple of years back, up in Park Lane. They make it in different shapes, not just bars, but cups and saucers, telephones, handcuffs. She'd come up to the caravan the day after her birthday, my present all wrapped up, with a bottle of champagne and a little cake with a candle on it beside it. When she'd got over showing me her new pair of boots and her new earrings that Iss and Ted had given her and was blowing out the candle, holding her hair back so it didn't get in the flame, I told her that I'd bought her a set of DIY tools, so she could learn to be a bit practical, and she'd wrinkled her nose up, all puzzled, tearing at the ribbon like the kid she still was, and there they were, a chocolate hammer, a

pair of chocolate pincers and three six-inch chocolate
nails lying in a little wooden box. She'd nearly brained
me, trying to bang one of them in, giggling all over me
with her scent and her young weight, and her laughing
looks. Best birthday party I'd ever been to, Miranda
and me and that chocolate hammer. We were so close, it
hurt. Here old Poke Nose had bought one shaped like a
lighthouse on a bunch of rocks. Only when I took it out
I saw it wasn't a lighthouse at all, but something else
entirely, something that Fortnum and Mason's wouldn't
ever dream of selling, not even if they could charge two
hundred quid an inch for it. A chocolate Tonto, that's
what it was, a chocolate Tonto, large as life, uncannily
accurate and with the top bitten clean off.

I held it there for a moment, looking at it, wondering
where she'd got it from, who the hell had made such a
thing, wondering too what it tasted like. I mean, it looked
good, but it was hard to contemplate, putting a chocolate
Tonto in my mouth. I know it was only confectionery, but
still, it didn't seem right, especially not alone, as if it was
something I could only do when no one was watching. I
must have held it for a good minute, my hand was getting
all warm and sticky, turning it this way and that, looking
underneath for the maker's stamp wondering whether it
was taken from real life or imagination, wondering, even,
if it was Duncan's. No, she wouldn't have bitten Duncan's
off like that, not if that photo was anything to go by. I
gave it a little lick, where the chocolate had started to
melt. Fabulous. Would I? Could I? 'Oh, fuck it,' I said,
closed my eyes and bit into it, took a bit more than I
meant to, but it slipped in so easy, it was hard to judge

how much I'd got in. It was brilliant, just what a chocolate Tonto should be, all bitter and sweet and softer than I'd thought possible. It was all I could do to keep myself from gobbling it off there and then. I gave it a little lick and put it back. Time for the LPs.

Took me half an hour to go through them all, taking them out handful by handful, but there was nothing there. She didn't half have a collection though, loads of them signed on the back, this from Mick, that from Janis, even one from Steve, the Small Face himself, bless him. She had all the Cohens, natch, but not one of them inked. Not a thing you'd ask someone like Leonard Cohen, I suppose, not unless you want to appear a prize prat. Still it didn't help with the frustration. No signed Leonard Cohen, no weed, and the chocolate Tonto out of bounds. Perhaps another drink. Perhaps not. I sat down on the sofa by the window, the one she'd crashed out on, and looked around. The fireplace? The speakers? Where else hadn't I looked. Was there a trap door or something? I shifted in my seat, re-arranging the cushion, trying to get comfortable. It was all spiky and scratchy, horsehair sticking into the small of my back. Not pleasant at all. Barely a cushion. More like a bale of . . .

I had it open in a jiffy, the zip along the top peeling back. There it was, Poke Nose's stash. Three cushions full she had in all, enough to float a whole tank regiment a couple of feet off the ground for a week. I took out her little tobacco tin and stuffed it to the gills, put a couple of handfuls in my pocket too.

Time to relax. Time to think things through. I rolled a big one. I opened the fridge door, took another swig,

another nibble and lit it, turned off the light and watched
it flare in the dark, sprawling out on that big comfy sofa,
the vodka, the cocoa beans, the weed, all washing in
and out my head like warm water. I still was no nearer
knowing what had happened than three days ago, where
Audrey went, who I pushed off, what happened to
Miranda and yet I was. In myself I was, even though none
of those questions had been answered. I felt, not in control
exactly, but as if nothing could happen to me, that it
would all pass over me, whatever it was, like a wave. The
coming weekend, Audrey and I would drive to Salisbury.
I'd treat her gentle, like Alice Blackstock's lock, my fingers
like feathers, my voice like massage oil running down her
back. I'd get it out of her, where she'd gone. Then I'd find
out what it was they'd found on the beach, Miranda's or
no. What could it be? A scarf, that boot I saw, a yellow
coat? And if it was hers, if I had done it to her, then I'd
done it to her, and that was that. And if it wasn't her, it
wasn't her, and that was that too. I mean what was it that
I had done really? Just the push of a hand, that's all. One
push. It's not a lot, is it, just one push. The pressure of
someone's fingertips upon another person for two sec-
onds, maybe three. Hardly any contact at all. Then there
was Miranda's bag. I should get rid of it, I knew that, let
the Major sort it out, but it didn't sit easy on me, just
handing it over. I wasn't convinced by what he told me,
not a hundred per cent. What if instead of leaving all
lovely-dovey that Sunday, they'd had a quarrel, she
wouldn't leave or something and the wife was coming
back. What if he'd killed her and I'd caught him trying to
get rid of her clobber? What if I *should* take it to the police?

I mean, he did leave it in my taxi. If only there wasn't the caravan.

I had a lot to think about.

I lay back. The moon had come out and the outside was lit up, all cold and blue, like time had frozen in its tracks. I lay there in the dark, blowing smoke into the air. You could see everything from that window, her lawn and her little border plants, the funny little shrine we'd sometimes smell her burning incense on; Audrey's alpine rockery, the dip in the lawn where poor old Monty was buried, the path leading to the fish pond where Torvill and Dean would be moving slowly about, nudging at their last bits of feed. Across the fence lay Kim Stokie's back garden, the back porch that stuck out further than the rest on account of the kitchen extension he built, the yard and the open outhouse where the gas cylinders stood alongside the cauldron where he cooked up his lobsters. You could even see the dark outline of the Beacon, way in the distance, blotting out the sky. From somewhere like this, Poke Nose would have seen me skulking back that afternoon, after pushing whoever it was off that cliff. God, what must I have looked like, searching this way and that, making sure no one was about. And there she was, up a fucking tree and me with the mark of murder upon me. Yes, I could leave it behind, but that's what I had on me now, on account of those fingertips. The mark of murder. And it stains, I knew it, whatever I wanted, whatever I hoped for. Whatever happened, it would always be there, what I'd done.

Suddenly, across the way, light flooded out onto Kim Stokie's yard, two long shadows caught in the frame, before the door shut again. I sat up. One was Kim Stokie. I recognized the way his bullet-shaped head sat upon his shoulders, but his companion? Kim seemed to be guiding whoever it was, his hand firm across their back. I couldn't see who it was, as Kim was blocking my view, but there was something furtive about the two of them, hurried, like they didn't want to be seen, like they shouldn't be there. That didn't look right. Kim was bare-headed, but the other fellow had a hat on, pulled firm over his eyes. They hurried across the yard towards the fence at the back, Kim looking this way and that, making sure no one was about, me in my garden, or Pat Fowler on the other side. Could that be Jacko with him, I thought, remembering that smirk on his face. I knew they were quite thick, the pair of them. It would be typical of him to get dressed up for a bit of villainy. They seemed to be carrying some sort of rope between them, I could see coils of it looped in Kim's hands, the other chap's too. Smuggling, that's what sprang to mind, good old-fashioned customs-and-excise knockabout, stuff coming in on the high tide, beached on one of those inaccessible beaches past Durdle Door, and Kim and his fellow reprobate ready to haul it up the cliff face.

Then they came to the fence, Kim heaving himself over, turning to help the other one over. As he did, the light shone down clearly on the other's head and all thoughts of smuggling went clean away. I could see the shape of him now, the swell of his bust beneath the coat, see his long hair hanging long and thick, like a woman's. It wasn't a hat he was wearing but an oilskin, a yellow one like the fishermen wear, with the hood up, and he had glasses on, dark glasses, to hide God knows what. I was on my feet now, hands pressed against the window. It couldn't be, but it was. Miranda, Miranda, holding her hair back and taking the fence easy and supple like only she could. But still something wasn't right, the chemistry between them, the way they set off across the field, her wanting to go fast, him slowing it down. Then I saw it. They weren't carrying the rope. He'd *tied* her to it, tied it fast round her waist, while he held on to the other end. He was holding her prisoner, like something in Roman times, like she was his slave, like he owned her!

It all made sense now. She'd told him it was all over. He couldn't take it. I know how something like that can build up inside a man, the injustice of it all, losing something that you think is yours. And then he saw her that Sunday afternoon, sheltering from the rain, or walking up from the cove, and he thought, Right, this is it, chum, just like I did Audrey, jumped out of his Peugeot and bundled her in, no one any the wiser. Perhaps he knew where she was going, saw all that wasn't his any more writ on her face and just flipped. I hadn't killed her at all. No one had. Kim Stokie had kidnapped her, taken her back to his place, shoved her in some room or other and bolted the door – which meant Gaynor must have been in on it too. No wonder she wasn't too happy to see Audrey that afternoon. Miranda had been locked up all this time, right under my very nose. And I'd found her. Me. Her dad, the real dad, the one that didn't exist. I'd found her, no one else, and now I was coming to her rescue!

I took the stairs two at a time, knocking hubby clean off the wall, the picture frame bouncing corner to corner

in front of me as I jumped down, glass cracking underfoot. Then I was out the front door and running round
the back, up towards the fence. They were in the middle
of the field now, walking up towards the path and the
Beacon, Miranda running ahead, trying to escape, Kim
yanking her back, almost pulling her over, squeals and
warnings filling the air. I slipped in between the two top
wires and ran, crouched and quiet, my feet soft under the
grass. He didn't hear me, concentrating as he was on my
poor girl twisting and turning like a fish on a hook, didn't
realize I was there until I was nearly on top of him, my
heart busting out my mouth, and then he turned, hand
up, palm out, like he was going to ward me off, but it was
too late for that, too late for him to see what or who was
going on, and I crashed into him, slammed my body into
his gut, my arms wrapping around his legs, feeling the
weight of him hitting the ground as he toppled over,
scrambling on top of him, belting him around the head
with my fists, my knees pinning down his arms. He was
younger than me, stronger than me, but I had the anger,
the upper hand, the God-given right to finish it there and
then. I wanted to kill him, felt the need for it growing
in my bones with every blow I landed. I wanted to
kill him, not like with Audrey or Alice Blackstock, but
to hurt him real bad, kick his head in, make him suffer,
watch him die, nothing but a bloody mess, face, dignity,
who he was, all gone, do it to him like I've wanted to do
it to someone all my rotten life. I knew who it really was
at the receiving end, even while I was hitting him, I knew
who it was, but it didn't matter. This was good enough.

Then someone kicked me in the side, right in the

kidneys, and Kim jerked up, banging his head on my nose, throwing me off onto the ground. I rolled over onto all fours but a foot came up hard under my ribs, knocking what little wind I had left out of me. I rolled over again and sat up, trying to get my breath. I wasn't as fit as I thought. And my hand! I hadn't felt a thing, but now, Christ. I blew on it, trying to ease the stabbing pain. Kim was four foot away, nursing his nose, Miranda standing between us.

'Miranda,' I gasped, wondering what they'd been feeding her that her legs should look like that. 'What the fuck did you do that for?'

She took no notice, but walked over to Kim, helped him sit up, rubbing the blood off with her sleeve. I couldn't understand it. Her hair seemed to be slipping off her head, like she'd been scalped. Then she threw back the hood, and tore it off, wiping his face clean with it, and I saw her head, the peroxide crew cut shining over her shades like a second moon.

'Gaynor?'

Kim got to his feet. I scrambled to mine, though it hurt. If we were going to have another scrap, I wasn't going to take it sitting down. He didn't look too pleased with me, took a step forward, fists hanging down by his side. She pulled him back.

'Gaynor,' I said again, my eyes darting from one to the other. 'Is that you?'

Kim placed a finger against his left nostril and honked bloody phlegm out onto the ground, wiping his nose on the back of his sleeve.

'Course it's fucking her,' he said, touching the side of

his face. 'Who'd you think it was?' He stooped to gather the rope up again, Gaynor stepping out the tangled coils. She was shaking.

'It's OK, love,' he said, his voice all calm and soft. 'Go on now. It'll be all right.'

Gaynor put her wig back on, then started to walk across the field again, hesitant at first, the rope trailing after her.

'Go on,' he said again, all reassuring. 'Nothing to worry about.'

'Kim,' I said, still panting, 'what the fuck's going on?'

He picked up the other end of the rope, tied it round his hand. She'd got into her stride now, half walk, half trot, like she couldn't quite decide which.

'Gaynor's going for a walk,' he said, picking up the slack. 'Not that it's any of your damn business.'

'On a lead?' I said, not quite believing what I was seeing. She was trotting round on the end of the rope, like a horse at the circus, her hands pawing the air.

'Why not?'

''Cause she's a human being, Kim, not a dog.' He stopped.

'You don't understand,' he said, watching her like a trainer might. 'The rope makes her feel safe. Go on, girl,' he whispered loudly. 'Go on.'

She started to somersault, run and somersault, no hands, just the jumping roll. She was an ungainly girl, Gaynor, but there was a beauty to what I was seeing, the way she ran so strong and sturdy, enjoying it so, cart-wheeling across the grass, laughing to herself. Thirty feet away and I could feel the ground shake. And I'd mistaken her for Miranda!

'I don't get it, Kim. I thought she couldn't go outside, she was, what-you-call-it, agoraphobic, housebound.' Kim pulled on the rope, pulling her in a little. There was a change to his voice, soft like a memory, brought out under dark.

'That's what we all thought. But then one night I got her to go out into the yard. She liked it as long as I was there, as long as she could see her way back. We started to go out every night, right as rain as long as I was with her, as long as she could see her way back. Then one night, after about a year or so, I thought I'd try her out here. Spooked her. I had to pick her up and carry her back, her screaming all the way.'

'About this time last year?' I said. 'We thought you were cooking lobsters.'

He nodded.

'Terrified, she were. Wouldn't go out for a month. So I had this idea. If she were tied to me, she'd know she could always get back, 'cause I would always be there to haul her back in, see her safe. That's what she's afraid of. It's not the outside as such. It's the thought of not being able to get back in, of being cut loose. So after a month of coaxing, we tried it, first the field, and then, further out. She can go for walks now, up to the Beacon, over to the old caravan site. We even been across the other way, over the army range. As long as the rope's there, as long as she's tied to me, she feels safe. See now why I could never leave her? I'm her passport to a bit of freedom.'

She'd stopped running and was walking along the path that cut the field in two, her running her hand over the uncut grass, reaching round every now and again to check the rope was still there. If it wasn't for that dark line snaking behind her, it would have looked almost normal.

'Wouldn't it be easier in the daytime, not as frightening for her? If she could see it all, see you.'

'What, and lose the disability allowance? She don't want the daytime any road, people looking at her, asking questions. Neither of us do. Daytime's for inside. Night time is . . .'

'The right time, yeah I know. And the wig and stuff?'

'We came across a couple once. They weren't bothered with us, but they could have been, could have recognized her, got the village talking. So ever since then she dresses up, long hair, dark glasses, so when we do come across anyone, we go into a cuddle and they all think I got a new bird or think it's the old one, Miranda.' He laughed. 'Miranda, true to me at last.'

'That's who I thought it was,' I told him, 'I thought you'd kidnapped her.'

'That'd be the day!'

Gaynor had reached the stile at the far end. She stood on the wooden step, ready to climb over. Was it cruel what he was doing, was it kind? I couldn't work it out.

'Time we were off,' he said, setting after her. 'If that's all right with you.' He stopped and spoke without turning. 'It is all right with you, isn't it? Audrey's drinking, Gaynor's walks, best kept to ourselves, don't you think?

Things like that get out and anything can happen. Your car, those fish of yours.'

'No need to threaten me, Kim. I won't tell. It's not what I do. You should know that.'

He nodded, not looking back.

'Sorry about the fisticuffs.'

He shrugged his shoulders.

'I'll say goodnight, then. Tell Gaynor I'm . . .' He stopped, inclined his head, listening. 'I'm sorry not to have seen her.'

I went back, closed Alice's door, and returned to the bungalow, tripping over that blasted ornament of Audrey's dad. She'd polished it again and not put it back properly. I kicked it back to where it should be. What was it with Audrey and that thing? I mean who needs a doorstop anyway?

Back in the kitchen I ran my hand under cold water, splashed my face clean. I was aching all over, hand, chest, nose, kidney, and now a stubbed toe. Daytime, night-time, was there any end to it?

'I hoped you locked it again.'

Jesus!

Mrs Poke Nose was sitting in the conservatory, World War One still wrapped around her head, her hands folded over one of our best plates. She hadn't moved an inch, or so it seemed. I dabbed myself dry, blood on the towel.

'Shouldn't you be in bed, Mrs Blackstock,' I said, walking through, 'after what you've been through?'

She waved the suggestion away.

'Duncan's room. I saw a light go on. Did you lock it again?'

I nodded. God, what else did she see? The fridge light going on, the glow as I lit up that joint?

'And the tobacco tin?'

I pulled it out of my pocket. She took it like it was the first pint, Saturday lunchtime, the whole afternoon ahead of her. She'd been waiting for this. She turned it in her hands, shook it like she expected it to rattle. Maybe I'd filled it too full.

'Where was it?' She sniffed at the lid, reassured, then slid it down beside her, next to the plate.

'Down the back of the sofa. What's that you got there?'

'Ham sandwich. Hope you don't mind. I found some in the fridge. And what happened to you? Don't say you tripped down the stairs as well.' She was smiling, as if she'd watched every move I'd made, as if she *knew it all*.

'I thought you were a vegetarian,' I said, remembering my lobster.

'I am, have been for twenty-seven years, but I don't know. Suddenly I feel all . . .' She bit into the second half, chewing hard, the bandage slipping down over one eye, making her look like a Passchendaele pirate. 'This ham is really piggy. I wouldn't mind another one if there's enough to go round. I seem to have got the munchies.'

I went into the kitchen, made her another. Made myself one too. When I got back she had a spliff stuck fat in her mouth.

'You don't mind?' she said.

'Liberty Hall, our bungalow, as far as you're concerned,

Mrs Blackstock.' She took a deep drag, hot ash falling onto the Titian cushion.

'I've told you before, *Alice*.'

'Right. It's good to see you so at home here, Alice, I must say. So many people would have stood on ceremony, felt obliged to ask before helping themselves as the fancy took them. Pleased you're not one of them. Glad you're making yourself comfortable.'

'Oh, I am.' She let the smoke out slow and easy. You could almost see the gyroscope in her head taking on a new setting. 'Though I must say, I miss the view from my upstairs windows. You can see everything from there, the Beacon at the back, the hills at the front. The whole village goes past those windows one time or another. Man, woman, beast.'

I didn't like the way she said that last word, the way she looked at me. She was playing with me, I could feel it.

'Yes, whether they like it or not I see it all,' she said, taking another drag. 'You talking to your fish, Pat doing his keep-fit routine, not to mention the midnight ramblers.' She caught my questioning eye. 'Kim and Gaynor?'

'You know about them?'

'How could I not, out every night after they think everyone's gone to sleep. Just because a light goes out doesn't mean you've turned yourself off. I spend hours there sometimes, staring into the dark.'

'Is that a fact.'

'Just like you. There am I upstairs in my room, there you are, down by the pond. Sometimes I feel like opening the window, calling down. But I don't. We should all have our private moments.'

I wish. I hadn't had a private moment since coming back from the cliff.

'And twice a month I can watch the tanks practising. Like bonfire night. I love it.'

'I wouldn't have thought you would have approved, Mrs Blackstock, instruments of war like that.'

'Oh, guns don't bother me. Daddy taught me to shoot when I was fourteen. And when we were in the States, Duncan always carried a gun in the Impala, some of the places we went to. Still got it, as a matter of fact. Now, about this deal of ours.'

'Sorry?'

'On the way back from the dentist, didn't you suggest giving me free taxi rides in exchange for some French lessons?'

There it came again, the wink.

'I thought you couldn't remember anything, Mrs Blackstock.'

'It's coming back to me. Bit by bit. We had a drink at that pub. You wouldn't let me smoke in your car. We started talking about the old days, isn't that right?'

The order might be jumbled up, but it was coming back to her, there was no denying it. That is if it ever left her.

'You weren't all that easy to understand, Alice, not afterwards. The French lesson thing we'd talked about in the pub. On the way over.'

'Yes, I remember now. And when we got back I showed my photographs on the piano, when I was a bad girl.'

'I wouldn't say that, Mrs Blackstock.'

'Bad, bad, bad. Know what bad is in French?' She took another pull, her eyes filling up. 'Méchant. Even without thinking, any number of useful phrases spring to mind. Here, have a drag of this and repeat after me. Je suis un garçon méchant. I am a bad boy.'

'I don't know if this is quite the right time for this.'

'Nonsense,' she said sharply. 'Come on. Sit up. Hands together. I am a bad boy. Je suis un garçon méchant.'

'Je suis un garçon méchant.'

'Garçon,' she said. 'Think nasal. Imagine you're going to sneeze.'

'Garçon.'

'That's better. Now here's another phrase with bad in it. J'en ai grand besoin. I want badly.' She stretched out her hand, wriggled her fingers. I handed it back.

'I want badly.'

'In *French*, Al. J'en ai grand besoin.'

'J'en ai grand besoin.'

'Now say them together. I am a bad boy and I want it badly. Je suis un garçon méchant et j'en ai grand besoin.'

'Je suis un garçon méchant et j'en ai grand besoin.'

'Now two more and it's off to bed for both of us. You are badly off, Vous êtes mal loti, and I am badly wounded, Je suis gravement blessé. Come on, come on.'

I did as I was told. I was a bad boy. I was badly off and badly wounded, several times over. At the end of it she gave me the joint to finish off. I was badly in need of it, but there was nothing there. She'd smoked it all.

'I'll test you in the morning,' she said. 'Do you think you can remember all that?'

'I very much doubt it, Mrs Blackstock.'

'Too bad. Dommage. I'll say goodnight, then.'

She went to bed, her little tin tucked safely in her bag. I rolled another myself, didn't even bother to open the window I was that whacked. What was I to do with her? What would happen when the grass ran out, or when she went back home, when a bit more memory broke through, when she remembered seeing the yellow oilskin, when she remembered seeing me? When she told Adam Rump all that, then what? What would I say? I'd just popped out to look for Audrey, Inspector? That I didn't think of it as going out as such? To look for your wife, he'd say, when you knew where she'd gone? Ah, but I didn't, I'd reply. She went out without telling me, to surprise me with the hot toddy. So you went out one door and she came back another, like a Whitehall farce. If you like, Inspector. He might humph and hurrah, but it would stand up, wouldn't it? Wouldn't it? But the yellow oilskin, the path to the Beacon round the back, he'd know all about that. Seen me up there too, a couple of days later. I should never have gone there. Never.

I knew I wouldn't get a wink of sleep that night. And yet . . .

# Ten

'What happened to you?'

I rubbed my eyes. Audrey was sitting on the side of the bed, holding a cup of tea. She was fully dressed, tartan trousers, red jacket, a white blouse with a bow tie at the front.

'That heirloom of yours. Nearly broke my ankle coming in last night. You'd moved it.'

'Alice said I should show it off a little more. She says it's too unusual to shove behind the door. It's a talking point, that ammunition shell.'

'It's a doorstop, Audrey. It's where it's meant to be. Anyway, talking point for who.'

'Guests. We're changing, Al, remember. Going to the gym, sailing down the Nile, bungee jumping, that's just the start. No reason why we can't entertain too, have people round to dinner.'

'Well, put it on the mantelpiece, somewhere where they won't break their leg and sue us for negligence. I know. Hang it up upside down in the porch, use it as a bell for when they call. That'll get them talking.'

She ruffled my hair. 'My, we are creative this morning. Would it ring?'

'If you had something to hit it with it would, like one

of those triangle things. It would make some sort of noise anyhow.'

'A bell! It's a thought.' She rattled the cup and saucer at me. 'Come on, drink up.'

I took the tea. There were a couple of biscuits on the saucer. She got to her feet turning sideways onto the mirror, patting her stomach, tucking the blouse in. She'd lost a bit of weight.

'This is all very cosy, Audrey, all very *Homes and Garden*.' She turned, smiling. Her lips were that red again, but this time they had a glow to them, generous, welcoming, almost plush, like a hothouse plant. Audrey Greenwood all spruced up, ready for the fray.

'I'm driving today, remember,' she said, mussing up her hair. 'I thought we'd start off on the right foot.'

I patted the duvet. 'Why don't you get the left one over here then, get the motor running.'

'Al!' She bent down, let me breathe in her perfume. 'Plenty of time for that later. Besides, Alice is up. I said you'd pop down to the shops, get her some bacon.'

Petit déjeuner, that's what breakfast is called in French. Butter is buerre, jam is confiture and bread is pain, same as the English word pain, which is what Alice Poke Nose was in the arse all that breakfast. Plus de lard, s'il vous plaît, she kept on saying, likewise plus de free range eggs, plus de pork sausages and plus de slices of fried bread. I could handle most of the words, oeufs and saucissons, but lard just stuck in my throat. Didn't seem right, to call bacon, lard. Lard is lard. Bacon is bacon. But lard or bacon, she had two whole platefuls, along with a pot of my best coffee, a glass of grapefruit juice and a handful of Audrey's vitamin pills.

We were due to pick the Colemans up around eleven, take them over to Salisbury. They owned the Bindon Hotel near the cove. Sheila ran it. Donald, her husband, had had a stroke a couple of years back and wasn't driving any more. They were in their sixties, wary about their comfort, what they had, how they'd keep it.

Audrey went down to the supermarket to get Poke Nose a pork pie for her lunch. I spent a good hour with Torvill and Dean, cleaning the pond out, having a bit of a chat. I'd been neglecting them, what with one thing and another. I brought an orange with me, and did what Rump had suggested, cut it in half, chucked them both in. They'd never seen an orange before, but they knew what to do, sticking their faces in, nibbling away. They even seemed to have a little race between them, up to the nymph and back, dribbling the two halves across the water like they were basketballs. Torvill was the more agile of the two, but then she always had been. I loved that fish, almost as much as I'd loved anybody, anything, moving and weaving and twisting her tail, gentle, complicated patterns like one of those country dances I used to see. Across the fence Gaynor stood busy at her sink scowling at me, washing her pet dog, a Peke or something. I didn't know they had a dog. It was only when she started to wring its neck I realized that it wasn't a dog at all. It was that damn wig.

Audrey called me in at ten to. She was in the kitchen polishing her best handbag. It was like her hair, big and shiny. I got changed. We walked out to the car, the sun flicking off the boot. I handed her the car keys. She held them like they were jewels. It was a big moment. We got in. It felt all topsy-turvy, me on the left side with no pedals underfoot, her on the right at the controls. She stuck the ignition in. Her hand was shaking.

'Now remember, Audrey,' I said. 'Nice and steady does it. Don't chat unless they want to. Nothing worse than a driver yapping like a small dog all day.'

'Monty was a small dog. He didn't yap.'

She started playing about with the air-conditioning vents. It had taken me a long time to set them up exactly how I like them. It was the towels all over again.

'Actually, he did. You just didn't call it that. You thought he was talking to you.'

'He was in his own way. He loved me, that dog. And he died, just over there.'

She shoved the gear into reverse. I put my hand on hers.

'Audrey, Audrey. This is no time to get emotional. You're nervous, I can tell, and if you're not careful, we'll start to have an argument, about your backing out, or parking skills.'

'What's wrong with my backing out? I'm not the one who ran him over.'

She sat there, clutching the wheel, like it was about to fly off. I took a deep breath.

'There's nothing wrong with your backing out. There's nothing wrong with your parking skills either. It's just that we're both a bit tense, this being your first time out, official. I'm tense on your behalf. You're tense on mine. And we're both tense on behalf of this old beauty. It's a big car, big engine, big girth. It can run away with you if you let it. You got to stay focused, you got to stay calm.'

'I am focused. I am calm.'

'That breakfast didn't help either. Passez-moi this, passez-moi that. How long is Madame staying?'

'As long as it takes, Al. She's had a nasty accident. Anyway, you're the one who said it was open house as far as she was concerned. Not me.'

'I said that?'

'Her third fried egg.'

'That was irony, Audrey. Irony or sarcasm, I can't remember which. Not that she seemed to notice. Now, let's go and pick up your first fare, shall we?'

They were a bit taken aback when they saw Audrey grinning at them over the steering wheel. They'd never seen her behind the wheel of the Vanden Plas before, hardly anybody had. Sheila had a piece of fox over her shoulder even though it was warm. He was more relaxed; nice blue cotton shirt, good shoes, a stick to help him walk. They were off for a few days in Salisbury, top hotel. Business and pleasure, she said.

I helped him in first, then her. Usually it should be the other way around, but I was letting her know that I knew who wore the trousers. She liked that, settled back already three-quarters there. That's how it should be, everything done and dusted, even before they'd strapped the seat belt on.

We set off. I was pleasantly surprised, the way Audrey handled the car, the way she sat in it, worked it. I mean, she had driven it before, but not regular, not as a performance, not like it was part of her, like it was of me. But from setting the wing mirrors to the way she clocked the speed trap, it was like she'd been born to it. She was good with the Colemans too, glancing in the mirror to see if they were all right, making the odd comment, concentrating on the road. And then, halfway through:

'I hear you've had some activity down in the cove the last few days, Mrs Coleman? The police.'

Mrs Coleman clacked her mouth. 'Didn't help trade much, the way they sealed the beach off. No one was allowed on it for the whole day.'

'I would have thought that would have helped trade, Mrs Coleman. Kept your guests inside.'

Sheila Coleman sniffed. I nudged Audrey's knee, frowning. Not a good thing to contradict customers like that, particularly a self-made woman like her. There's nothing the self-made man or woman doesn't know, particularly about their own show. If the police on the beach was bad for trade it was bad for trade. Simple as that.

'Though I suppose it's not something you want to be associated with,' Audrey added, 'a hotel of your standing.'

That was more like it. That was a sentiment Sheila Coleman appreciated.

'It's that Miranda Grogan,' she said, with a voice like she'd just put her rubber gloves on to clean the toilet. 'Seems like they found something of hers, on the beach. They had her parents down, to see if they could identify it. That poor mother.'

'What was it, do you know?' Audrey glanced at me.

'They wouldn't say. Not beachwear, apparently.'

'Not a yellow oilskin, then,' I put in.

'Oilskin?'

'It's what she was wearing that afternoon. A yellow one.'

'Not that I know of.'

'It was a shoe.'

We all turned, even Audrey. Donald was staring ahead, a drop of saliva running down his chin. Sheila wiped it clean.

'A shoe, Donald? How do you know?'

The right side of his mouth opened, to let the words fall out.

'They were talking about it in front of me, Dave Stone and some woman PC. People do that, you know, talk as if I'm not there.'

'What kind of shoe?' Audrey asked. He puckered his lips. You could feel him getting them ready.

'Tarty, that's what he said. That's why it got noticed in the first place.'

'That doesn't surprise me,' his wife sniffed. 'She worked with us for a short time, you know. The number of times I had words with her about dress code, the blouses she wore. It's not what you want, in a family hotel. We had to let her go in the end.'

I remembered. It was her first job almost, just turned eighteen. The Spread Eagle was empty for six months. Everyone was down in the hotel's public bar, watching her pull pints.

'Really.' Audrey's ears pricked up.

'Yes.' Sheila Coleman sniffed again. 'There was nothing we could prove, of course, just the takings going down.'

With that extra custom? I couldn't let that go, her sitting in the back all la-di-da, slagging Miranda off like that.

'She worked for me too,' I said, 'and I never had no complaints. Hard-working, good with people, fun to be with. Wish there were more like her, myself.' Audrey revved the engine. I'd jumped in too hard, I knew it, but still.

'Well, you don't get the opportunities in a business like ours, do you?' she said. 'Not like a hotel, all that cash around. Isn't that right, Mrs Coleman?'

Mrs Coleman nodded. That was right.

We didn't say much after that. The Colemans sat in the back going through some legal papers. Audrey drove, cut up a cyclist just outside Blandford Forum. Beautiful. Couldn't have done it better myself. Miranda was getting closer and closer to the Beacon and my treacherous hands, Miranda who had once seemed so brimming with it all, so full of everything you would want a girl like Miranda to be. Now there was a different Miranda walking up that path towards me, a Miranda I never knew and yet knew only too well.

We dropped the Colemans at their hotel. We parked round the back, and started to have a wander about. It had been a long time since we'd done that aimless together sort of stuff. I was glad to be there, out of the bungalow, out of the village, where everywhere I turned reminded me of who I was, and what I had done. We went sightseeing, took in the old town, the cathedral. It was like getting lost in memories I'd never had. Audrey wanted to go inside, but I didn't. I had enough going on inside me without God shoving his oar in. So I stood on the green while she went in, gazed at the crazy splendour of it, the way it sat on the ground like a ship, ready to set sail on the joys and sorrows of this world, that mast stretched to the sky. She was there a good half-hour, and I was glad of it wondering what the hell it was that made us do the things we did to each other, what we did to ourselves. When she came out she had a bunch of postcards clutched in her hand.

'You should have gone in,' she said. 'It might have done you good.'

'I don't need God, Audrey, not with you around. Who are all the postcards for?'

'I don't know. Anybody. Carol, Aunty Vi, Tina.'

'Tina!'

'Why ever not. I'm tired of ... Look,' and she pulled the biro out of my top pocket and wrote 'Wish you were here!' on all three of them.

'Do you,' I said, 'wish they were here?'

'Oh, Al,' she said, touching my lip with her finger. 'Don't be jealous. Enjoy it while you can, enjoy the day.'

So I did. I bought a new cap, flat, tweed, good for the winter, also a pair of new gloves from the same shop, leather with white stitching up the fingers. Audrey found an antiques clothes store, parasols and ball gowns and Hardy Amies cocktail dresses, bought herself one of those little veiled hats, like they used to wear in the twenties. It didn't fit on her head proper, but she didn't seem to mind, just blew the veil up over her nose and grinned, like a monkey with a fez.

'Where are you going to wear a thing like that?' I said. 'The circus?'

'Your funeral?'

'Very funny.'

'No, seriously, Al. Wouldn't it look good if I have to drive a client to the crematorium? Winter's coming on. You know how business picks up, cemetery-wise, after a cold spell.'

It was true. A good blast from Siberia, an unheated bedroom with only a couple of thin blankets on the bed, and off they pop. January, February, more than October, November, when their resistance is low, but still, I liked the way she was thinking. We bought it, thirty-five quid, on account of the Belgium lace. It fired her up, having that tucked up under her arm. Shop after shop we went, clothes, confectioners, beauty salons – it was all I could do to stop her buying a four-foot painting of a cross-eyed elephant with its tusks akimbo from some poncy art gallery.

'It would be another talking point,' she said, fingering the eighty-five-quid price tag.

'I wouldn't want to talk about it,' I said. 'I'd want to shoot it. Anyway, where would we put it?'

'Why not the mantelpiece?'

'What, and get rid of Torvill and Dean? I'm sorry, dearest, but the mantelpiece is a no-go area as far as the depiction of wildlife is concerned. Torvill and Dean are there to stay.'

She was a bit put out, but soon perked up in the shop next door, a junk shop, all kinds of rusty tat scattered about. One thing they did have though, stuck in a bucket, was a big brass hammer with a leather strap at the end, like for a gong that had got lost.

'Look, Al,' she said, squeezing my arm, 'for Dad's brass shell. It's just perfect. All you need now is to hang it up, and we'll have our own personalized doorbell. What do you think?'

And so it went on, me and Audrey parading up and down arm in arm like a couple of swells in some feel-good movie. For the first time since that Sunday, for a couple of hours I forgot all about what I had done, what I might have done, the two of us just soaking it all in, the cobbles, the bendy buildings, the fun of just being there, topping it off with a clotted-cream tea with a painting of an angry-looking bishop staring down at us. I could have shot him too.

'Perhaps we should have saved some for Alice,' I said, popping the last scone in. 'She must be starving, with only the contents of our fridge to keep her going. And you'd better not be having any of these any more. Not if you're going to the gym.'

'That's where you're wrong, Al.' She beckoned to the waitress, pointing to the empty plate. 'Now I'm going to the gym I can have as many cream teas as I like.'

Who was I to say no to that?

We took our time coming back too, stopped off at the pub at Tarrant Monkton, a pint for me and a virgin Mary for her. It was all beginning to make sense, Audrey doing her bit. Maybe I'd been wrong. Maybe we could take on the Newdicks after all, beat them at their own game. We knew the area, we knew the people, we'd just never thought about it like that, like it was a team effort, these lives of ours. Fred and Ginger, Torvill and Dean, why not Al and Audrey? I felt almost sad when the Larches turn-off came into view, as if something had happened that afternoon that should have happened a long time ago and was now coming to an end. We were saying goodbye to a world that wasn't there, a world that could have been, should have been, if only we'd seen sense. Perhaps we could find it somewhere back here, but back here there were things I had to sort out, things that might turn this afternoon into an impossible memory, a dream.

She turned into the drive, parked the car in the garage, sat back, satisfied. A day well done. Almost perfect. I unbuckled.

'I must say, Audrey, that was as good a piece of driving as I've seen. You're made for this line of work.'

'Al. You're just saying that.'

'No. It's true. This is the beginning of something new, Audrey, a new venture. You know that Renault, the one I got for Miranda? I never did get rid of it. First thing tomorrow, we go down to the lock-up, see if it suits. What do you say?'

'I don't know, Al. It's all a bit sudden. I'd have to buy some new clothes, of course.' She put her hands back on the steering wheel, staring straight through the bricks and mortar. Sideways on she looked like a ship's figure-head, ploughing into the future. I patted her knee. It was a shame to spoil it, but it had to be done.

'Of course you would. A whole new wardrobe, winter and summer. A whole new wardrobe, a trip down the Nile, who knows what else is in store. There's just one thing, if we want to start with a clean slate. I need to know where you went last Sunday.'

I could feel her stiffen, see her knuckles whiten.

'I told you, Al. The Beacon.' Her voice had gone flat.

'No you didn't.'

'What do you mean I didn't. After all we've done today . . .'

'Audrey, Audrey. I know you didn't.'

'How do you know?'

I took a deep breath. This was a big moment for me, not a leap in the dark, but an act of inspiration, a kind of crossing over, from one world to the next. I was putting myself in a minefield, but I knew the way out. Audrey didn't. It had come to me, driving back, how I could out-manoeuvre her, and I felt sort of great, sort of invulnerable.

''Cause I went there.'

I could almost feel the inrush of air as she sucked it into her lungs, all the oxygen she needed. Yes, Audrey. Got you now, my ruby-lipped beauty, my cracked china queen.

'You!'

It was all she could say, throwing the confession back in my face. I could see her mind working overtime, what she could say next, the possible excuses flipping through her head like cards on a rolodex. Truth or lies? Quick now. I decided to give her more time, let her wriggle on the hook a bit longer. Yes, I might be happy with a new Audrey, willing to give the new me a try, but God, I was going to make sure we'd start off on the right foot this time, with yours truly in the driving seat, home *and* work.

'Yes. I was walking up to the caravan. I was going to spend the night there. I was in a mood, remember.'

'I remember all your moods that day, Al.' She fidgeted with her hair. Tumble, tumble, tumble, went her insides.

'Then I thought, bugger it. This is no good, this thing between Audrey and me. It's been going on too long. It's got to stop. So I came back.'

'Yes. I never asked you, when you came back, when you almost jumped into the house, you said something peculiar, very odd.'

It was clever of her, to try and turn the tables on me, give herself more time to think her way out of it. I was happy to oblige.

'Did I?'

'Yes. You said, "Bonsai!"'

'Bonsai? Well I never.'

'All the evening while we were, you know, I could hear it ringing in my head. Bonsai! Bonsai! as if Tonto was moving to the rhythm of it. I've been meaning to ask you why Bonsai, ever since.'

I closed my eyes. God, that Bonsai moment, how great it felt, how unbelievably, irretrievably great. Too great for it to be true. I understood that now.

'Tell you the truth, Audrey, I don't rightly know. I guess it was just coming back, you know, with the new me in tow.'

'And there was I waiting for you, in a mood.'

'More in a mood than I can say. Perhaps I should say it more often. Bonsai!'

I was wondering whether she would try and lead me off the scent, start loosening her vowels, undo her consonants, but no. She was on a bit of a search-and-destroy mission herself now and I could sense it.

'And the expression on your face, Al, when you saw

me, in a mood, a kind of bewildered concentration. Reminded me of Carol filling her nappies.'

I'd given her enough slack. It was time to reel her in.

'Audrey, this is all very interesting, but it doesn't get to the point, does it?'

'The point?'

'Yes. The point being that you weren't up at the Beacon and I was, up by the pimple, where the bodies are hidden.'

'Oh. That point. No, I wasn't there. I was . . . I went over to Tina's.' She said it hurriedly, to get it over with, like jumping into a frozen sea. Tina again.

'Tina!'

'Yes. I didn't like to tell you because I was afraid you'd think I was betraying you, all the trouble you've had. The truth was I'd wanted to be friends with her again for ages. It was stupid, me not seeing her any more just because of you and Ian. So I went round the back, like I used to, poked my head in the kitchen door like I used to. Do you know what I saw? Two new uniforms, hanging on the kitchen door. New uniforms, Al, and us always waiting for the next cancellation. And then I heard them. They were having a flaming row, Ian accusing her of all sorts of terrible things, making eyes at everyone up at the camp, coming back at all hours from where he could only guess, and she was screaming back at him. I could hear things being thrown, glass and heaven knows what, and then a scream, not a scream, a bellow, like a cow with its throat cut or something, followed by a terrible quiet, like something dreadful had happened. And then a moan.'

'He'd hit her?'

'Not that sort of moan. The other sort, passionate, bruising, like a kiss. You know how it is when all you hear is that sort of movement, furtive and desperate even when there's no one else about. You can just feel it, can't you, like a smell in the air. I knew what they were doing, what they were going to do. So I left, all jealous and angry and that moan, stirring up everything inside of me. I came back. But the house was empty. You'd gone out. I didn't like it. It didn't seem right. I panicked. I thought you might have gone round to Kim's, for a drink or something, so I went round, knocked on the door, made some excuse wanting some whisky. I didn't know where you were, rang the pub even. But then I noticed your weatherproof wasn't there and I thought you must have gone out, maybe gone out to find me and I suddenly thought how marvellous it would be if, like in that book with Heathcliff and that girl, with the storm all raging around, how great it would be if you found me and got hold of me, held me, made me moan too. So I said to myself, right then, this is it, I'll wait for him like I haven't waited for him in a long time, all churned up, so I got the champagne out and showered and put the perfume on, the one you like, had the kettle on the grate, just off the boil, like I was.'

'Hence the mood.'

'Yes. Hence all the moods, you and me, the parcel, everything.'

She turned.

'All for you, Al, all for you.'

And she kissed me hard, like she meant it.

It was time for the coup de grâce. I pulled myself free.

'I'm glad you told me, Audrey, but now I must tell you something.'

'Oh?' She wasn't really listening. She'd made her bed, now she wanted me to lie in it.

'Yes. I lied. I didn't go up to the Beacon that day at all.'

'But . . .'

'I know. I just said that to get you to tell me where you were, to flush the truth out of you.'

'Oh, Al.' She put her hand to her mouth.

'I knew you hadn't gone to the Beacon. Don't ask me how. I just knew it. Inside here.' I patted my stomach. She nodded.

'Just like I can you.'

Or so she thought.

'So where were you? You weren't round the back like you said you were. Not when I came back. I mean I looked for you. Couldn't find you anywhere.'

'Did you look in the garden? The pond?'

'Of course I did. It was the first place I thought of, you telling your troubles to Torvill and Dean.'

'The garage? Did you look in the garage?'

'Probably. I can't remember.'

'Ah,' I said, thinking fast, 'but you didn't look here, in the car, did you?'

'No. Why should I?'

''Cause that's where I was. Taking a nap.'

'You were here, in the Vanden Plas?'

'You know how it is with me and this car, Audrey. I did go out, went down the pond in a rage, but it was pouring down. I thought about going for a drive. I got in, settled down, and it just came over me, a kind of weariness, where we were going. And when I woke up, I kind of saw a light, like you must have done. The Bonsai moment, Audrey. Bonsai.'

'Your car,' she said. 'Your precious Vanden Plas. You slept in it, like a baby in his cot.'

'Yes.'

'Oh, Al,' she said smiling. 'Come here.'

She pressed her bosom into me, stroked my head. It felt good, my head on her breasts, her fingers in my hair. There was a smell about her, more like bread than any perfume, soft and white and comforting, like the warmth of rising dough. Things were happening between me and Audrey, good things, proper things, things that had never happened before. And I thought, with my head buried in her flesh, that if I hadn't tried to kill her, hadn't tried to push her off that cliff, my head wouldn't be where it was, all safe and peaceful. I'd be alone and pill-popping nervous, wired and happy in a horrible, old-Al sort of way. And I was glad I'd tried, glad that it was someone else rather than her that I'd pushed off, even if it was Miranda. I could never bury my head in Miranda like this, never feel this comfort from her hand. Yes, I was glad I had tried, glad I hadn't succeeded, glad that there was this peace in the world for such an undeserver like me, in this car, this bungalow, with its fluffy carpets and glass ornaments.

'Audrey,' I said, 'why don't we nip out and lie out under the stars. No funny business. Just you, me, the moon and the Lourdes blanket. When we see a shooting star we can both shout Bonsai together.'

She tickled my nose. 'What about old Poke Nose? Do you want her to shout Bonsai too?'

I half sat up.

'Christ, I forgot about her.' I lay back down again then opened my eyes. 'You called her Poke Nose,' I said, looking up. 'You called Mrs Blackstock, old Poke Nose.'

She tickled my nose again. 'That's because we're drawing closer, Al. You're a little bit me, and I'm a little bit you. Like the song.'

And she stroked my head some more and I closed my eyes again. It was the best thing I'd felt for ever, I think. A moment of pure peace. And this was the woman I'd tried to kill. I must have been mad. So what if she wasn't who I thought I wanted. No one was.

A little shudder woke me, the Vanden Plas bouncing up on its springs. Audrey wasn't next to me any more. I'd slumped down, my head on the empty driver's seat. I looked up through the garage window, Alice sitting in the conservatory, a light coming from the kitchen. Audrey must be cooking supper. We'd bought some chops on the way back. More pig.

It came again, a shudder, followed by a sort of hollow tearing sound, like when a ship groans. Someone was trying to break into my car. Looking through the back window I could see a figure hunched down by the boot, hear the scrape of metal as he tried to jam something back under the lock. I put my hand over the catch, opened up the door nice and gentle, slid my feet out. It was a tight squeeze, but I did it, edged along, crouched and quiet, picking up an old barbie fork that was leant up against the wall. He was muttering to himself, getting impatient. That lock wasn't giving up easy. It was a Vanden Plas, for Christ sake. He started to bang at it. I couldn't bear it, the damage done.

'Drop it!'

He jerked his head up, throwing a tyre iron at me as I lunged forward. I ducked it, banging into him as he turned, driving that fork deep into his buttocks. He jumped up, squealing, and started to leg it down the drive, the fork flipping up and down out of his backside like a flag on a pole. I gave chase, tripping up over an old bit of carpet stacked against the wall. Out the drive he went, turning up into the lane, up to where a car was parked on the brow of the hill, just past Alice's house. I got halfway and then stopped. I didn't need to go any further. I recognized the car. If you're on the road all day like me, you know the back end of cars, every one of them. You've driven behind them long enough, wanting to pass.

He pulled out the fork and jumped in. That must have hurt. The car skidded. I gave a little wave. I knew what kind of car it was. And I knew who was driving it.

Back inside, Audrey was at the stove, cutting open a packet of frozen peas. Alice Blackstock was up at the dining table, drumming on the tablecloth with her knife and fork. I could smell the chops sizzling under the grill. The dining table was laid, best plates, wine glasses, the fox-hunting serving mats.

'What was that?' Audrey said, barely looking up. 'You run over another dog?'

'It was tomorrow's pig,' I told her, 'getting ready for Alice's breakfast. What's all this in aid of?'

'Alice is going back in the morning. She feels so much better. So we're having a farewell dinner. She's bought us some wine. Isn't that kind?' She raised her glass. 'Cheers!' she shouted.

Poke Nose looked up, pulled the earpiece out.

'What?'

'I was saying, you've been a presence, Alice.' Audrey's lips were quite red. She'd already had a couple, thanks to our little chat. I was pleased. 'A house with the same two people in it day in, day out, can get so dreary. Especially if one of them's my husband.'

It was a joke, but not in very good taste.

'I wouldn't mind a house with another person in it,' Alice said. 'Make yours a happy home, as the song goes.'

Her mouth took a downturn. She was thinking about that room, poor old thing. She didn't want to go back at all.

'Have a glass of wine, Mrs Blackstock, before Audrey drinks it all.'

I filled hers up. Mine too.

'What you do today?' I asked, trying to cheer her up. 'Took it nice and easy, I hope.'

She shook her head, her eyes floating about like peas in saucers of milk. Any minute they'd drop out. If there was any weed left in that tin, it wasn't for want of trying.

'All week something's been niggling me, and then, this lunchtime, I suddenly realized what it was.'

'What? Pork isn't a vegetable?'

Audrey scowled at me, then poured herself another.

'That Sunday afternoon, when Miranda Grogan went missing, I saw someone up at the Beacon, in a yellow oilskin. That's what you told me she was wearing, wasn't it, Al?'

Audrey and I exchanged glances. 'Did I? I'm not sure,' I said.

'On the way back from the dentist, or maybe in the house, it doesn't matter. The fall had knocked it clean out of me. But seeing Audrey's hanging in the hall, it all came back to me. So, I did what I was going to do. I rang the police this morning, apologized for the delay. Adam couldn't have been nicer, said it might prove very valuable, my information. He wants to take a statement. He's coming round this evening, if that's all right. I didn't think you'd mind.'

Of course we didn't mind. Open house, our bungalow.

Audrey hauled out the chops, dumped the mash and the onion gravy onto the table. She makes good mash, Audrey, grain mustard, butter, a dollop of salad cream. Cauliflower cheese and peas followed, and then, from out the oven, a tray full of stuffing balls. I wasn't expecting stuffing balls. Stuffing balls don't go with chops. Stuffing balls are strictly roast chicken. Our conversation had clearly unsettled her.

One look at them told me by how much. These looked more like old Father Time's testicles than stuffing balls, oval in shape, and covered in wisps of straggly hair, where she hadn't cut up the parsley proper. I couldn't help thinking of the chocolate Tonto back in Poke Nose's fridge. Bit like the seven ages of man, only whittled down to two: the promise of youth, the disappointment of old age. Audrey shoved a couple onto my plate, then doled out the chops. Though Alice got the biggest, I got the one with the kidney.

I spooned out the mash next to the chop, made a little hole in the centre like it was a volcano and poured in the gravy. I've always done that, let it stew there for a while, while I have a taste of the mash and the peas and the cauli. Then, when all the juices are running, I stab a great hole in the mash and watch the gravy run all over the plate. I do the same when it's roast beef and Yorkshire pudding. There's no point in having meat without a decent amount of gravy to float the whole thing off. Alice was fascinated, started making a mash mountain of her own.

'Make sure the walls are thick enough,' I told her, 'otherwise it'll just seep through.' She nodded, grateful for the advice. It was just like playing sandcastles at the beach.

The doorbell rang. I leant over and pulled back the curtain. Adam Rump was standing on the porch.

'Oh good,' I said. 'Guess who's coming to dinner?' I banked up the mash and went to the front door. He had a hat in his hand.

'Mr Greenwood. Official this time, I'm afraid. I under-stand that Mrs Blackstock is staying with you.'

'That's right. She had a nasty fall. She's a tough old bird, but . . .'

He nodded, anxious to get on with it. He had a home to go to, a wife to see, fish to feed. He passed the rim of the hat round his fingers, like he was reading Braille.

'I don't know if she's told you, but I need to take a statement from her. I hope this isn't an inconvenient time.'

'Not at all. You can watch me pop Vesuvius.'

'I'm sorry?'

'Audrey's gravy,' I said. 'It's like lava, destroys everything in its path. Come in, come in.'

I led him in. Audrey was up out of her seat, laying another plate.

'Adam!' Poke Nose threw her arms open. He had no choice but to bend down and offer himself up. She didn't even wait for his face to arrive, just went for the first bit of flesh within striking distance, her lips clamping onto his neck like a couple of lampreys, specks of mashed potato falling into his collar. He jerked himself free, the mark burning on his skin like a branding iron.

'You've just started dinner,' he said, wishing he'd never come. 'I'll come back tomorrow.'

'Don't be so stand-offish, Adam,' Alice piped up. 'Tuck in. There's plenty for everyone. Take my statement afterwards. You don't mind, do you, Al, if Adam has some of yours?'

She got up, leant across the table and started to cut my chop in half, straggles of her hair trailing into my gravy. We all stood there, thinking the same thing. Rump looked at me. I looked at Audrey. Audrey looked at Rump, a little conversation going on between the three of us. I turned out my hands. What can we do? Audrey threw a sympathetic smile. Humour the old dear. Rump hung his head, then sat down.

For our first dinner party, the conversation was a bit stilted. None of us were properly prepared. If I'd let Audrey buy that elephant, we'd have had a talking point. I began to understand that for a dinner party to succeed, you didn't have to have something nice to hang on the wall at all. In fact the more horrible the talking point was, the better, for then the more you'd have to talk about. That elephant would have been perfect. The cross eyes alone would have been good for a couple of hours. But I hadn't. For the first twenty minutes we concentrated on the grub, despite the fact there wasn't as much to go around as there should have been. My plate in particular looked particularly vacant. Luckily Audrey had made enough stuffing balls to sink the *Mary Rose*. Visually on the vulgar side, once in the mouth they were OK, though the funny thing was, the more you chewed them, the chewier they got. I timed the second one by the electric Sun King clock above the microwave. Seven and a half minutes from mouth to throat. Seven and a half minutes and a belt of plonk to soften it up. Yet despite the jaw ache, once you'd finished one, you kind of hankered after another. Twenty minutes in and Audrey was tucking into her third. Some dinner hostess she. She'd barely said a word since we'd sat down. It was time to break the ice.

'Alice tells me she taught you when you were a kid, Inspector,' I said. They all looked up, startled, as if I'd broken wind in a public library. Adam put his knife down and drank a glass of water. He wasn't drinking any wine, which was just as well. Audrey was drinking his share.

'That's right. Maths, in the main. A proper tartar she was.'

'I taught you the piano too.' Alice's voice was shrill, like she still had her iPod clamped to her ear. Underneath the table her foot was going up and down like a jackhammer.

'So you did, Mrs Blackstock. I'd clean forgotten. It's years since I've played the piano.'

'It's years since I've taught it. Can you play, Audrey?'

'No. We bought a xylophone for Carol once.'

'I have a baby grand in my living room. Duncan gave it to me for my . . .' Her voiced trailed off into memory.

'Birthday?' I suggested.

'Divorce. My first and only. He gave me a piano the day the papers came through, tap-danced on the top of it while I played. Tap shoes. Nothing else.'

Adam kept his eyes firmly on his plate. Audrey was trying not to laugh.

'A very vivid memory, I'm sure,' I offered. 'Was that how it lost its leg?'

She shook the question away. 'He had lovely hands.'

'Duncan?'

'Adam. As a boy. He had lovely hands. Look at them now. There was a song I used to sing.'

We all looked at his hands. They seemed all right to me, a bit fat round the knuckles. We carried on eating. Being with people I didn't know, I began to see what a complicated procedure a dinner party was, all that eating and talking at the same time. I mean it's much easier to do one or the other. Eat or talk. But all this business round a table . . .

We went another couple of rounds with the grub. The stuffing balls were surprisingly buoyant. If you dipped them in the gravy they were easier to chew, tasted nicer that way too. I demolished another one. The talking was drying up again. Poke Nose slapped the table.

'Adam and the Hand Jive!' she shouted, waving her knife about.

'What?' I gulped, a stalk of parsley sticking in my throat.

'The song I used to sing. Adam and the Hand Jive. I was always reminded of it, whenever Adam came.'

'I don't think it was Adam,' I said.

'Who I was reminded of?'

'The title of the song, Alice. I don't think it was Adam.'

She nodded, not caring if it was Adam or not. No one cared. It was becoming that sort of evening.

'I'm teaching Al now, Adam, did you know? French.'

'French?' Audrey looked at me.

'I thought we might take the Vanden Plas on holiday next year.'

'To France?'

'It was just a thought, Audrey.'

'Willy!' Alice banged her knife down on her plate. 'Willy and the Hand Jive. I used to make you play it on the piano, don't you remember, Adam, every time you . . .'

'How are the fish?' Rump said suddenly. I was as relieved as he was.

'Top form. I did what you suggested, gave them half an orange each. They loved it.'

'They all do. I've tried other things, peaches, avocados, kumquats, but nothing delivers like the humble orange. In my pond, there's quite a tussle to get hold of them.'

'How many fish do you have?' Audrey asked. She leant her elbow on the table, as if she was interested in the answer. That was more like it.

'Thirty,' he said.

'Isn't that an awful lot?'

He paused. 'Well, it's not as many as forty.'

We thought about this, thought about it for quite a while. It seemed strangely profound, thirty not being as many as forty.

'And Mrs Rump? What does she think of them?' Audrey put her hands together. 'She's from South Africa, I gather.'

I tried to kick her under the table, but missed. Alice gave a little squeal. Adam mashed at his potato.

'Cape Town. Her family left after it all changed. She's the great-great-something of Dr Verwoerd.'

'Doctor!' Audrey was impressed. 'I've seen her name on the gym noticeboard but I haven't had the pleasure.'

Rump wriggled uncomfortably. 'Nor will you. We've split up. She's left the country, flown back to the old country. Left me a letter.' He tapped his pocket. 'Said she'd rather be ruled by the rainbow nation than by rainbow trout.'

'Oh, I am sorry,' said Audrey. Silence descended.

'Of course,' Poke Nose said, trying to get things back on the rails again, 'before decimalization, the gap between thirty and forty was even greater, all the twists and turns it took. They could catch you out in those days, the numbers. Who's for another stuffing ball?'

We all reached out at the same time for the last four, popped them in our mouths, started on the long chew. Sounded like a bunch of horses trotting down the road. There was other food on our plate but none of it seemed to matter any more. It was stuffing balls or nothing. Ten minutes they took to demolish, ten long minutes. At the end Adam pushed his plate back, his forehead wet with perspiration. I was feeling it too, kind of shivery, not myself, like I was coming down with something. He wiped his forehead clean, took a little notebook from his inside pocket and laid it on the table.

'Now, Alice. If I could take your statement, I really should be getting back.'

'Should we leave?' Audrey asked.

Rump sat there, trying to work the answer out. There was something getting in the way, something getting in all our ways. A little bell started ringing in my ear.

'Probably,' he said.

Audrey made to move, but I put my hand out under the table, pressed her leg back down. It was as I thought. It didn't matter. Nothing did. Alice gathered herself together.

'It was like this. I only remembered this morning. The day of my accident, I'd been talking to Al here, and he mentioned Miranda Grogan and the yellow oilskin. And I suddenly remembered that I'd seen it.'

'Miranda Grogan?'

'The yellow oilskin, silly boy! Miranda Grogan's not an it. I saw one, a yellow oilskin, going up the Beacon that afternoon. Not by itself of course. It had a person inside it.' She giggled.

'What time?'

'Four thirty? I can't be sure exactly.'

'Towards the Beacon or away?'

'Towards.'

'Where were you?'

She giggled again. 'You'll never guess.'

'Mrs Blackstock, Alice, I really don't . . .'

'Go on, have a guess.'

'I really . . .'

'Just one.'

'In the kitchen?'

'No.'

'The drawing room?'

'No. These are very boring answers, Adam. You'll have to do better than that.'

'Alice.' He started to breathe heavily. 'I'm not feeling very well.' He gripped the table, like he was afraid of falling off his chair. He did look a bit pasty. 'Please. Just tell me.'

She looked around the table, triumphant.

'I was up a tree.'

She was getting it all wrong but what could I say. My mouth couldn't open. I was glued to my seat, to the room, like everyone else. We were stuck here, on the last train, time waving us goodbye.

'Up a tree,' Rump repeated.

'Rescuing my clothes. The wind had blown them all away, but the tree had caught them. There they were waving away in its branches. So up I went. And when I looked out I saw someone in a yellow oilskin going up the path. I thought it might be Audrey at first. She often used to go up the Beacon, when Monty was alive.'

'Monty?' Rump was confused. Audrey clutched her bosom.

'He was my closest friend, Adam. He got run over.'

'He wasn't wearing a yellow oilskin, then.'

'He was a dog, Inspector. It happened a long time ago.'

'A dog inspector? What's a dog inspector?'

'No. A dog. He was a dog. Monty, was a dog.'

'A dog?'

'I ran him over. In the Vanden Plas. Not deliberately, of course.'

'He's got nothing to do with the Beacon, then?'

'No. No one has. Alice just saw someone go up, that's all. Wearing a yellow oilskin.'

'Yes. I got that.' He thought for a moment. 'Was that all you saw?' Alice put her head to one side, like a bright little bird. She was enjoying it, the attention.

'Up on the Beacon? Yes.'

I held my breath. If he didn't ask another question I was out of it. Alice would have done her duty, Rump would have done his. If only he would leave it alone. I was watching him. He was struggling, staring at his notebook, trying to work it out, what he should do next. You could see there was a kind of fog covering him. There was a kind of fog covering us all, making it difficult for us to see our way. Then he pushed his hand out, broke through.

'And did you see anything else, apart from the Beacon?'

'The wind? The sky?'

He wrote it down.

'Anything else?'

'Nothing. Nothing apart from Al here. He wasn't up a

tree. He wasn't up on the Beacon. He wasn't even wearing a yellow coat. He was just outside, in the undergrowth. Weren't you, Al?'

I nodded. They were all looking at me.

'I'd gone out to call Monty in. For a moment I'd forgotten he was dead. Habit can do that to you, can't it. It was terrible weather and I thought I must get Monty in. Didn't you hear me call him, Alice? Monty! Monty! I felt such a fool.'

Adam was staring at the tablecloth. He didn't seem very interested. No one did. Audrey was ringing the edge of her plate with the last of her peas. Alice had picked up her chop and was gnawing at the bone. There was something going very wrong here. The size of the plates, for instance. They seemed have grown larger. There was a strange hum in the air like one of those tops that kiddies used to play with, like the room was being pumped up like a tyre. I could feel my head cracking, ready to pop open. Somehow a great big hand had come down from nowhere and sent us all in a spin.

Come down from nowhere?

'Who made them?' I asked Audrey suddenly.

'Made them?'

'The stuffing balls. Who made them?'

'That was Alice,' she said. 'Weren't they tasty?'

Tasty? That wasn't parsley! She must have mixed in a whole tin's worth. We'd just drugged a policeman. I slumped back in my chair. Rump waved his hand in the air, like he was trying to grab at something.

'Do you think,' he said, 'that I could take a look at your fish?'

We trooped out, all four of us. I switched on the pool light, and there they were all lit up. They began to swim and move about, like we were in the front row watching some Russian ballet, all the swans and ballerinas twirling before our eyes. None of us said a word, none of us. We just sat there, mesmerized, our lips thick, our tongues thick, the sky as big as I'd ever seen it, pattern folding into pattern, like a kaleidoscope. Audrey and me. That was a pattern. Adam and Alice that was another.

'That's what everyone is,' I said. 'A pattern.'

'A beautiful pattern,' Alice put in.

'A pattern only God can see,' Rump added.

'I feel strange,' Audrey said. 'I think I'm going to be sick.'

I led her inside, undressed her, her flesh lumpy and white and spread out on the bed like a beached jellyfish. The room was moving about, like we'd set sail and just reached the open sea. Keeping my balance I went back to see if Rump was all right, hadn't fallen in the pond or something, but when I got there, both he and Poke Nose had gone. She'd be all right, she was used to this sort of thing, and if Rump had any sense he'd stick his bonnet plumb on the white line and let the car drive him home. I turned all the lights off and went back to the bedroom. As I slid into bed, Audrey clutched onto me, quivering like a bed of mussels. It had been quite an evening.

'Has he gone?' she asked.

'No, he's joining us in a couple of minutes, after he's seen to Alice. Course he's gone.'

'Did it go all right?' She might have been stoned, but she was still trying to think straight.

'He's not going to give us any bother,' I told her. 'Do you know what old Poke Nose told me? He used to play with himself under the table. While she was giving him maths lessons. Willy and the Hand Jive, Audrey, Willy and the Hand Jive.'

And we laughed and laughed, clinging together like we were riding on a switchback, whirling round and round, up and down, mad fairground music ringing in our ears.

# *Eleven*

Things started to settle down after that. I'd been through the test. Rump knew I'd been out. He didn't care. Nobody did. I was clean.

The next day I drove Audrey to her first gym lesson, her gear all pressed and ironed in a brand-new sports bag.

'I feel a bit nervous,' she said, 'like my first day at school.'

'Nonsense. Sit in the back like you're a regular punter. That'll make you feel good. And when you come out I'll tip my hat to you and look at your legs, like I do to all my customers.'

'Al!' She settled down. 'Much on today?'

'Not a lot. I've an evening run. We could go together if you want. Have some fish and chips on the way back. Or a curry.'

Back at the bungalow I found an old chain in the shed out the back, drilled a hole in the base of her dad's shell and hung it up in the porch, the hammer hanging by its side. When Audrey came back she was thrilled, spent half an hour banging on it from top to bottom, just to see where it sounded best. It was duller than we'd expected, but she was right. It looked good, hanging there. Definitely a talking point. Even Alice approved. That afternoon we helped her move back in. I'd cleared

up the mess, hung Duncan back on the wall behind a new
sheet of glass. She was all excited, even though she'd only
been away a few days. First thing she did when she got
up the stairs there was to flop down, plump up the
cushion. She tried to hide it, but she was like a farmer at
an auction, feeling up livestock, the strength and weight
of it. She looked at me for a moment, as if she'd guessed,
but what the hell. It was her memory against mine.

'You know, Al,' she said, 'one night when you're down
there and I'm up here looking out, I just might open that
window, invite you up for a chat.'

'You do that, Mrs Blackstock. You could get out your
best vinyl. *Songs of Love and Hate.*'

'You like that?'

'My favourite words, Alice, on my favourite album.'

Audrey started going out with me, regular. I enjoyed it,
showing her the tricks of the trade, how to keep the
speed at a steady forty-five to maximize the mpg, how
you always take the longest way even when they know a
shorter, the sort of change you need to have handy, to
maximize your tip. She surprised me with suggestions
of her own, little things that would make customers feel
special, a box of coloured hankies in one corner, a bowl of
condiments in the armrest where the ashtray was, even a
little menu tacked on the back of the driver's seat with
a choice of CDs on offer, Herb Alpert, the three tenors,
waltzes from old Vienna. 'Bird on the Wire' or Brünnhilde
and her dad going up in flames, she drew the line.

There was no more news coming. It was like Miranda
had gone forever. I tried to phone Iss but she never

returned my calls. I walked down there once or twice, but the place was shut up. I left her a note saying I'd be up at the caravan the following week, eleven to half past, while Audrey was at the gym, but she never showed. She didn't want to talk to me. I could understand that. I was too near the bone. God damn it. I was the bone.

It was a Wednesday, three weeks after Miranda had gone. There'd been sightings of her of course, Guernsey, St Ives, some beach in Gozo. None of them were her, I knew that. I'd decided to give the Major the bag back. I had the bag in the car. I'd drop it off at the army base. So what if he was going to run off with her. I didn't blame him. If I'd been him, I'd have wanted to run off with her too. He'd messed about with the motor but it didn't bother me any more either. He wouldn't be sitting down in a hurry. It wasn't much, but it was enough. I'd done with mayhem.

I chucked the bag in the boot, took Audrey to the gym. It was something we did now. She'd driven Sheila Coleman to Dorchester the day before, all on her own, in the Renault, come back with the news that she was going to be designated the hotel's official taxi. It wasn't much, but it was a start.

I walked her in, like I always did. I didn't have to, but frankly, I looked forward to clocking the piece behind the counter. Audrey didn't mind. Old habits, she said. She was going to be there longer than usual that day, a session in the immersion tank and then her first yoga lesson. Someone from Wareham was doing it now. They'd even taken Miranda's picture down.

Audrey went off to get changed. The girl wasn't there. I hung about for a minute or two, hoping against hope, but no deal. She'd parked her arse somewhere else. I was about to leave when I saw her, treading down the stairs like a cat. Not the girl. The Major's wife, Mrs Fortingall, in a white top and white trainers and dinky little white socks. There was something unforgiving about her, something hard, something cruel, even in the way she ran her hand down the banisters. When she saw me, her mouth turned down, not much, but enough to notice. I repelled her, and something else too, something like when you see a snake, slithering through the grass, disgusted yet kind of fascinated. And suddenly I felt the old Al come awake again. If she hadn't looked down at me that way he would have stayed fast asleep, but here he was, full on, looking straight back at her.

'Mrs Fortingall. Remember me?'

She looked across.

'Mr Greenwood, isn't it. You called the other day.'

Yes and I didn't use the tradesman's entrance.

'That's what I've come to talk to you about, if you have a moment.'

'Oh?'

'Yes. Can we sit down, at the juice bar.'

She followed me through. There was no one there. I put some change in the drink dispenser, pulled out a couple of cranberries.

'My wife's just joined this place,' I said, setting the cans down. 'You might have met her. Very thick with Tina Newdick and the owner's wife, Gail.' She nodded.

'I know Gail, but I don't think I've met your . . . wife.' Disdain dripped from her mouth.

'Well, I'm sure you'll meet her in time. She's very sociable. But you're not, are you. Would that be right?'

'I'm sorry.' She blinked, uncertain if she'd heard right.

'You don't like people, Mrs Fortingall. Not the human variety, anyway.'

She took a deep breath, paused.

'What exactly do you want, Mr Greenwood.'

'I'm coming to that. I see from the noticeboard you're taking yoga lessons for the new intermediate class. Audrey Rainbird. That's you, isn't it?'

'Yes. It doesn't pay to advertise if you're army.'

'You were in Miranda Grogan's class too. She was very good I hear, very patient, very supple.'

'Yes she was. Look, what is this? I'll call the manager.'

'If you must. Pat and I go back a long way. I helped his mother out. And now I've come to help you out. You and that husband of yours. Neil, isn't it.'

'Do we need helping out, then?'

'He does. He's in a spot of bother.'

Her face changed, kind of questioning, but not in a worried way, more curious, like she detected a weak spot, a crack in someone's defences. She was like a dingo, thin, and hungry, the scent of wet meat in her nostrils. God it was good.

'It's about that bag, isn't it?' Her mouth seemed to grow as she said it, like the words were getting too big for her lips.

'Right first time, Mrs Fortingall. It's about that bag, the one I brought to you the other evening.'

'I knew it.'

'Of course you did. You know an awful lot of things, don't you, who's strong, who's weak. It's a kind of pack mentality you have, all of your own. This you might not know. You remember that Sunday, the Sunday you were away visiting your mum, the Sunday Miranda Grogan disappeared?'

'Of course I do, though I don't see . . .'

She stopped. She could see. Of course she could.

'That's right, Mrs Fortingall. The Sunday you were away, Miranda Grogan was showing how supple she could be to your husband. In your own house, according to him. Carpet, sofa, you name it, she was supple on it. What's the matter? You find this funny.'

She was smiling.

'You seem to think this is news to me, Mr Greenwood.'

'It isn't?'

'The carpet, maybe. It's very hard, even on the feet.'

'It doesn't seem to bother you much, whatever its condition.'

'No. It seems to bother you, though.'

'It's the moral dilemma I'm in, Mrs Fortingall. You see the holdall he didn't lose, the holdall he left in my taxi, is not full of running gear as he told you, it's full of Miranda's clothes, alongside a couple of your husband's shirts. They were going to run away together. She went back home to tell Dad the glad tidings. Never came back. Least, that's his story. I've got it in the back of the car. I could fetch it, if you don't believe me.'

She shook her head.

'I believe you, leastways the bag. I'm not so sure about the running off. The army wouldn't like him running off.

Still, it's possible I suppose. When she came for that second interview she was dressed more for the catwalk than for the waiting room.'

It was an observation rather than a criticism, like she had watched it all from afar, made notes.

'Whereas you, I imagine, dress for the waiting room nearly all of the time, starched, crisp, a little severe, a little intimidating.'

I brushed my hand against her leg. She moved it away.

'So you knew?'

'Not exactly. Though she was always very attentive in class, buttering me up, praising me. She was a good teacher, though. She had a good body.'

'Had?'

'It's a turn of phrase, Mr Greenwood. She has a good body. We all liked looking at it. My husband included, apparently.'

'Yet you took her up to the surgery to have that tooth out.'

'That was Gail's suggestion, not mine. I just went along for the ride. I enjoyed it, seeing them act out the innocents. They did it rather well, considering I was there with them. I'm a trained dental assistant, did you know.'

'I didn't.'

'Oh yes. My certificate's on the wall. I could have caused her real pain if I'd wanted to.'

She sat back, as if the conversation was over. What more was there for me to say?

'The thing is, Mrs Fortingall, this holdall I have, I should give it to the police, but . . . I'm trying not to.'

'Why?'

'Because of you.'

'Me?'

'After I saw you that evening, he came round to the pub that night, the Red Lion, you know the one off the main road? He wanted the bag back. I told him he could have it back, on one condition.'

'Which was?'

'That I could have you in return.'

Colour flushed up her neck. She shifted her legs.

'And what did he say?'

She kept her voice steady, but she was churning inside, I could tell.

'He said I was disgusting.'

'He was right.'

'I told him it couldn't be a simple exchange. He couldn't come up to you and say, "I've struck a deal with this chap to get me out of a tight spot. You do the business with him and I'll get this bag back, a bag that could wreck my career, possibly send me to jail." It wouldn't work, would it? Know what I said? I said, he didn't have to tell you about the bag. Or me. Or her. Or anything. All he had to do was to set me up with you, give me a few tips, what you like talking about, what makes you laugh, your interests, then I'd take my chances like any other bloke. He gets the bag. I get a crack at you. The swap of the century, I told him. No one need know. Least of all you.'

'So why are you telling me?'

'Because I wouldn't stand a chance, chatting you up, Mrs Fortingall, would I? I don't interest you at all. But what I could do for you does.'

'Which is?'

'Provide you with ammunition, castrating shears, anything you want really. Give you the opportunity to have the Major right where you want him.'

'And what makes you think I don't have that already?'

''Cause of women like Miranda Grogan. He's still got a pair of balls. Play your cards right and he soon won't have. Why, he wouldn't even pester you after this.'

She poured herself a drink, took a couple of sips, watching me all the time. It could have been blood she was drinking, Miranda's, the Major's, mine, it wouldn't have mattered, she was that calm. Even her hand wasn't shaking.

'So if I sleep with you, Neil will get the bag back, is that it?'

'Yes, only there's no sleeping involved, Mrs Fortingall. I want you to be quite clear on that.'

'And if I do, you won't go to the police, is that it?'

'Correct.'

'And if I don't sleep with you.'

'That's the beauty of it. I won't go to the police either. I'm not interested in the bag, or the Major. I'm just interested in the leverage it might bring the two of us. For me, it's about you, what you can do for me. For you, I hardly enter into it. I'd hardly even enter you. All the time you'd be thinking of all the humiliation you can pour on his head, the power you'd have over him.'

She put her hands together, businesslike.

'This would be definite, would it, if I did what you wanted me to do? You'd give me the bag right away?'

'Absolutely. I imagine that might give you a good deal of satisfaction, telling him what you had to do to get it.'

She leant back, eyes closed, thinking it through. I'd been right. I had nothing to do with it. She returned, face as straight as a plate.

'And do you have a timetable for this transaction?'

'As I said, the bag is in the car. Now would seem as good a time as any, if you've nothing else planned.'

'Where? Here? A hotel?'

'I was thinking your bedroom would be best.'

'Wouldn't it just. You're really not a very nice human being, Mr Greenwood.'

'It takes all sorts. Just two more things.'

'And they are?'

'One, I'd like you to keep those socks on.'

'And two?'

'Would you mind very much if I called you Audrey?'

Going out, I held the door for her, all polite. My car was parked three down from hers. I opened up the boot, took out the bag.

'Not on trust, surely?' she said. Our hands touched as she took it. Not a flicker.

'I'll follow you,' I said. 'When we get there, I'll wait in the car a couple of minutes, let you get ready. Just leave the door open, OK?'

We drove out, the morning traffic light. I kept close, bumper to bumper, even jumped a red so she could feel me, right behind her, almost touching. I could see her face in her mirror, tilting up every now and again, to look back at me. Oh, the thoughts going on in that car.

Fifteen minutes later we turned into the officers' quarters. A woman was weeding her front flowerbed; down the road some kid was banging a tennis ball against a garage door. It was a weekday morning, nothing special, everything nice and quiet, everything nice and regulated. Just right for a little mayhem. Mrs Fortingall parked her car in the drive, took out the bag, and let herself in.

She didn't quite close it. I could see the green of the wallpaper and the edge of the little gilt mirror that hung on the wall. I thought about her climbing the stairs, going into the bedroom, undressing. I thought about her lying there, in her little white socks, waiting for the door to open, the sound of my feet on the stairs. I thought about what she would be thinking, what she would be like, the expression on her face, the colour of her. I thought about her mouth, the size of it, just a little too big for her face and the little core of hatred that had burnt such a hole in her. I thought how easy it would all be, the memory I'd have of it. I thought and I thought and I thought. And then I drove away.

I felt great, a million dollars. I'd done it, seen the old Al off, done the right thing. OK, so I mixed it a bit, but Mrs Fortingall deserved that. They both did. And me? I deserved Audrey.

I had some time to kill. I found a fare at Dorchester station, drove him home, then went to pick up Audrey. Back at the gym the girl was behind the counter again. She got the biggest smile going. Life was good.

'Mr Greenwood. Your wife's been trying to reach you. She's been a bit delayed.'

I peered through the porthole window. Audrey was clinging on to some exercise machine, her legs pumping up and down like she was climbing the stairs. Gail Fowler stood over her, punching buttons.

'Al! You're here. We're running way behind. I was going to take her back.'

Tina was standing at the top of the stairs, a towel round her shoulders, her hair all wet.

'Sudden booking,' I said. 'I got held up. I don't mind waiting.' She didn't look at all bad, Tina, not just the flesh on the bone, but the light behind the eyes. I gestured to the swing doors.

'She seems to be taking to it.'

'There's no stopping her now. Treadmill, rowing machine, weights; she does the lot. We've asked her to join our Sunday club too.'

'Oh?'

'Nothing official. It was Gail's idea, to use the gym Sunday afternoon, when it's usually closed. Just a bunch of us women, getting fitter together, have a bit of a laugh, in private, when no one else is about.'

'Sunday?' I said, thinking of what I like doing on Sundays, when I haven't anything on. 'Every Sunday?'

'Yes. It's been going for about six months now. Of course it's rather put paid to Sunday lunch, but you know what, who wants to cook Sunday lunch? None of us.'

'It's a dying institution, regular meal times. Tell her I'm outside.'

I sat in the car, thinking. There was something about what she'd said that didn't seem right, but I couldn't put my finger on it. They came out together about an hour later, carrying identical bags, wearing identical shoes. Audrey gave Tina a little peck on the cheek before crossing over. She looked flushed and happy. She'd only been going a few weeks and already you could see the difference. She liked herself a bit more.

She opened the door and slid in.

'All right, love?'

'Never felt better. Why I never went years ago . . . And they're so good to be with, the girls.'

She pushed her skirt down, pulling the safety belt across her. I started her up. The mobile rang. I didn't recognize the number. It came on, over the speakers. Those bastards who drive with their phone jammed up against their ears deserve everything they get.

'Yes?'

'Mr Greenwood.'

The voice was all muffled, like he was talking through a pillow.

'Yes, can I help you? You'll have to speak up.'

'Mr Al Greenwood of 14 the Larches?'

'Yes, what is it, a booking? The line's very bad.' I took it off the holder, made a face. Audrey grinned back.

'Not exactly.'

'What, then?'

'It's about Sunday, Mr Greenwood.'

'Sunday?' I turned, feeling it all slowing down, like an old wind-up gramophone.

'Sunday afternoon to be precise. The afternoon Miranda Grogan went missing.'

I pressed the phone against my ear, hard as I could, terrified that Audrey might hear. I tried to place the voice, but couldn't.

'If you could be a little more specific, Mr . . .'

'A little more specific? How about this? Four forty-eight, Sunday 23rd September, you and Miranda Grogan. Together. On the record.'

On the record? What did he mean, on the record? The coastguard hut? They couldn't see the Beacon from there, could they, and in that weather?

'I'm afraid I don't quite follow, Mr . . .'

'How much plainer do you want it, Mr Greenwood. I saw her, how shall I put it, in a certain environment that very windy day, and therefore I saw you. Not for long, as I am sure you'll appreciate, but long enough to put a rope around your neck if ever they find a body. Is that plain enough?'

'I'm not sure if it is, Mr . . . If you tell me what you want?'

'What do you think I want? I want your money, Mr Greenwood, almost as much as you have. Either that or I go to the police and tell them what I saw. What do you say to that?'

I killed the call, sat back, punched out.

'Al. Are you all right?'

Audrey was squeezing my hand. I'd gone white. I knew I had. All the blood had run out of me. Every last drop.

'Yes. It's just, I'm having one of my giddy turns.'

'I better drive back, then. Come on, swap over.'

We got out the car. I felt all wobbly. Audrey helped me round. Tina was still in the car park.

'Everything all right,' she called, rolling down the window.

'It's Al,' Audrey called back. 'He's having one of his funny turns.'

'Anything I can do?'

'No. I'm taking him home.'

'Is that wise?'

'Best place for him. You'll be all right, won't you, Al?'

I didn't think I would, but I nodded anyway. We set off. Tina overtook us, after the first bend. The wear and tear on that car.

'Who was that on the phone?' Audrey asked.

'Some customer. We were cut off before he gave his name.'

'What did he want?'

'Next Sunday. Bournemouth. The afternoon.'

'We could do that, couldn't we?'

'I think so. Give me the phone, Audrey, in case he rings back. The line was terrible.'

I sat there, the mobile sitting in my lap like a bomb waiting to explode, Audrey glancing over to see if I was all right. There was a tightness in my chest, my heart lurching about inside like it had lost its balance. Someone had seen me, seen me push Miranda off the cliff, some-one as heartless as I could be, who didn't care about her, who just saw her death as something he could turn to his advantage. But that wasn't it, that wasn't the thing that was killing me. It was not what he'd seen. It was what I knew I'd done. I'd killed my own daughter, murdered her, my own flesh and blood. If Rump had been there I'd have fallen on my knees right there and then, blabbed it all out. I had nothing left in me. Nothing.

Audrey parked the car, leant over, unbuckled me.

'Are you all right, Al? Perhaps Tina's right. Perhaps you should see a doctor.'

'Perhaps.'

The phone rang again. Same number.

'You go in,' I said, 'make me a strong cup of tea. Plenty of sugar. I'll take it out here, where the reception's best.'

I started to walk down towards the pond.

'Yes.'

'We got cut off, Mr Greenwood.'

'Is that right?'

I opened the gate. The nymph was looking the way she always looked, up to the sky, but now it looked as if she just couldn't bear the sight of me.

'We were getting to the important part of the conversation. The how and when and where of it. How much money, when you can get it, where you'll give it to me.'

I laughed, looking down into the water. Even the fish were avoiding me.

'Give it to you. I'll give it to you, all right. You think you've struck rich, don't you. Look closer my friend. You've got nothing but fool's gold in that pan, nothing but dross. Comprende?'

'Don't get clever with me, Mr Greenwood.'

'I'm not. I'm just saying. You've told me the one thing I never wanted to know. Do what you fucking like. I don't care any more.'

'You'd better care. Otherwise I'll make your life very unpleasant, even more than it already is.'

'Unpleasant! What could be more unpleasant than knowing . . .' I stopped. I couldn't tell him what I'd done.

'Yes, than knowing what?'

'Go to hell,' I said. 'Go to hell and come back and tell me what it's like, tell me what I need to pack. 'Cause I'll be going there too.'

There was a scream from inside. I knew who it was. She'd screamed like that when she'd discovered Monty gasping his guts. Then it started up in earnest, like the pull on a mower, throttle out, scream after scream, running full tilt. I charged back up the path, crashing through the backdoor. Audrey was standing in the corner, pointing down. Torvill and Dean were lying dead on the linoleum, a great hole in Torvill's head where she'd been stabbed in the eye, her mouth all open when she'd breathed her last. Dean was lying next to her, his tail flopped over her body as if he'd been trying to protect her. Audrey was panting like a dog.

'Someone's in here, Al. I heard him.'

I picked up one of her golf clubs and went from room to room. There was no one about. I checked the outside doors. They hadn't been forced, front or back.

'There's no one here, Audrey. Did you lock the doors, going out?'

'The back was open just now. Didn't you feed them this morning?'

Did I? I couldn't remember.

I bent down, picked them both up, Torvill, then Dean. They weighed real heavy, dead. I laid them out on the kitchen table, Audrey sobbing behind me. It was hard to believe that neither of them would never do the dip and dive again.

'Who could have done this?' I said.

'Someone who really hates you, Al. I'm frightened.'
She sounded all trembly and faint. I felt stronger. The
blood was coming back up.

She walked over to the phone.

'What are you doing?' I asked.

'What do you think I'm doing. I'm calling the police!'

'Are you fucking mad?' I put my hand down over hers.
She was looking at me, fear deep in her eyes. 'I know who
did this. The police won't help.'

'Who?'

'Someone I crossed. It doesn't matter, Audrey. He's
done what he wanted. He won't be back.'

I wrapped them up in cling film and made a bed for
them in the freezer so that they could lie nice and flat.
It was horrible, to think of them lying in there, so cold
and still. Later I'd have them stuffed, get rid of the glass
ornament and have them up on the sideboard, put that
music on, and think about them, moving about, in and
out of one another. I'd get other fish, but there would
never be another Torvill and Dean.

'What now?'

Audrey was on her hands and knees, wringing a cloth
into the bucket. The floor was clean but you could still
smell them, smell their fishy death. They must have been
writhing on that floor, wondering what the fuck was going
on. All the beauty.

'I need a drink, Audrey. Not here, though.'

'Don't leave me alone, Al, not after this.'

'Come with me if you want but I can't stay here,
Audrey. I can still see them lying there. Torvill and Dean,

Audrey, your present to me, the best I ever had in my life.'

I walked down in a kind of daze, alone. I didn't care now if I was caught or not. I just wanted enough time to even up the score. He wasn't going to get away with that. OK. I messed with his wife, but there was no call for this. Down the Spread, Doc was on his usual stool.

'What's the matter, Al? You look done in.'

'Torvill and Dean are dead.'

'What was it? A car crash?' He giggled. 'They skidded on ice?'

'Not the skaters!' I shouted. 'My fucking fish. They've been murdered. And I know who.'

He bought me a whisky. And another. I started buying them for myself after that. People came, people went. I talked to them, I didn't talk to them. I can't remember. Then Jacko walked in, all on his lonesome.

'Jacko,' I said. 'Drink?'

He nodded to the lager pump.

'About them grenades. You still got them?'

He looked alarmed. 'What do you want with a grenade?'

'Someone's done something very bad, Jacko. A grenade would remind them how bad.'

'This sounds very personal. Would you no rather buy the sat-nav?'

'Jacko, you offered me a grenade and now I'm willing to buy one. How much? Fifty. Hundred?'

He shook his head. 'I'm no selling you a grenade. What sort of person do you think I am?'

'How about a gun, then? You said you had a gun.'

'Of course I have a gun. I'm a soldier. I'm supposed to have a gun. Leave me alone, Al.'

Then I remembered. Poke Nose had said she had a gun, or rather her husband, Duncan, had. It would be somewhere in that room of his. I'd get the gun and shoot the bastard. Walk into his surgery and shoot him. Perhaps drill a couple of holes in his jaw first, like in that film with Dustin Hoffman. Just because I got his wife to lay herself out. What's worse? Doing that or killing a bloke's fish?

I walked up. I still had her spare key. I let myself in. Guitars were thrashing in the room above. I eased myself up the stairs. Poke Nose was laid out on the couch, a haze hanging over her head, her eyes closed. This is what she did every day, listened to her music, smoked her weed. All I had to do was to get past her, work that key, and take a look around. Under the white suit would be my guess. Sort of James Bondish. I took a couple of steps down the corridor.

'Who's there?'

I came back into the room.

'It's me, Mrs Blackstock. Al Greenwood.'

She raised herself up, blinking, squashing the last of the spliff into the ashtray.

'What do you want?'

'Just came to see if you were all right, settled in like.'

'You shouldn't come in without asking.'

'Just being neighbourly, Mrs Blackstock. Brought you your key back.'

She took it reluctantly, questions in her eyes.

'Everything all right? Need anything?'

'Nothing, Al, thank you.' She wasn't quite as friendly as before. After all we'd done for her.

'I'll be getting along, then. Do you think I could use the loo, Mrs Blackstock? Seem to be caught short.'

'If you must.'

I went back down the corridor, made a good show of opening and shutting the bathroom door. Duncan's room was opposite. I bent down, worked the key, pulled the bell pull.

She'd been in. There were flowers on the sideboard, white heavy-smelling numbers, the room ponging like she was trying to hide a corpse. The curtains were still closed. I got the impression that this room never saw the light of day, a bit like her really. She was closed off too, like this room, curtains drawn, memories packed away, wrapped in tissue paper. Every now and again she dusted herself with food.

I opened the chest's drawers one by one, proper like a burglar does, from the bottom up. I was right first time. It lay underneath a pocket, as if he was still carrying it, wrapped up in a leather pouch, what they call a snub nose, bluey grey, wicked-looking, easy on the grip. I'd never taken up with guns. I knew plenty of blokes that had, but me, never, always been wary of them, how they weighed in your hand, like you were already laid out in the morgue. Dead things, that's what guns are. There's nothing that feels as heavy as the weight of a gun. But in that moment I wished I'd taken the trouble to get acquainted. I didn't know what to do, how to check it for bullets or trigger guards, whether it was safe to carry. I tried to open it up, pressed the barrel up and down, looking for a catch, trying to remember what they did in the films, and then it sort of flipped open, like a toy, showed itself, clean and shiny and empty. I stuffed it in my jacket pocket, shut the drawer with my knee, started in on the others. Nothing under the cashmeres, nothing under the shirts. Then in the top drawer came all the little boxes. Of course. The bullets were at the back. I dropped them in my pocket, then picked up the little cufflink box, took another peek. I was tempted.

'Aspreys. He bought them after his first gold record.'

I whipped round.

'Alice.'

'Grass, vodka, chocolate. Haven't you had enough?' She held her hand out. 'Come on, give them back.'

I hesitated. I could have picked her up, thrown her down the stairs, done anything I liked, we both knew it, the size of me, the size of her, but I couldn't move. I'm a coward really, when it comes down to it. I handed them back. She wagged her finger at me, her face all stern, schoolmarmy. If she'd had a ruler, she'd have rapped my knuckles with it.

'This isn't good, Al. What, you thought I wouldn't notice, wouldn't know who'd taken them? All that time you were up here that evening, the light on while you were rummaging through. I'm surprised you didn't take them then.'

'I don't know what to say, Mrs Blackstock.'

'Neither do I. I thought we were friends, Al.'

'I didn't mean anything bad by it. It's just . . . I wondered what they'd look like, on my wrists, driving the Vanden Plas. Al Greenwood, a bit of class.'

She studied my face.

'You've been drinking, haven't you?'

'A little.'

'It's not a good idea, if you don't know who you are.'

She stepped round me, put it back, touching his picture as she closed the drawer.

'He was a good man, Duncan.'

'I can see that. You can tell by his smile.'

'You're not a good man. You could be, but there's a bad man on your shoulder, whispering into your ear. I've always thought it, even though there've been moments . . .'

'Moments?'

'When another Al comes through. Methuselah, Torvill and Dean, the way you helped me at the dentist's. But then there's the other Al, the Al with his anger barely in check, the Al with his isolation and contempt, the Al I saw in the undergrowth that Sunday. What were you doing then, Al? You weren't looking for Monty.'

'It was Torvill and Dean,' I said. 'Someone's been trying to get at them, tampering with their filters, buggering up the water. I've been trying to catch him for weeks. It's too late now, though. You know what? He's killed them, Alice, killed my lovely fish. Spiked their heads in, left them dead on the kitchen floor for me and Audrey to find. Can you believe it, that anybody could be so cruel. I'm not myself, Alice. I swear to God. I'm not myself. When I think about it, how they died.'

I felt tears coming up inside of me. It wasn't just my fish I was talking about. Alice touched my shoulder.

'Killed them? Oh you poor man. Come, sit down. I've got some coffee somewhere.'

I shook my head, gulping the words.

'No. I've got to go. I'll make it up to you, Alice, promise. Just, don't tell Audrey. Please. We're getting on so well at the moment.'

I left her, picked up the car, flashed past the roads, the gun heavy in my pocket. It was one of those late September evenings when all the swallows and stuff gather on the wire, ready to fly off to the sun. Looked like they were all watching me, hundreds and thousands of them, flapping their wings in acknowledgement. I didn't have any choice in the matter either. I parked the car a street away, walked up. The surgery was closed, the house mostly dark, save for the flickering light of a TV. I peered through. She was sitting there, bottle of wine on the carpet, flipping through the channels. I rang the bell. When she opened the door the snub nose was pointing straight at her. She didn't even blink. God, she had nerve.

'Mr Greenwood. Come in. You're a little late.'

She stepped back, as if I'd been invited. She didn't dress for indoors like you and me. It was almost formal, the skirt, the jacket, the little tight shoes.

'Now, what can I do for you?'

'What did you do? Tell him that I made you do it?'

I waved the gun around, pointing at the rooms and stairs. I'd loaded it by this time. It felt dangerous. I felt dangerous, like I could go off at any time. I was pumped up, you know, even down there.

'Your husband. Where is he?'

'Neil? What do you want with him? I thought your transaction was with me.'

'And you couldn't wait to tell him, could you. Made it

sound a bit more than it was. So he thought he'd get his own back.' I held my breath, listening. The house was empty. She was alone. Bad thoughts hammered in my head.

'What are you talking about, Mr Greenwood?'

'I'm talking about my fish, Torvill and Dean. Your husband came round and killed my fish. And now I've come round to . . .'

'To what? Is that a Webley?'

'What?'

'The gun. Is it a Webley?'

'How the fuck should I know.' I glanced down. An arm came out of nowhere, banged the gun straight up, as she turned, grabbing my other hand, swivelling her back to me. Then I was rolling over her, crashing into the table at the other end of the corridor and she was back upright, facing me, shutting the door with the back of her foot. The gun was on the floor. She picked it up, checked the cylinder, snapped it back, caught me watching her.

'I've been around guns all my life, Mr Greenwood. Get up.'

I got up, rubbing my elbow where it had caught on the table.

'I suppose you learnt that at the gym.'

'You suppose wrong. Now, what's this all about?'

'Your husband. He killed my fish. In retaliation for this afternoon.'

'And you were going to come round and shoot him?'

'Something like that.'

'And me, what were you going to do to me?'

'Nothing.'

'No? You're a reckless man, Mr Greenwood, driven by instinct. You'd do anything if you thought you'd get away with it.'

'I've done all I was going to do with you, Mrs Fortingall. You should know that.'

'So you've just come round to shoot my husband. That seems extreme, despite his shortcomings. Tell me, when did he do this, kill your fish?'

'Straight after the little tale you told. Drove round and spiked them in the head.'

She crossed her arms, the gun nestling against her bosom. It looked at home there.

'Mr Greenwood, my husband has been in surgery all day. A late sandwich for lunch and then in the afternoon, one crown, three fillings, two check-ups, a false-teeth fitting, one spit and polish and a stage-two root-canal treatment. I helped him with the last. The girl had to go off early. As for the little tale, as you put it, this evening, at around six, we had a little talk, Miranda, the bag, it all had a thorough airing. He's driving to his mother's now, for a rest. When he comes back, we'll see.'

God, she was cold. And he slept next to her. What must that be like?

'You're sure about all this. You're not just . . .'

'Protecting him?' She shook her head. 'I've protected him quite enough for one week. He didn't kill your fish, Mr Greenwood. And neither did I, if that's what you're thinking.'

I was thinking of it, as a matter of fact. I could see her doing it too, in return for what I put her through, knocking them on the head, bang, bang, bang. I had to come back at that. I couldn't let her have it all her own way.

'Perhaps he'll run off anyway, Mrs Fortingall, Miranda or no Miranda. Take his chance in gay Paree. Did you think of that?'

'Without his passport? It was in her bag. Did you see them? In the side pocket?'

'No.'

'Just as well I did, otherwise it would have gone up in the army incinerator, along with the bag and all the other medical waste. Now go home, Mr Greenwood. Go home, and leave us alone, before I call the police.'

Back at the bungalow there was a note stuck to the front door. 'Staying at the Bindon'. I should have gone over there, brought her back, but I couldn't face the thought of being in the bungalow that night, not with Torvill and Dean stiff only a few feet away. I drove up to the caravan, lit the gas lights, pulled out the bottle of whisky I kept tucked under the window seat, sat it on the table with a cup and saucer and a packet of fags. I still had some weed left but I needed a clearer head than that. Whisky and smoke. Whisky and smoke. It was dark now, the moon up, rain clouds coming in low from the sea, salt air seeping in under the door. If it wasn't the Major who murdered my fish, then who? I tried to think. It was a way of blocking out what I'd done, I guess. All that innocent beauty, all that movement, that flash of blue, their heads coming up whenever I drew near, gone. It could have been Kim I supposed, Kim and Gaynor, but it didn't seem likely, not if they wanted to keep me on the right side. It could have been the Major's wife, whatever she said, but how did she know I kept fish or where I lived? Then there was this bloke who'd phoned me, the one with the handkerchief over his face. He wanted money. I'd told him I wasn't going to give him any, but only the second time he phoned. He'd have had to have killed them already. What was that, a sort of *Godfather* thing? I tried to work it out, Miranda, Miranda, running through.

It got bad that night, surrounded by what I thought we were, Miranda and me. Halfway through the wind got up, the cups rattling above my head, like there was a ghostly tea party going on, a kind of wake, her and me, at the end of the road. I sat where I used to sit, looking across at the empty space that she had filled, elbows on the table, head in cupped hands, that glossy hair trailing over her face in a dark wavy frame. I poured two cups' worth then, one for her, one for me, lit two cigarettes, one in each saucer.

'Well, here we are, monkey-face,' I said. 'You and me. I can tell you everything now.'

And I did, about her mum and me, how it was between us, about the first time I saw her, in the pram, when she took hold of my finger, clutched it, like she *knew*, even then, who I was, and what I was to her. Later I went through the caravan, bit by bit, trying to find traces of her, things that I could hold, but we never left much behind, her and me, like we understood it had to be secret, what we were doing. There were a couple of things, though, another celebrity mag of hers, stuffed down the side of the bed, every page defaced, all John Lennon glasses and

Dracula teeth. It used to make me laugh, the things she drew, now I could hardly bear to look, such life in those drawings, such sure, insolent life. I found one of her hair bands, what she used when doing the washing-up, and tucked in behind the front door, in a crack between the wall and the fittings, a bottle of nail polish. I remembered that, how she'd sat on the steps one afternoon, painting her toenails, skirt hitched up, the tip of her tongue poking out as she concentrated on nice clean strokes. So I sat there by that table and painted my nails too, five fingers' and two thumbs' worth, dark glistening red, the gas light flickering on and off like my hands were pumping blood.

Then dawn was coming up, sucking the colour out of me, mist rolling over the grass. I fell asleep, woke to the sound of the gas jets dying, the sun well up, the clouds blown away. I looked at my watch. Ten to eleven. Nearly the whole morning gone. I knew who'd killed my fish then, the moment I opened my eyes I knew. Perhaps I'd dreamt the answer, perhaps I'd known it all along. It was Audrey's fault, her and that damn parcel of hers. It had backfired, backfired on me, Ian taking revenge on the bra and the letter and all the other things I'd done over the years. He knew about Torvill and Dean, knew what they meant to me.

I washed my face in the little sink, the soap hard, the water thin and cold, dried myself on the curtain. I opened the door, felt the stale air rush outside. Iss was standing at the bottom of the steps. Looked like she'd been up half the night too.

'Audrey said I might find you here.'
She pushed me aside.

'What do you want, Iss?'

'The truth.'

She picked up the whisky bottle.

'What's this, Al? Drowning your guilty conscience?'

She threw a crumpled magazine down at me. There were drawings all over the front, eye patches and Pinocchio noses and devil's horns.

'It was in her room,' she said, her voice all flat, weary. 'Look on the inside page.'

I turned. In her handwriting, a bubble coming out of Catherine Zeta Jones's mouth. Al. 4.30. Tuesday.

'Something to do with the taxi?' I said. 'When she was working.'

'Nice try, Al. Look at the date.'

'Ah.'

'What four thirty, Al? What Tuesday?'

'Honest, Iss. I have no idea.'

Then she saw them, lying on the table, the other magazines, the other doodles, and next to them the hair band and the dark red nail polish. She put her hand to her mouth.

'My God. She was here, wasn't she? That was what the twitch was that morning, you lying bastard. It was nothing to do with Audrey's yellow coat. It was Miranda. You've been seeing her here.'

Then she saw my hands, the fingernails shiny red, realized what I had done. She started choking, terrible thoughts rising up. 'Oh Jesus, Al! Not her.'

'Not like that, Iss. Not like that.' Her eyes were spinning wild. I couldn't let her think that. Even knowing what I'd done, I couldn't let her think that.

'Tell me I'm not right, Al. Not Miranda. Not your own daughter.'

'No. On my life, Iss.'

'But she's been here. I'm right, aren't I. Aren't I?'

'She used to come here, yes.'

'Used to come here!' She started to scream, her eyes popping out her head, neck all knotted and twisted like rope, like someone had his hands round her throat. She lashed out. I grabbed her wrists, held them firm.

'Listen to me, Iss. Listen.'

I let go. She hit me once, right across the face. Hard. I was glad of it.

'Listen to me, Iss. She came here, like I do, to get away. We'd meet up, have a chin wag. She liked my company.'

'Bastard.' She hit me again.

'That's all, Iss. On my life. It was our way of getting to know each other. It's something we both wanted, both needed. We got on, Iss. You know that. Ever since she was a toddler. Me and Monkey-face. You've always known that.'

'Why did you never tell me, then?'

'It's a private thing. If I'd told you, it would have been like asking your permission, opening doors to rooms we don't want to go into.'

'How long? How long have you been seeing her here?'

'Couple of years. Don't look at me like that, Iss. It wasn't like every week. I gave her a key in case she turned up early. Didn't want her hanging around outside, not if the weather's . . .'

'Like Sunday.'

I let that one lie. I couldn't admit to Sunday. Not to Iss.

Not to her mother. I could feel a kind of shield closing round me. I hadn't meant it, had I? I had to make her understand, I always had Miranda's best interests at heart. Always. I never meant to harm her. Never.

'We had something special here, Iss. She could feel, like I could. The only difference was she didn't know why.'

'You never told her . . .'

'Of course not. Not even hinted. But we were close, there's no denying it.'

'Could she have come here that Sunday? Have you checked?'

'Course I did. There was no sign.' I hesitated. I was on delicate ground. 'Her perfume. It lingered, you know, after she'd gone.'

'You checked straight away?'

'Not straight away. I never thought . . .'

'You never thought! A place she comes to, a refuge, and you never thought.'

What could I say? I was running out of words.

'God, Al. I don't know. I find this all . . . You and her, alone here. It doesn't sound right.' She gathered herself up. 'You'll have to tell the police. That she comes here.'

Did I? Self-preservation was kicking in. After all, I didn't mean to kill her, did I? There was just a chance, just a chance, if she kept her mouth shut, if I dealt with the joker on the phone . . .

'You sure, Iss? Think about it for a moment. They'll pull the place apart, search the bungalow. If Miranda and me are placed any closer, there's no knowing what might come out, or who might hear it, if you get my drift.'

'You mean Ted?'

'He doesn't deserve that, Iss. Not right now.'

She stared out, battling with it, the past and the present.

'It's too late for that, Al. They've got to know. I'll tell them if you won't. Tell them everything.'

I watched her drive away. I didn't have much time.

Audrey was back home, calm like floating in oil, dressed up neat too. I felt all gritty, out of place. The kitchen smelt of disinfectant.

'You OK?' I said. 'You stayed at the Bindon?'

'Yes. They were very understanding. You?'

'The caravan.'

'I thought as much. Did Iris find you?'

'Yes. Tell me, have you seen Ian recently?'

'Ian? No. Why?'

'Just wondered. Look, I've got a job on, might be away for a while.'

'What sort of a while?'

'Most of today. Courier job, for the army, could be as far as Wiltshire. Don't wait up for me.'

You see, it comes easy to me, the lying. Audrey was staring at me.

'Are you all right, Al?'

'Not really. I'm sorry, Audrey.'

'What for?'

'Being me.'

Out in the garden Alice Blackstock was fussing about by that little shrine of hers.

'Al,' she said, beckoning me over. 'Just the chap.' She

waited until I got to the fence. She had that little lace cap on, the one Audrey had bought.

'We'll forget about last night.'

'That's very kind of you, Mrs Blackstock.'

'See this? Audrey lent it to me. I've been sorting out my wood.'

'Oh?'

'Yes. I found some sandalwood and some sweet-smelling rose. I thought it would be nice if we held a little funeral service for Torvill and Dean. You could say a few words, I could sing a song. You could even lay them upon it, if you wanted.'

'What, burn them!'

'Or not. That's just the Eastern way. A remembrance service would be just as good. We could play Ravel's *Bolero* too, think of them, swimming about in the afterlife.'

'Do they have fish in the afterlife, Mrs Blackstock?'

'I think goodness and beauty survives in its essence everywhere, don't you, Al? Duncan, Leonard Cohen, Torvill and Dean, they're all there together, somewhere, on the stairway to heaven.'

'Leonard isn't dead yet,' I reminded her.

'No, but he will be.'

I left her to it, picked up a couple of petrol cans and the tyre iron the Major had left behind, got in the car. After I'd dealt with Ian, I'd make a run for it. Better than facing them all, knowing what I'd done. There were plenty of ways I could try. Go up to London, knock on a few doors. Borrow Kim's boat, or take a Channel ferry, do a Lord Lucan, jump overboard halfway across, my decision. Maybe not. Maybe get down to Tangiers, start afresh, try and be a better Al this time. But not before I'd seen right by Torvill, by Dean.

There were no cars in their drive. Too busy being successful. I kicked open the kitchen door. Their new uniforms were hanging on the back, like Audrey had said. I took them out onto the back lawn, poured petrol over them, watched them burn into the ground, the imprint of their suits burnt into the grass, like they were already dead. It wasn't enough, but it was a start. I began walking through the house, splashing petrol here and there, over the carpets, the sofa. The fumes were stinging my eyes.

The mobile rang.

'Good afternoon, Mr Greenwood. This is your friendly blackmailer calling. About my money, did you get my warning?'

I nearly dropped the phone.

'Is that you, Ian?'

'Ian? You can call me any name you like, Mr Greenwood, as long as you come up with the money.' He paused. 'You did get my warning, I hope? I mean business, Mr Greenwood. I hope you can see that now.'

I clutched my forehead, trying to think what to do. This wasn't Ian. Even disguised, it wasn't Ian. He didn't kill my fish. And I was going to burn his house down.

'Yes, I got your warning. You sick bastard.'

'The things you love, Mr Greenwood. They have a way of getting to a man. I'll be moving on up, if you don't come across.'

Moving on up? He was threatening Audrey now.

'You mean Audrey?'

'Your wife?' He sounded surprised. 'Yeah, why not?

Her face wouldn't look too good, would it, after a couple of visits from me. She might start awkward questions, as to the why and wherefore. I don't want to, Mr Greenwood. I don't want to do anything. Harm your wife, go to the police. All I want is your money.'

I tried to think quick. I was going to pay him all right. Pay him big time.

'How much?'

'That's more like it. Ten thousand would seem a fair sum for what I saw.'

'Ten thousand! I haven't got ten thousand.'

'I'm sure if you put your mind to it you could make a stab at it. That motor of yours would make a sizeable contribution.'

'Yeah, and how do I live afterwards?'

'Out of prison, Mr Greenwood, a free man.'

I paused, let him think I was crumbling.

'I'm waiting, Mr Greenwood.'

'It would take me some time, ten thousand. How about a down payment, to put a stop to all this aggro?'

'What sort of down payment?'

'I could get you a thousand.'

'When?' The question was spat out, like he couldn't wait for the answer, like he could already see the money in his hands. He hadn't planned this at all. He was winging it, sensing an opportunity, amateur night at the Blackmailers' Ball.

'Tomorrow. I could get a thousand tomorrow.'

'As long as you're clear. This is a down payment.'

'Yeah, yeah. Just tell me where.'

'Do you think I'm stupid, Mr Greenwood. I'll let you

know where. And don't worry about the wife. She's OK for the moment. For the moment, you ken.'

He rang off. Oh, I kenned all right. And he'd taken all the trouble to stuff a handkerchief over his face. I phoned home.

'Audrey. I'm off now. Did you see what old Poke Nose is doing?'

'Yes. She asked me to dress in blue.'

I laughed. Probably the last time I did.

'Why not? You look nice in blue. Take care of yourself, Audrey, do you hear?'

I blew her a kiss, went back to the car. The thought of that bastard taking a knife to her churned my guts. I knew where he'd be if he wasn't on duty, and he hadn't sounded as if he was on duty. Come lunchtime he'd be where they all were, down the pub. So what if he had all his mates with him. So what if he had the whole fucking army with him. I drove over to the Spread Eagle. No show. I went down to the cove, tried the one there. Kim Stokie was lording it over a bunch of fishermen, but no sign of Jacko. Then I noticed, on the small TV up in the corner, there was a football match coming on. He'd be up at the Red Lion, in front of the giant plasma, along with the bouncy maids and the crap food, with all the other wankers.

I called into Mr Singh's Curry House before going in, had a quick lager while he took my order and did that special favour for me, only too happy to oblige. Didn't realize it was the last time he'd see me there? Twenty minutes later I'd parked the car near the car-park exit and walked in. I was right. They were all there, standing in gawping clusters, listening to the pre-match prattle. There was a lot of beer being put away, a lot of cock in the air, you could tell by the sour smell and the slop on the floor and the chants crashing in and out like waves. Jacko was leant up at the end of the bar, his mate Rodney, a bunch of others too. Tattoos and haircuts. I threaded my way through, careful not to spill anyone's drink, careful to keep my eyes to myself. Jar a man's pint or his ego here, and you could lose most of your teeth and all your credibility. Jacko took his elbow off the counter as he saw me coming through. He wasn't expecting this, didn't quite know what to make of it, a fleck of wariness in his eyes. I nodded, friendly like, like I didn't suspect a thing. As I said before, I should have taken up acting.

'Mr Greenwood. Fancy seeing you here, in the lion's den.'

'I called in on the off chance of seeing you, Jacko.'

'Oh?'

I gestured him aside. 'I was out of order last night. Apologies. The thing is, I'm thinking of going away.'

He was intrigued, bless him.

'Are you now?'

'Yeah. That sat-nav you were on about. I thought it might come in handy.'

'The sat-nav?'

'For the Vanden Plas. I'm selling the other car, selling the bungalow, raising some cash and getting out altogether. Me and Audrey are going travelling.'

'This is very sudden, Mr Greenwood. When do you plan on going?'

'Not straight away. Next week, next month. I've got a few things to settle up, then we're off. Time for a fresh start. Who knows where we'll end up. Now this sat-nav, Jacko. How much?'

He was watching me closely. I made kind of sense. Who'd want to stick around with blackmail and murder hanging over him? And I'd just told the one person I shouldn't have. I could almost see it, the smile he was hiding.

'Three hundred. As I said, it's a quality product.'

'How about two twenty?'

'How about two seventy-five?'

'Split the difference?'

We shook hands. He thought himself so clever. A thousand pounds tomorrow, two fifty today.

I tapped my wallet.

'I brought some readies.' I knew his methods.

'Not here,' he said. 'I'll meet you out the back.'

'I'll be by the car.'

When he came out I was waiting for him, behind the wall leading to the disused gents, the Major's burglary kit in hand, the back door already open. I whacked him hard on the back of the knees as he passed, and then smack, on the back of the head as he fell down. I pulled him inside. We were out of the car park and out on the main road before he'd had time to bleed.

When he came to he was propped up in the caravan, tied to the spare gas cylinder. I was at the table, the takeaway spread out, the chicken, the rice, the nan bread, the two Cobras, and the little jar of germ killers by their side. I was wearing pink rubber gloves, the picture of hygiene. Jacko looked around, trying to work out where he was.

'What's going on?'

'We're having a takeaway, Jacko, Mr Singh's special, all the accoutrements. Fancy a bite?'

I leant over, offered him a spoonful, but he twisted his head this way and that, slopping it all over his face.

'Careful,' I said. 'Stings a bit, vindaloo.'

He tried to wipe his face clean with his shoulder. Made him look like shit.

'What's this all about, Al?'

'Don't you know?'

'No, I don't. Is it the sat-nav? I could do it for less.'

'You could have given it to me for nothing and you'd still have that bump on your head. Really, Jacko, you seem to have lost a sense of direction yourself. Never mind. This will help you find it.'

I picked up the little jar, unscrewed the cap. Jacko looked from the jar to me, and back to the jar again.

'What's that?'

'This, Jacko, is Mr Singh's renowned lime pickle. Not for the faint-hearted, Mr Singh's lime pickle. Been known to burn a novice's stomach lining clean through before he's finished his first popadom. Get it on your fingers, and ooh, you better not wipe your arse for a good week after. Here, have a sniff.'

I held it under his nose. He started to wriggle, rocking the cylinder back and forth, shaking the caravan.

'What are you going to do with it?'

'Well. I'm not going to wipe your arse with it, Jacko. Try and think back, where I might choose to put it.'

'What's all this about?'

'You know what it's about, Jacko. You killed my fish. You killed my fucking fish.'

I dipped my fingers in. I could feel the heat coming through the rubber. This was going to hurt.

'I don't know what you're talking about.'

'Yes you do. You killed my fish. What sort of person are you?'

'Honest, Al. I never killed no fish. I didn't even know you had any fish.'

'Torvill and Dean, the most beautiful things you've ever seen in your fucking life, and you killed them, just because I hung up on you.'

His eyes fell.

'Oh, I know Jacko. Your friendly blackmailer, *you ken*. Couldn't even disguise your voice properly, you Scots prat. A warning. My fish a fucking warning.'

I smeared some over his lips and gums. His mouth started moving about, like he had a couple of eels in there.

'Jesus Christ, Al, honest to God, I don't know what you're on about. I never touched nobody's fish.' He tried to spit it out. He wouldn't be worried about his mouth soon.

'You're going to tell me next you didn't make those phone calls.' I reached in, fished out his mobile. 'If I scroll down here I won't find my number on it, is that it?'

'OK. OK. I made the calls.'

'Audrey next, you said. My fish and then my wife. My fucking wife!'

I yanked his head back and taking a good dollop, rubbed it into his left eye, thorough, like I was giving my boots a good dubbin. He started to scream, all high and excited, like a snared rabbit, like he couldn't believe what was happening to him, the eyeball contracting with the pain.

'I never said your wife. Jesus, Al. You said that. I never thought of her. What type of man do you think I am? I just did your car, thought it would make you see reason.'

His head was batting back and forth like he was trying to shake his eye out, fingers twitching like a piano player, feet dancing in the air.

'What are you talking about, my car?'

'The wee bevels. At the back. God, water, Al, please, for the love of God. I'm going blind here.'

'Wee bevels?' I turned round, looked out the window. There were two great scratches down the boot, like King Kong had taken his fingernails to them.

'You did that?'

'That was the warning. No fish involved at all, on my life. I was just trying to make a little money, Al. That was all. You know that. I like fish. The way they swim and everything.'

He looked up at me, all the tattoos, all the beer boasts washed clean out of him.

'What are you going to do?'

'I don't know yet. Do a little more basting, set light to the caravan. Roll it over the edge. You in it.'

'Al, I swear to God. I was never going to tell the police. You got to believe me. After all, what did I see? Not much. Just her in the passenger seat, that's all. I didn't think anything of it, until you told me that night in the pub, that she'd gone. What happened after that, only you know.

Probably nothing. You just didn't want to get involved. I can understand that.'

'Passenger seat? What the fuck are you talking about, Jacko?'

'Miranda Grogan in the passenger seat of your car, that Sunday afternoon. I saw you both. Water, please. I can't . . .'

I tipped his head back, chugged the lager over him, wiped the eye clear with the front of his shirt. It didn't help much.

'Now tell me,' I said, 'before I do the other eye.'

'I saw your car, that was all. You know what we have to do now, standing in that sodding box all day, on account of the terrorist threat? Note all the cars going past, registration numbers, time, direction. Four forty-eight, that's when I saw yours, heading in the direction of Wool station, Miranda Grogan in the passenger seat.'

'You're making all this up. I wasn't even in the car. Anyway, how could you see a passenger? You're on the wrong side of the road, in the box of yours.'

'I'd just seen a convoy out. I was on the other side. It was Miss Grogan all right, and it was your car. I didn't even bother to read the number plate. I know it off by heart. It's in my pocket book. Take a look.'

He nodded towards the inside of his jacket. I took it out, a little notebook he had, his name and number written inside. I flicked through. Sunday. September 23. There it was. 4.48. Reg AL 123.

'But . . .'

'Yes?'

My car, the car that was in the garage, the car that I'd

told Audrey I'd been sleeping in. The car that had been in the garage while I'd been up on the Beacon, while Audrey had . . .

Jesus Christ. Jesus H. Christ.

I untied him, threw him down the steps. He stood there, uncertain, not knowing what to do. The Vanden Plas. Jesus Christ, the Vanden Plas.

'Go on, Jacko. Before I change my mind.'

I got into the car and drove, drove for I don't know how long, out along the back roads, parked up by the lay-by, looking out across the army range, the firing positions, the dummy tanks, the ground all scorched and blasted apart like the rest of my life. They'd be coming for me soon, thanks to Iss and Ian and now probably Jacko. Who knows, maybe even Poke Nose would make a contribution. It was up to me to set the record straight, whatever they thought, whatever else I had done. I hadn't killed her. I'd killed someone but not her. Miranda had been sitting in this very car that afternoon, next to where I was sitting now, there on the passenger seat, the rain lashing down, wipers going like buggery, thankful that she'd got this lift, that it was going to be all right, that she was going to Paris with her new bloke, with her new life. She must have felt so great, so relieved. What had happened then? There was only one person who could tell me.

'Audrey!'

I stepped into the hall. There was a quiet to the place, but not an empty quiet. I walked through to the living room, the kitchen, looked through to the conservatory. Then I heard the sloshing, someone getting out of the bath. I took the yellow oilskin off the hook and walked through. She was standing on the bath mat, a towel wrapped round her.

'Al.' She looked surprised. 'You're back early. What happened to the army job?'

'Bombed out.' I held out her coat.

'What's that for?'

'You're going for a short walk,' I said. 'You may get a little wet.'

'In this weather?'

I held it out.

'Put it on, Audrey, please.'

'What is this, some sort of game?' She was all smiles.

'If you like.'

She put it on, the towel falling to the floor. Her feet looked really big, poking out underneath it.

'There. Satisfied?'

'Take a look in the mirror. Remind you of anyone, wet hair, yellow raincoat? That's what she looked like, wasn't it?'

'Who? And what you done to your nails?'

'Never mind my fucking nails, Audrey. Miranda. Miranda Grogan. This is what she was wearing, wasn't it, that Sunday. Just like you now.'

She pulled the coat tight around her, suddenly aware of the state of her, the state of me.

'I don't know what you're talking about.'

'Don't give me that. I know what you did. My daughter. My fucking daughter. These fingernails? I'm in the devil's pay now, Audrey, come to take you down to hell.'

I lunged forward, grabbed her head in the crook of my

arm, her fist flailing at my back. I marched her down the hall, her feet skittering along the tiles, her body all warm and loose. She could smell the lime pickle and the rubber, didn't know what to make of it, didn't know what was in store for her.

'Al,' she said, her breath coming through. 'For God's sake.'

I dragged her out the back door, down the path, kicking and struggling but there was nothing she could do. Gaynor was at the sink, staring at us, but I didn't care. I forced her down on her knees, pushed her head under, her body nearly sliding in after her. I held her like she was a huge fish, writhing and gasping and flapping her fins. She came up, the dank of the pond stinking on her.

'You knew I was lying when I said I was having a kip in the car, didn't you? You knew because you were driving it. Driving Miranda Grogan to God knows where. What happened, Audrey, what happened?'

I ducked her again, the water churned up. She came up all lank, hair like weed. Gaynor was standing by her open door, poking her head out.

'All right. I admit it. I gave her a lift. So what?'

'So what? I'll tell you so what.'

I pushed her up and down, up and down, her teeth banging against the stone. Gaynor had run back inside. Time was running out.

'Come on, Audrey, out with it.' Up she came, her lips split, words spilling out with the water.

'I took her to the station, that's all. After our row I was going up to the Beacon, but I bumped into her, by the bus stop, crying her eyes out. She'd had a row with Ted, gone

down to the cove to cry it off and missed the bus to Wool.
She had to get to Wool, she said. She was hysterical, out
of it. I was worried for her.'

'Worried? You? About Miranda?'

'She asked if you were around, to drive her to the
station. I said you probably were. So we came back.'

'You too?'

'I thought you might have hit the bottle, gone on a
bender. But you weren't there. So I drove her, then came
back. You know the rest.'

'That's what put you in the mood? I don't believe you.
What train did she catch?'

I was poised right over her, ready to start in again.
There was no pretence now.

'I didn't wave her goodbye, Al. I just dropped her, glad
to see the back of her.'

I put my hands in front of her face, fingernails facing.

'If you don't stop telling me lies, Audrey, so help me,
I'll drown you here and now. You didn't drop her at
the station. Someone was waiting for her, but she never
turned up. They were running away together, Audrey.
That's what she was all worked up about. She'd missed
the bus. They were going to miss the train. What happened, Audrey? You meant to take her to the station but
you didn't. What happened? What happened?'

I made to duck her again.

'I saw you!' she screamed.

'What?' I stopped, a kind of panic rising in my face.
'Saw me? Saw me how?'

'In *her*, plain as if it was written on her forehead, her
voice, the little twist of her mouth, your bastard child

sitting right next to me, twiddling her hair, acting as if there was no history between us. I was trying to keep things under control trying not to think of the humiliation all these years, half the village knowing, going on about the weather, how bad it was. We were driving past the lay-by. Do you know what she said with that dirty smirk on her face and her eyebrows raised, just like you raise yours? Do you know what she said? "You should get out more, Audrey. Live a little!" What you'd just said, not ten minutes before. Twenty years I'd had of it. I couldn't take it any more. "Live a little!" The pair of you. "Live a little!"'

She started to scream at the top of her voice, at least I think she did, for it all became mingled with the police sirens and doors slamming, Poke Nose yelling out her window, pointing a shotgun down at me, Gaynor rushing out, banging on two saucepan lids. I ran down the path, through the house. Adam Rump was charging down the path, Dave Stone and a crowd of others behind him. I swung the door open.

'Adam. Thank God you're here. I would have killed her. So help me. I would have killed her.'

Dave Stone slammed into me, spinning me round, my head banging up against the artillery shell as he grabbed my wrists, hiking them up behind my back, snapping the handcuffs on. He pushed me back against the wall. Adam Rump stood in front of me, his face like a block of stone.

'Alan Greenwood. I am arresting you on suspicion of abducting and causing grievous bodily harm to Miranda Grogan on Sunday, 23rd September, 2007. You do not have to . . .'

'What are you talking about. I had nothing to do with it.'

He took no notice, babbling on, policemen pushing past him, warrant cards being waved. I tried to make him see sense but he wasn't having any of it. Audrey was being led in from the garden, her face all bruised.

'Ask her,' I said. 'Ask her.'

'Ask me what?'

'Miranda Grogan, Mrs Greenwood. We've had information that leads us to believe your husband is connected with her disappearance.'

'Miranda? Your god-daughter. Not her too, Al.'

They searched my pockets first, Dave Stone breathing in my face, nostrils all worked up, like he'd like to punch me senseless, Rump going through them one by one. He found the tooth straight away, dropped it on the carpet in his surprise, Audrey running out the room, sobbing. Rump asked me whose it was. I told him, natch, told him how I'd got hold of it, told him how it had nothing to do with what had happened to her, but he wasn't listening, just bagged it and labelled it, and had someone take it out to the car. They were like a pack of beagles after that, running and rooting through everything they could lay their hands on, little whoops of delight coming from wherever they uncovered another nail in my coffin. Miranda's black bra came next, stuffed right at the back, behind Torvill and Dean's winter feed. No parcel, no letter to Ian Newdick, just some grass cuttings in the cups, and, later, from forensics, a wisp of hair where the clasp had caught my wrist. Audrey had lied to me about that too. She'd bottled out just like I'd wanted to. Hadn't known whose it was, of course, but she was lucky that way. Again I tried to tell them, how I came by it, but it didn't look good. Audrey was back in the room, her face fixed up.

'Audrey, tell them for Christ's sake,' I said. 'I'm sure, with a good lawyer . . .'

'I'll tell them all right,' and the way she said it made my blood run cold, like all this time she must have been thinking how she'd get out of it, if it ever came to it. And here it all was, out on a plate. Her eyes fell onto the black lace.

'Is that hers, Inspector?' Rump nodded. Her eyes went all wide, looking at me like this was the first time she'd really seen me. God, she was as good as me, maybe better, and I'd never realized it before.

A shout came from the bedroom. Rump got up and left. Audrey and me were left alone, Dave Stone looking over us. We looked at each other, reading each other's faces, so much silent stuff to say. I tried to reason with her, plead with her, make her see the injustice of it all, but she never moved a muscle, stared back in defiance, the room behind her eyes admitting everything, her face saying nothing. I could almost see it, read the story in her eyes, how she'd have slammed on the brakes, the words ringing in her ear. I could feel it too, the strength in her as she hauled her out, Miranda all surprised, not expecting it, fighting her off perhaps. God, she'd have been a giant then, Audrey, wouldn't even have known her own power. What had she done, wrapped her hands round her throat, lashed out, picked something up, hit her?

'It was an accident, right?' I said.

'Isn't everything? Look at you, Al. You're an accident, a bad one.'

'What, a rock?'

'You a rock? More like something underneath it.'

'Not a rock, then.' Then I remembered that stone, the way she'd played the headlights on it, and what she'd said.

'The milestone,' I said. 'She bang her head on it?' That unsettled her, her face suddenly pale. Dave Stone saw it too.

'See that, Dave?' I urged him. 'Ask her about the lay-by.'

Rump re-appeared. He was holding up a shoe, high heels, leopardskin print, flash. He was holding it high, triumphant.

'How do you account for this, Mr Greenwood? Under the bed. Any idea how it got there?'

'I don't account for it at all. Ask Audrey. It's probably hers.'

Rump shook his head.

'This shoe belongs to Miranda Grogan. We found its partner on the beach.' He turned it in his hands, peering closely at the heel. 'Looks like there's blood on it.'

Audrey stepped forward.

'I think you'll find that's fish blood, Inspector.'

'Fish blood?'

'Yes. I used it to kill my husband's fish, Torvill and Dean.'

'Audrey?' I couldn't quite believe what I was hearing. Neither could Rump.

'Mrs Greenwood?'

'I found it in the car under the front seat, a couple of days ago. I thought he must be up to his old tricks again. All my life I've had to live with it. Then yesterday, I saw him chatting up some woman in the gym. I just couldn't take it any more. So I borrowed my friend's car, drove back, killed them right there on the kitchen floor. I didn't want to do it.'

'Didn't want to do it!'

I lunged up, but Dave Stone just pushed me down. Rump was looking at her with distaste.

'That is a very serious offence, Mrs Greenwood.'

'Yes. I'm sorry for it. Perhaps if I hadn't found the shoe, hadn't seen him with the girl. Only, the day before I'd found that bra in his pocket, in the same jacket where you found the tooth. He told me it had fallen out of a customer's bag. I wanted to believe him, God knows I wanted to. Then came the shoe. His latest conquest I thought. I never imagined they belonged to—'

She broke off, biting a handkerchief.

'It's all bloody lies,' I was shouting. 'I've never seen this shoe in my life before. Ask her about the lay-by.'

'The lay-by?' Rump was flummoxed. Dave Stone piped up. His big moment.

'He was talking about the lay-by, sir, just before you came in. Something about a milestone. It's where I saw him about two weeks ago, when I warned him about the Peeping Toms. He said he was having a smoke, but I didn't see none. I thought he might have been a bit of a Peeping Tom himself.'

'It's where he takes all the girls, Inspector,' Audrey offered. 'It's where he took me.'

They led me to the bathroom, made me take my clothes off, put them in a bag, all the unwashed stuff too, even took a clipping off my fingernails. Iss had been on to them, the moment she'd left me.

They didn't find anything else in the bungalow. There was nothing more to find. I'd forgotten about the car. The first thing they saw was the scratches down the boot, the bent lock.

'Having a bit of a struggle here were we, Mr Green-wood?'

Rump took the keys and placed them in the lock. Up it came. It was empty enough, but when they lifted the carpet covering, peeking out from the spare tyre cover was a tug of material. Tartan. I didn't own any tartan, not even a rug. Stuffed in the empty hub, the lining half showing, lay a crumpled oilskin, bright yellow, still damp. Rump lifted it out with a suspicious hand. There was a label on the inside, under where the coat hook should have been, a name on it, written in one of those indelible pencils that leak all over your fingers. Ted Grogan it said, in blurred capital letters. There was a tear in the right-hand pocket. This was the coat Miranda was wear-ing when she ran out of the house. She wouldn't have wanted to get the car wet, she knew how much I hated that. So she put it in the boot. Later Audrey hid it under-neath. She must have been thinking of me all the time.

They led me out to the car. Rump led the way, Dave Stone bringing up the rear. He had a smirk on his face the size of Wales. The biggest thing that had ever happened in the village and he was right in on it.

'Don't forget, Dave,' I urged him. 'Don't forget.'

Rump opened the door for me, placed his hand on my head.

'Don't forget what, Dave?' he asked.

'My cap,' he said, patting his bare head. 'I've left it behind.' He plodded back down the path, embarrassed. Rump guided me down.

'She shouldn't have done that to your fish, Mr Greenwood. There was no cause for that. I'd have found good homes for them, even put them up myself. They'd have looked nice in my pond. I'll throw the book at her, don't you worry. Where are they, by the way?'

'In the freezer. I was going to get them stuffed.'

'That'll have to wait. We'll need them for evidence. But later on, I could arrange it for you if you want. Be company for you, in your cell.'

We waited. Dave Stone was standing inside the porch, knocking on the door. No one came.

'I don't suppose you'll want Mrs Greenwood visiting you. Not after what she's done.'

'No, I suppose not.'

'Wives.' He let out a sigh. 'Mine left me. Did I tell you?'

'Yes.'

'The house seemed a bit empty without her, so I bought a big tank, put it in the drawing room, filled it with angel fish.'

'That must be nice.'

'It is. You should come round and see it some . . .' He stopped. 'Sorry. I wasn't thinking.' He leant back.

'You know, you nearly got away with it.'

'I keep telling you. It wasn't me. I haven't done any-thing.' He wasn't listening.

'Had my mind not been distracted I'd have caught you a lot quicker, only what with Michaela walking out on me that weekend . . .'

Something stirred in the corner of my brain.

'How do you mean, walking off that weekend?'

'That's the weekend she left me. Propped the letter on the mantelpiece and walked out. One last walk where we used to be a couple, it said, and then she was off, back to the land of her fathers. It's a shock, you know, after seven years. When I saw you up on the cliff top ready to jump off, I should have realized that the awfulness of what you'd done was finally sinking in. It was all there, in your eyes. But my mind was elsewhere. She'd only been there herself, a couple of days before.'

I couldn't quite believe what he was saying, he was speaking so matter-of-fact. I gripped the seat in front of me, like I was behind the wheel of the Vanden Plas, the brake cables cut. I could feel it all running away from me.

'You sure that's where she went? It's not exactly next door.'

'Oh yes. She loved it up there. Practically lived there in the summer. She was brought up near the sea, needed to be near it. That's why I never understood, the thing she had against my fish. They had so much in common.'

'What day, do you know?' I tried to make as light of it as I could.

'I'm not exactly sure. Could have been the Saturday, might have been the Sunday. I was helping Freddy

Lanchester disinfect his three ponds that weekend. Couldn't go home. Couldn't take the risk.' He caught my puzzled expression. 'The herpes outbreak I told you about? Very virulent strain, the worst in thirty years.'

'Right.' I was getting a funny feeling about this. Mrs Rump. Michaela.

'Have you heard from her since?'

'Not a dickey bird. She never was one for writing.'

'Mobile?'

'She refused to have one. Said they gave you cancer.'

'What about friends?'

'She didn't have any. Truth be told, she wasn't a liked woman, Mr Greenwood. The fish didn't think very much of her either. They can always tell. They're a good judge of character, carp.' He banged on the window. 'What's that idiot doing?'

I peered out. Dave Stone had picked up the hammer, and was banging on the bell, the dull clang of it falling to the ground like lead. It might have been good as a talking point, but it was bloody hopeless as a bell. Adam Rump was watching him too.

'That wasn't here when I came last, was it?' he said. 'Those marvellous stuffing balls.'

'I put it up the next day. Making yours a happy home and all that.'

'What is it, exactly, something from a ship?'

PC Corn-Plaster was still hard at it. I thought about yellow oilskins and what Audrey had said, how everybody wore them, like a uniform.

'No. Look, about your wife, Inspector. Do you know what she was . . .'

There was a flash and a rush of air, like my ears had gone. The car was blown sideways across the road. When I looked out again, Audrey and Tina were standing in front of a great hole where the porch had been. Rump was crawling out the bushes, his hair half alight. Of Police Constable David Stone, there was nothing to be seen.

It doesn't help, does it, when you're being arrested for murder, to blow up one of the arresting officers. Didn't help the bungalow either, the front half blown to bits. Audrey had the whole thing pulled down, filled in the pond while she was at it, put in a hot tub. She could afford it, the publicity she was getting. Her dad's artillery shell. All those years of me tripping over it, all those mornings of her polishing it, rolling it up and down the kitchen table. It could have taken her out any time.

After that things went from bad to worse. Up on the lay-by, they found blood on the milestone, where Audrey had shone the light, Miranda's blood, natch. I'd taken her there, of course. Jacko had seen me driving the car, hadn't he, seen Miranda in the passenger seat. He made a good witness too, pensioned out the army, his left eye blinded, the blackmail charges never pursued. There'd been plenty of squaddies seen me in the pub. Even Mr Singh came forward, his hands clasped in horror over what I'd done with his lime pickle. The Major came up trumps too, admitting the affair, admitting that weekend with her, how they planned to run away, Mrs Fortingall all prim and proper in the public gallery, white top, white skirt and little white socks. I like to think she wore the little white socks for me. Perhaps we should have done it after all. There were other witnesses at the station who saw the

Major waiting for Miranda to turn up, CCTV pictures of him too, pacing up and down in the forecourt until way past seven. I called Poke Nose in my defence, trying to put myself back in the undergrowth, but three thirty, four thirty, how could the old dear be sure? Audrey had been very helpful too, my haunts, my habits, what passed for my psyche. Out on the army range, past the disused cottage, they found footprints matching my Wellington boots. In the remains of one of the dummy tanks, across the way, fragments of bone. They made a reconstruction some time later, showed it on Channel Five. I watched it. It made perfect sense, the clout on the head, the falling back, brain and blood on the stone, the ride in the boot, to the empty army range, out of sight, out of mind, when not in use. It was all quite accurate save in one important respect, viz. that they had the wrong person carrying her the half-mile in the fireman's lift, tipping her into the tank dummy, before racing back home, finding me gone, all fired up, ready for the Bonsai moment. The Bonsai moment. God, that night, when we'd stopped halfway through and she'd stood stark naked by the window, watching the shells smash Miranda to smithereens, I'd run my hands up her flanks, her flesh all trembling like an animal at the abattoir. 'How do you feel,' she'd said, when we were back at it, 'like it isn't you, like it isn't me?' and it was true, we were both somewhere else. No wonder we'd gone at it like knives, cutting bloody slices out of each other. She was just like me and I'd never really known it. While I was up on the Beacon, pushing her off the cliff, Audrey was out getting rid of Miranda. If only I had succeeded and she hadn't. I might be still in prison, but my daughter would be alive.

Yes, I was Miranda's father. At least that made a kind of warped sense. If I hadn't been, Audrey would have killed her for nothing. Ted didn't take it well. He didn't deserve something like this. I wrote him a letter, begging him to come and see me, let him tell me what I knew, but he never replied. No one wanted to know. I was monster enough. I don't mind any more. I don't mind about anything. Miranda's dead and that's all that matters. My girl. My lovely Monkey-face. She had a future, but the little bits of me inside her got in the way.

So now I'm inside, twenty-five years for the murder of my own daughter that I didn't do. Kim and Gaynor sold their story to the papers. Living next door to a murderer. Audrey's been asked to write a book. Lying underneath one. She doesn't visit very often. Doesn't visit at all, as a matter of fact. They have the business now, Audrey and Tina. Ian's long gone. Back to Scotland from whence he came. They're doing very well. Alice Poke Nose has joined them, looking after the books. Last Christmas she sent me a photograph of the three of them, arms around each other, standing on this dirty great platform, all togged up in jump suits and helmets, swigging a glass of champagne after their bungee jumps.

And Rump? I hadn't the heart to tell him. What could I say? No, I didn't kill my daughter but it looks like I might have done for your wife. It would only have confused the issue, and I'm sure if I had he wouldn't have had Torvill and Dean stuffed, like he promised, and sent them to me, stuck up on a little wooden plinth, lips just kissing, like for the first time. He even had their names writ underneath, only he got them the wrong way round, Dean under Torvill and Torvill under Dean. Still, I don't mind. I can still look at them, remembering how they used to do the dip and dive, as if it was just for me. They were special, those two.

So that's it. My life story. Not much is it? I don't mind for myself, but sometimes I think of Mum, and then it hurts. What would she think of me now, her boy, gone so rotten. I'm a wrong 'un. I know that, always did, like that song that came out when I was a kiddie. I've written to Carol, asking her to make sure it's put on my grave, but I doubt if she'll do it. She's always been stubborn that way. But as I said in my letter, she should, if only to bring her boys over, have them take a look at their grand-dad's grave, hear about the debris that's strewn around his life, make them think about what they do before they do it. Here's what it should say, just in case she doesn't.

*Here Lies Al Greenwood, husband of Audrey,*
*father of Carol, father of Miranda.*
*He was No Good*